W9-CNW-342

summer
society

WITHDRAWN

ELIZABETH
BROMKE

Created with Vellum

For Lela, Vicki, and Lisa

Prologue

Sophia

Picture it:

Gull's Landing. Summer of 1983.

Wrinkles didn't exist yet—not that *we* knew. Not then.

Shoulder pads were all the rage, and perms were a safe bet. But disco was out.

And the boardwalk was the only ticket on the east coast. It was our slice of heaven, our hamlet down the shore for every single summer since we could successfully tug a wet swimsuit over our own fannies.

Aunt Lil licked the tip of a bejeweled finger and slid a tarot card into position on her folding table. She stabbed at it. "See that? Seven of swords. That's no good." She shook her head and her earrings clanged like wind chimes. "No good at all."

Next to me, Sue sucked in a deep breath, her fleshy stomach expanding like a balloon beneath her one-piece.

She let out the sigh on a shudder, but her stomach stayed sticking out.

Diane sat mesmerized. "Whaddya mean *no good?*"

Bea yawned. I snapped my fingers at my hip. "It's a crock, Diane. Come on; let's go."

Aunt Lil ran her hand over the cards, ordering them in one quick shuffle and slotting them back into a wooden box where she kept everything from postcards to coupons. "No drinking, no smoking, and *no boys.*" She picked up a long-burning cigarette from a seashell ashtray and gave it a good flick.

"Hey, I wanted the rest of my reading," Diane protested, but it was too late. If we were going to sneak over to Wildwood, we didn't have time for games.

I gave her the eye then drew a cross over my chest. "Swear to God, Aunt Lil. We'll be good."

"Oh, for the love of God, *no* taking the Lord's name in vain!" the old woman added, standing with her hands on the hips of her saggy bathing suit. I muttered an apology until she lifted a Russo eyebrow at us then turned away, babbling to herself as she shuffled past the television set. She eased into the crook of the corduroy couch and punched the remote. *The Price is Right* blared to life.

That's how our summer looked since forever. Our folks and Diane's mom and Sue's dad would shuttle us down from Philly and we'd stay the whole summer, living on the beach and falling asleep to *The Price is Right* on Aunt Lil's musty old couch. As we got older, falling asleep got swapped out for flagging down a cab to the next town over. Swear to God, though, I think Bea would have rather stayed in the shore house with old Lil. Sue, too. Me and Diane, though? We were looking for a love connection, what can I say? I'm not talking about a

2

summer fling, either. True love, truly. That's all we wanted.

"I happen to agree with the Lord's-name-in-vain part," Sue whispered.

"You agree with all of it," Diane pointed out. Me and Bea shared an eye-roll, even though we were more Catholic than anyone.

I crossed the shag carpet and bent down to give Aunt Lil a kiss on the cheek. "I promise, Aunt Lil. We'll be good."

She held her cigarette over my shoulder and pressed her mouth to the side of my face, then looked past me to my sister. "You take care of them, Bea," Aunt Lil said, smudging the pink stamp of her lips from my cheek.

Bea took my place at the sofa, lowering herself to kiss our aunt and make the same promise. The thing was, Bea meant every word. She really did. She was the oldest. She was *that* one. The good one. The smart one.

After all, Bea was the reason we were still there together. She was the one who started it all when we were just kids, years before we were wiping Aunt Lil's lipstick off our faces and sneaking off to Wildwood every night of the week.

Years back, Bea grabbed our sunburnt shoulders and huddled us into a circle and told us we had to make a pact. Now that I think of it, that was probably the first time I ever swore to anything. So, I should really blame Bea for the nasty habit.

But anyway, you see, that's why when me and Diane wanted to go to Wildwood, Bea would drag Sue with us. And when Sue wanted to make it over to Ocean City for the library, well, Bea would drag me and Diane over there, too.

It was like that for two whole months year after year,

Bea making us all stick around together even when we got older and me and Diane were into boys and Sue was into books and Bea wanted to spend the day on the tram car just people watching.

If any one of us ever needed anything—if there was a natural disaster or if we were in trouble or if the world *was* ending—we would meet there. Down the shore at Aunt Lil's, in our designated bedroom on the second floor. The one with the view of the beach. The one with two twin beds and an ancient creaking dresser. The one where we spent most of our nights together—good nights giggling and hard nights crying and every other kind of night there ever was.

That was the pact.

And if you had a pact then you had to have a club. A *secret* one, usually, to go along with the secret *pact*.

So, we had named ourselves The Summer Society.

The only problem?

Some of us had other secrets, too.

Chapter 1

Bea, 2018

A sob crawled up Beatrice Russo's throat as she stood at the casket.

Sophia's eyes were closed.

That's how it worked, Bea knew. She'd stood at other caskets, too. Aunt Lil's. And even her own father's. His eyes had been closed, too. Brown, though. Not green. And back then Bea had been too coward to stand there more than a perfunctory moment.

Were Sophia's still green?

She clawed through her brain searching for the last moment she *really* looked her little sister in the eye. She couldn't picture it. *Oh no.* She couldn't see her sister's green eyes. *Were they still green?*

She swallowed the sob and leaned against the polished wood, her nostrils flaring, the air coursing in and out in steady beats.

No one would see her do it. She could just discreetly lean forward and place her hand on her sister's cold forehead and press her thumb in the right position and sort of maneuver—

"It's time, honey." Diane's hand slipped around Bea's shoulders. "They want to begin."

She looked up at Diane, her eyes glassy, her head throbbing. "I can't remember her eyes," she whispered on a choke.

Diane cleared her throat and pinched the bridge of her nose, her eyes filling, too. "Bea, they want to start. You have to come sit down."

A single tear rolled down Bea's cheek, joining a wet spot at the hollow of her collar bone.

She didn't budge.

"We'll find a picture, Bea," Diane whispered more urgently now.

Bea slowly allowed the woman to shuffle her away from the coffin, her gaze falling across the church. Mourners had shown up en masse. Bea didn't know a fraction of them.

As she found herself back in the front row, she stared at the memorial photograph settled in a leafy, elegant wreath.

Greg had chosen it. The wreath was too distracting and garish, and Bea could hardly make out her sister's face behind all the green lifeless foliage. So amazing how a plant could be shorn away from its roots and stick around for a while. You could water it, and it would pretend to be alive for days—weeks if you were really good.

Maybe that had been Sophia's secret, too. The pretending.

The photo was a great one, actually; stunning—Sophia's honey-blonde hair in tangles around her olive face. White teeth flashed for the camera as she laughed at something or someone beyond the lens. But Sophia's eyes were squinty and you couldn't even see them at all. What a terrible choice for a memorial. Just terrible.

Bea glared at Greg as she lowered herself next to him.

The priest began the ceremony, and Bea tuned out, focusing every bit of her energy on the fight against weeping with wild abandonment.

Not soon enough, it was over. Diane's mother—Bea's aunt—ushered everyone to the wake.

————

THE ONLY ONE worse off than Bea was her mother, of course. She'd been rendered not paralyzed but instead a jittering mess. Now, she sat on her own threadbare recliner in her own house where she had *insisted* on hosting the service. She sat there staring dully out the front window, fortified with drugs to the point where she probably had no store of tears whatsoever.

Bea knelt beside her, one hand on her mother's knee, the other holding a framed photograph from Sophia's wedding. Her eyes were green then, at least.

"I was with Soph a month ago. We met for lunch in the city, Ma," she spoke as others swirled around the wake, entirely immune to the heartache at the center of the whole thing, and yet still there, breathing their air and eating their food and offering their lukewarm condolences over *a life cut short* and every other idiom in the book.

Her mother had no reply, but Bea went on. "I can't remember if she ever took her sunglasses off. We ate outside." Her eyes welled up again, and she cleared her throat, laying the frame on her mother's lap and standing.

Without another word, she walked off and squeezed through the crowds of people who probably didn't even know the beautiful, too-young Sophia Angelos even *had* a sister.

The kitchen was empty save for one tired, nearly foreign face.

"Hi, Bea." It was Sue, in a loose black blouse and stiff black slacks, sitting at the table. Her blonde hair, dishwater—not honey like Sophia's—had been combed neatly and pinned back, and Bea liked focusing on those details. Sue fidgeted, her eyes red, one finger drawn to her mouth as she chewed on the nailbed. She lowered her hand. "How are you doing, Bea?"

Bea sighed and then, inexplicably, chuckled. "Oh, you know. Just awful."

Sue stood and took a tentative step nearer, her hand making its way awkwardly to Bea's arm. "Where are you staying tonight? Do you need a place? I can kick Joe to the sofa—"

"I'll stay here with my mom. Thanks, Sue." Bea tried to affect a smile, but who knew what her face looked like? A blur of features, probably.

"Been a while, hasn't it?" Diane had joined them now, and Bea wanted out of there. She squeezed the plastic cup that had suddenly appeared in her hand. It was the fanciest plastic cup she'd ever held in her life, probably. Courtesy of Greg, who refused to spare any expense for the whole affair. At least Sophia had that—a nice funeral. Even if all the beautiful florals and pretty plastic cups were smooshed into Dolores Russo's dated rowhouse, at least they had the pretty crap to hide the dust and the sorrow. *Right?*

Sue and Diane tried for a normal conversation, pretending to do the math on *just how many years it had been*. Too many, was the correct answer, apparently.

Even though they were blood relatives, Diane, Bea, and Sophia hadn't gotten together since the last family Christmas, which was years and years before. Around the same time as Sue's wedding. Sue, the childhood friend Sophia had dragged home after dress rehearsal for her First Communion.

"How's Matt holding up?" one of them asked. Bea just shrugged.

"Sophia was his *mother*." It was all she could muster. A brittle, weak reply, nearly a question, as though she was asking for confirmation. *Sophia was a mother, right? And Matt her son?*

"I'm sorry," Sue offered quietly.

Bea's throat closed up as memories of Sophia's pregnancy cropped up.

She looked up at her cousin and her old friend, two faces that had grown all but unfamiliar. She forced herself to smile through a new wave of tears. "Will it always be like this?" she pointed to her head, but they apparently figured she was pointing to her wet eyes and therefore patted her hands and shushed her and told her that *no*, the tears would dry and it would get better.

And then, right when Bea was ready to kick them both out for their inability to read her mind and know that she didn't mean the *crying*, she meant the unstoppable memories and their total control over her brain… Diane laughed.

A loud, bursting belly laugh that started in the woman's paunchy belly and bellowed out from her oversized red-stained lips.

"What in the *world* is so funny?" Sue asked, catching Bea's eye and frowning apologetically.

But Diane kept laughing until her tears were both happy and sad, probably, and she was wiping them with any dry patch of skin she could find along the back of her fingers and hands. At last, she replied with a question, still struggling with the laughter. "Do you girls remember that one year, on the boardwalk?"

Bea's vision blurred and she shook her head, pushing a finger into the center of her head where the ache throbbed endlessly.

"Diane," Sue whispered, "Now's not the—"

"Yes, it is," Diane batted her away, a laugh creeping out again. "Now is the perfect time. Don't you *remember*? That one summer?"

Bea squeezed her eyes shut then peeked out and glanced around the kitchen looking for an escape route. From the past, the present, and everything else. She began to excuse herself and took a step toward the back door, but Diane grabbed her wrist.

"It was that summer down the shore when we met the boys," she said, her voice only a degree softer and still full of life and fondness, and Bea *did* of course remember that summer. She swallowed and stood still, crossing her arms at last, accepting that she'd be forced to relive it and wondering what might happen if she, too, laughed? Would God strike her down? Would Sophia's ghost slither into the kitchen and shake a finger at her? Would Bea's heartache turn into full-on heartbreak? Would she die, too?

Sue's eyes had grown wide, and a groan escaped her lips. "That was the worst night of my life."

"It was the best night of *mine*," Diane answered, her

face softening as she ran her fingers once more beneath her heavy eyeliner. *Who wore makeup to a funeral?*

Bea's throat had slowly begun to clear of the eternal threat of a sob. "I remember," she managed weakly.

"We were singing karaoke with the boys, and Doug made Sophia sing a duet with him," Diane went on.

A little smile crept along Bea's mouth. It was an earlier phase of that night—before the Ferris wheel. Before they went back to Lil's. She nodded, and all of a sudden those green eyes blazed into her mind. She could see the whole evening perfectly. Sophia and her deep tan and sun-bleached hair and white tank top glowing in the lights of the Pier as she made her way on stage with her summer boyfriend, Sophia reluctant and slow.

"'I Got You Babe,'" Bea murmured.

"Huh?" Diane asked, pausing in her recounting.

"That's what they sang. 'I Got You Babe.'"

"Oh, right," Diane went on. "And it was like… *perfect*. I mean they could have been Sonny and Cher up there. Everyone cheered, remember? The whole dang bar was whooping, and I swear I think someone offered to buy rounds after that. Or maybe a Hollywood agent came over and gave his card to Soph. I swear."

Bea nodded along. "Then…" she began.

And Sue chimed in, her lined face growing a shade younger. "Oh, I remember! One of the Canadians asked you to do a duet after, right?" She pointed a bare finger at Diane, who bent over and laughed again.

"Yes!" Diane shrieked, standing back up, her face flushed and dark hair wild about her face. Bea studied her for a moment. Diane was the sort who didn't really age. A little extra weight and the exact same makeup she'd worn since she was thirty gelled together in a timeless result that turned her into a cheery, chubby divorcee, frozen in time and everlasting laughter.

"What was it you sang, again?" Bea asked, her unease starting to wash farther away.

"That was the hilarious thing," Diane roared again. "'Friends in Low Places!' He was this stuffy dime-store cowboy from the great white north with a penchant for American country music. And totally tone deaf."

"Oh, right," Bea dove into the memory. Restrained laughter bubbled up in her chest. "He sort of just breathed heavily into the mic for two minutes while you giggled next to him."

"And then he grabbed *me* and took me to the dance floor," Sue added.

"And he tried to two-step!" Diane cackled.

Bea was laughing now, too, in spite of herself. "And then he did one of those fancy moves," she said through short breaths.

"He tried to *flip* me," Sue cried, her face mottled but her voice happy.

"And *boom!*" Diane roared anew. "He dropped you! I mean if it were me, I'd get it," she grabbed the flesh around her waist and then pointed at Sue's skinny build, "but *you?*"

"I can't believe you didn't have a brain injury after that," Bea remarked.

Sue nodded her head through tears of laughter or sorrow—it was unclear which. "I blame that whole night on why I ever said yes to Joe. It was like a gateway moment to my inability to say *no* to anything."

The laughter slowly died off, and Diane and Sue started in on a whole different conversation about Joe. But Bea was picturing Sophia again, there in the shadows of Pelican Pier, cuddling against her boyfriend,

Doug, who snuck peeks at Bea over her sister's shoulder. She shook her head. "I think that was the last time we all went to the shore house for the summer, huh?" She swallowed, breaking up the others' conversation.

Sue nodded. "Yes, it was. The last summer."

"What the hell happened to us?" Diane asked, but by then, Bea had fallen back down into the hole of grief, uncomfortable and forlorn and indifferent to anything other than her own pain. Her sister's pain.

When no one had a good enough answer, the conversation cut back to Sophia's death, as if the whole comedic interlude were a way to butter Bea up and get her to spill all the gory details.

Bea wanted no part of the drama and the shock and Diane's bold speculation and Sue's hushed whispers. So, she extricated herself to the back porch, leaving her old friends for good.

There was nothing any of them could do to turn the tides back to those good old days. Not now. Not ever.

Eventually, the wake curled to an end. Greg and Matt bid farewell and left in their black SUV. Other family trickled away back to their normal, not-sad lives, and Diane and Sue helped clean up and made empty promises about getting back together soon. Before long, it was just Bea and her mother again.

Bea drove home the next morning, her eyes bloodshot and her insides hollow. And there was no one to call on the way home. No one to gossip with about the cousins who didn't show up. No one to share in surmising about what Aunt Lil would have worn to the funeral if she were still alive—a bathing suit, no doubt.

And then Bea was alone.

———

SHE COULD HAVE CALLED out of school. Even if it was the final week, her principal understood, certainly, but Bea needed the distraction. Especially since she was going to spend the afternoons at her sister's.

All Monday, she'd dreaded the final bell, even going so far as to grab a knubby handful of pencils and begin hand-cranking them in the sharpener.

But Greg called her at exactly five minutes after three and asked when they could get started. Matt had plans to go to a friend's house, and Greg wanted him to be there for the first hour or so.

At that, Bea had grunted.

It was all rushed. Too much too soon, for her and for Matt—who shouldn't be hanging out with friends the Monday after his mother's funeral.

Greg reasoned that it was good to start sooner. It would help everyone with closure. *Sophia would have wanted it this way*. It was a line Bea refused to accept from the man who clearly had no idea what his wife wanted.

Although, he was right. Sophia was the sort to put away the Christmas tree on January seventh, every single year.

Easter baskets were stored at noon the following Monday.

Trash from their annual Fourth of July party was dragged out to the cans not five minutes after the fireworks finale.

Bea knew all this because she was the same way. And now she regretted it all. Why not leave the Christmas lights up until Valentine's Day? Why not decorate an extra dozen eggs with the leftover dye? Why not let things go on a little?

She drove the forty-five minutes to Westboro, craggy

city streets giving way to green tree-lined country roads and smooth acres of white fencing.

"Bea!" Greg greeted her as though he wasn't quite expecting company. It was a rich person habit, she figured—the polite surprise act. Sophia had started doing the same thing in the past couple of years.

He ushered her inside and upstairs, though Bea wondered aloud if they might start in the kitchen, instead?

"Sophia didn't cook much. You know that," he replied as they landed on a thick oriental rug on the second floor. Who cared if she cooked? Surely, she had a favorite apron Greg and Matt couldn't stand to look at. Surely, they'd want Bea to sweep away the coffee mug Sophia claimed as her own each morning. Surely, the two boys needed good ol' Aunt Bea to come in and both hide and protect even little trinkets such as those?

"Listen, Bea," he began.

Bea cut him off. "Where's my mother? I thought she was coming, too?"

He shook his head sadly, his dark hair remaining in its perfect Greek coif. "She called, and—" Greg shook his head, his face breaking. The first indication of his pain even after the funeral, where he'd hardly shed a tear. Maybe there was more to her brother-in-law than she'd given him credit for. Bea almost regretted her ill assumptions about him. Almost.

Swallowing, Bea nodded. "And Matt?"

Greg pointed his finger toward the door at the middle of the hall. Matt's bedroom. "He won't come out."

Bea considered how she'd handle doling out advice to Greg if Matt were one of her students, a surly teenager in the throes of complicated and brutal heartache.

"He needs time, Greg. It's too soon."

He ran his hands up his face and through his hair. "Well," he began. "Maybe you're right, but we can't live here like this. With her things and—" A sob fell from his mouth, and he raised his hands and dropped them before cocking each wrist at his hips and waiting for Bea to offer some magical answer.

So that was it. They didn't want to move on so quickly. They *couldn't*.

Bea considered what she would do if she'd lived with Sophia. How would she stand to be in the same four walls? Sleep there? Wake up there? She wouldn't. She would go down the shore and stay in the shore house. It's what she would do. It's what she wanted to do now, even.

But Bea couldn't suggest that to Greg and Matt. She couldn't even do it herself. Because even worse than waking up in the house where her sister had lived would be to wake up in the house where she had died.

Chapter 2

Diane

Diane De Luca accidentally swiped left.

Right? Left? Who could keep track of how to accept or reject an online suitor? Not Diane. Only once the handsome stranger's profile disappeared into cyber space did she recall that *left* was *no*. *Right* was *yes*.

She had an hour before Book Club, and she *should* be skimming the last half of Jane Austen's *Persuasion*, but why on earth would a group of otherwise reasonable, modern women choose a classic for Book Club? Why?

So, instead of even pretending this month, she'd set out the wine glasses and the cheese plate and then grabbed her phone and fiddled around with her dating app.

Her daughter had recommended a matchmaking service for Diane, but that was not the divorcee's style. She liked the cutting edge, and she wasn't afraid of technology. Not like some of the girls in her various weeknight groups. Now, there she sat, frequently forgetting which way to swipe if she liked what she saw on the screen.

"Stupid thing," she muttered under her breath, trying to thumb backwards and undo her mistake until the doorbell rang. Diane set her phone on the coffee table and rose to answer it, ushering in the first few arrivals with their books and drinks of preference, then returning again and again to the door until the seven of them were all present and accounted for.

Soon enough, everyone was seated and cracking into the appetizers and sipping away at their drinks and gushing over the book.

Meanwhile, Diane hid her phone and held her book at the sort of angle that she hoped would suggest that not only had she read the darn thing but had, in fact, *re-read* it, too. This took a little discreet bending of the spine and crinkling of the pages, however.

"Diane, how was the funeral?" someone asked between discussion questions.

She was taken aback by the question, which was a silly reaction since Diane had well and truly put the funeral and all its horrors in the past. She shook her head. "Oh, right. Thanks. It was fine. I mean… well, it was just terrible. Really awful, you know? She was so *young*. We were really close when we were kids. All the way until college." Diane pressed her lips into a line and batted her eyes until the watering was an effect of her own making and not some deep-down sorrow she couldn't seem to shake.

"Oh, did you go to Drexel, too?" another one asked.

Diane lifted an Italian eyebrow at the offender and laughed. "Like Sophia, you mean?"

"Her obituary said she graduated from Drexel. That's where I went."

Diane's mouth turned into a deep frown. "Right. She and her sister both got scholarships there. Not me, though," Diane laughed. "I tried my hand at Penn State." She took a long swig of her wine, then waved a hand around her living room. "Another one of Craig's gifts."

The others twittered in response, some giggling at her easy approach to the topic.

"Do you ever regret divorcing him?" someone asked, rapt.

Diane didn't mind the attention. Playing a role in so many charities for so many years, she wasn't shy about her face in the paper for this fundraiser or that. And anyway, once the divorce went through, her lifestyle didn't change.

She said as much, and again the group murmured excitedly.

No one could argue that Diane didn't do well for herself.

She'd actually given college a go. Two years at Hatsburg Community. Then Craig dragged her into Penn State with him, but she didn't quite finish, instead focusing her efforts on figuring out how they were going to pay the ungodly amounts of student loans it took to cover what his scholarships and part-time jobs did not. As smart and hard working as he was, Craig wasn't great with managing money.

Then he graduated Penn State, moved on to the Beasley School of Law at Temple, finished top of his class and promptly took up with the best firm in Briar Creek. Soon after, the last remaining partner of the two who founded the place retired. He bequeathed the whole thing to Craig, and *badda bing, badda boom,* they were set for good.

Money poured in, and Diane made it her full-time job to track their finances and ensure they didn't lose their grip.

It worked for a while. They had Brittany and did the whole *live, laugh, love* thing. Then, after Brittany *aged out* (one of Craig's funnier dad jokes), they came to the decision that they were nothing more than a stereotype—the well-appointed suburban couple who stayed together for the kids, or *kid*—singular—in their case.

Bored with each other and edgy about everything, the *live, laugh, love* adage that adorned their foyer wall was suddenly out of style and irrelevant.

And like a wet Band-Aid in the shower, the marriage slipped off.

Craig saw to it that Diane didn't miss a beat with regards to weekend shopping sprees and her housewife hobbies, as she called her evenings. She had never been good at the staying-at-home part of being a stay-at-home mom.

Still, Craig had agreed that it's what made her a good mom. She was always at school, volunteering loudly and embarrassing Brittany to her friends. She organized block parties and cut oranges for soccer practice by day and hosted fundraisers and cocktail hours by night. To outsiders, Diane and Craig made the perfect pair. But the only thing between them was a lifestyle, not love.

Now, they were friends. And Craig still footed the bill (despite her heartfelt and gracious declinations), but Diane was beginning to grow tired of the plump, pampered homemaker role, especially with no one to make the home for.

She'd taken up a few volunteer positions but still had a deep need for something more. A new man or a new hobby or *something* more than her various commitments. Then she realized what might fill the void.

A grandbaby.

Brittany flat out refused. She had no viable prospects, for one, and she wasn't about to turn into a baby farm just so Diane could have something else to do when Book Club wasn't in session.

So, instead, Diane turned to looking for a job. Something befitting a woman in her position: a woman who was sitting pretty on a pile of alimony and busy enough with this and that.

She'd applied at the library to run adult activities, and then she threw in an application at the local humane society, too, just to see. When both places called back and offered her part-time positions, she accepted quickly, splitting her time between books and fur babies, a decent consolation prize for a wannabe MomMom. And now, she was adding online dating. For fun. Her minimum wages would cover that monthly subscription. Diane was better than to make poor ol' Craig pay for her pursuit of a new man, especially when they sometimes went to dinner together.

But, all in all, Diane had everything a woman in the prime of her life could or should have. All of it. Really, she did.

As she took another swig of wine and returned her attention to her still-stiff copy of *Persuasion*, one of the Book Club women cleared her voice and lowered it. "Diane, what exactly *happened?*"

"You mean with my divorce?" she asked, her eyes dancing along the back-cover blurb and culling as much info as she could in order to come up with a new discussion question.

"No," the woman answered. "Your cousin. I mean, *Westboro?*"

Diane lifted an eyebrow. *Here they go again.* Another weeknight meeting, another gossip sesh.

There, in Diane's leisure community of Lynnecliff, Westboro was the competition. It was an ongoing dance between who had more money and who had more dramatic, glamorous lives. And though Diane never took part in the pretense, she now saw that her high-society cousin's death continued to make waves across the greater Philadelphia area. And to her various friend groups—the Bunco Babes, the Taco Tuesday Troop, and now clearly the Bookies—Diane De Luca was at the center of the scandal.

Scandal, however, wasn't the perfect word. And she took issue with it.

"Oh," she replied, her voice turning like a screw. "Well, I can tell you that the good community of Westboro had nothing to do with it. Nothing whatsoever."

Nervous laughter rippled across her sectional and the women fell in half an inch closer to the coffee table.

Diane smiled, but it had been just two months, and the whole thing still stung like a nightmare you couldn't quite shake and to engage in these women's yearning for some juicy secret was to betray her own family.

The expectant silence, however, tugged her deeper. Diane held up a hand. "A tragedy, really. Very sad." Her smile fell away, and she slapped her book onto the coffee table. "What say we go with a Reese book next month?"

The others twittered in quick agreement and soon enough *Persuasion* had lost the group's interest all together.

Thank God.

Diane excused herself to the kitchen to refill the

hummus. There, privately, she woke her phone and navigated out of the dating app and over to her texts. She scrolled below Brittany and their daily message thread, a quick thank-you note to Craig, and down past other names until she found Bea.

She started to type a generic *Hanging in there?* but quickly thought better of it, and instead, an idea caught fire in her head.

Exiting Bea's message, she composed a new text, adding both Bea and Sue.

Ladies—I need a break from reality. Shore soon?

As she hit send, she bit down on her lower lip. The message carried weight. But that's exactly what Diane De Luca needed. Okay, well, she definitely didn't need extra weight, literally, but she needed something more than adoption fairs and Adult Coloring Club. She needed more than the cookie-cutter group of girlfriends who asked for *a little less tequila in my marg, please, Diane!* and demanded that they choose *books that matter!* every damn month.

Three dots appeared as one of the two wrote back. They disappeared, reappeared.

Finally, Bea's name popped up.

School, remember? No break until Christmas. Sorry.

Diane's shoulders fell, and then Sue's name materialized.

Sounds fun…

Hope returned, and Diane punched out a quick reply as she glanced through to the living room, where the women squabbled lightly over Oprah and Reese.

Spring Break?

Bea responded. *March? Too cold.*

Sue agreed, apparently. *Maybe summer?*

But Bea shot that down, too. *Play by ear, okay?*

A sigh filled Diane's chest, and she wondered what was to blame for this evident dissolution of a friendship. Was it really Sophia's death? Or had the break-up started earlier... years before when they floated across the invisible threshold from girlhood to womanhood? If that were the case, then what a shame. What a boring excuse to let go of the best relationships any one of them had ever had.

Without an answer and more frustrated than ever, Diane left the message thread and opened her dating app.

And then, she swiped left on a perfectly handsome man.

Chapter 3

Sue

Sue Bleckert apologized and turned the volume down on her CD player.

"It's not that I don't like Rod Stewart," the front-desk girl complained to her, "it's that I don't like Rod Stewart on repeat all day every day."

Flushing deeper, Sue hit the power button and returned to her computer screen, punching in student I.D. numbers and D.O.B.s and all the initialisms and digits that corresponded to a college student's school identity.

She'd worked in the Office for Students with Disabilities for the past ten years, and it wasn't until now that they'd hired a student to run the front desk. It wasn't until now that anyone had complained about Rod Stewart's greatest hits, either.

Holding in a sigh, Sue felt her phone vibrate in the top drawer of her desk. She slid it out to take a peek—no phones allowed during office hours, after all (thus, the CD player).

Glancing briefly up at the student worker in front of her, she confirmed that she was alone with her little secret peek and slid the drawer out further, slipping her hand to the phone screen and opening the message to see that she had two new conversations.

One from her husband.

One from Diane. Frowning, she glanced up again to verify again that the coast was still clear, then she opened the second message with a quick tap. A girls' trip. It sounded amazing. But Bea was out, and if Bea was out, then the shore house was out.

If the shore house was out, then of course there would be no girls' trip. That was the best and most logical locale, especially for Sue who wasn't about to ask her husband to foot the bill for a hotel. Not in their current circumstances, what with him working well into the night with and for his clients.

Disappointed, she left the conversation as soon as it died out, which was quickly.

Then, Sue clicked on her husband's name, dread and hope pooling in her stomach in equal measure. When it came to unexpected text messages from Joe, Sue couldn't always predict what he had on his mind, nor could she adequately judge his tone. That disconnect in their marriage—that fine staticky disruption of their inability to get and stay on the same page—had begun to grow into more than a little fissure. It was becoming a crevasse.

And so, when she read this particular message, she couldn't tell if he was disappointed to disappoint her or if she'd done something to upset him or if he was slammed at work again or *what*.

I'll probably be home late tonight. Plan to eat without me.

Quickly, worried she may lose his attention in the distractible world of texting, she answered. *I was making Shepherd's pie… ;)*

His favorite.

No immediate reply came through. And five minutes later, still nothing. Then another twenty minutes, and *still* nothing.

Even so, she pulled out the used envelope where she'd begun to compose a grocery list and added carrots, corn, and ground beef.

Just in case.

As she refolded the envelope and tucked it back into her pants' pocket, the door to the testing room opened and a proctor emerged—another student employee, this one as nervous as Sue and dutiful about her job. The testing proctor was responsible for walking the testing room to ensure no one had their phone out and that each student put his or her pencil down when the little timer went off on that specific test.

The girl's face was stretched tight as she locked eyes with Sue and nodded her head behind her, whispering, "Integrity breach."

Integrity breach was not-so-subtle code for "cheater".

Sue glanced past the proctor to the tester following her, a pitiful, pimple-faced boy sweating behind a pair of Coke-bottle glasses.

Immediately, her heart ached for him and after the girl handed over the contraband, a crumbled sheet of notes, Sue waved the test-taker around the counter and to her desk. Aside from data entry, she oversaw testing accommodations and generally had the final say on when to report students and when to simply *redirect* them.

"What happened?" she asked, her voice soft and low as the proctor returned to the room.

His glasses fogged up, and Sue's gaze flitted down to the handwritten notes. They were nearly indecipherable, scratchy and too tiny for even her to make sense of. She looked back up at him. He adjusted his glasses, folding a knuckle up under a lens as he tried to dry his eyes behind the thick frames.

She gestured to the page, but he shrugged, tears falling down his cheeks.

Sue turned to her computer and searched for his name, learning within a few clicks that he was a freshman, legally blind. His accommodations included extended time, enlarged print on tests, and a student reader upon request. She frowned at the screen, then the page, then returned her gaze to the boy, holding his notes up. "Were you using these on your test?"

He dipped his chin and squinted at her over the frames, then lifted his head back and again looked through the mottled glass. He looked all of twelve years old, not eighteen.

Sue lowered the paper. "Tests are stressful, huh?"

He nodded, his chin quivering.

"Freshman year is hard. I know. We don't allow notes on tests unless it's in your plan, okay?"

He nodded again.

"Why didn't you request a student reader?" she asked.

The boy shrugged.

She knew why. It was the same reason nearly every other male underclassman waived that particular accommodation. Their pride was often fragile. New and underdeveloped. That was okay.

"Look," Sue went on. "The college takes academic

integrity very seriously. If you were using notes to cheat on your test, I can't ignore that, but—"

The boy dropped his head in his hands and pushed his fingers up beneath the glasses. Sue glanced again at the notes. They were truly impossible to make out. She glanced at him as he sat there, crying now and drawing the attention of the front-desk girl. "Oh, dear," Sue fretted. "Let me ask you this." She swallowed, uncertain if her next decision would be the right one but knowing full well that freshman boys with thick glasses and a jawline of pimples and scraggly notes weren't exactly on par with the half-drunk frat boys who Googled answers on their phones from inside their pockets.

Discretion. Sue had it. In more ways than one.

He hadn't looked up yet, but Sue smoothed the paper across her lap then held it at his elbow line so he could see it. "Can you read this for me?"

Sniffling, he dragged his hands down to his cheeks, his glasses foggy and smeared even worse. He took one finger and rubbed the insides of the lenses then pulled the frames against his eyes and stared hard at his own paper. He started to read, missing every other word and mixing up the ones he did get right. For that boy to have effectively cheated off the paper would have been a miracle. And with only having just begun his test, it was clear this was a false alarm.

Sue knew that the poor thing hadn't even had the chance to cheat. He could start over. She could use her maternal and professional judgment and simply have him start over. She'd file a note on the matter to indicate that next time around he'd require a special reminder. It would be fine.

And so, with nothing more than Sue's compassionate *redirection*, the boy scuttled back into the test room, a fresh copy of his test in hand. Once he was off, she typed up an email for her superior and copied his professor then slid the prohibited notes and the original test into a file to be submitted with the new test once he'd finished.

Within just half an hour, she received a reply to the email. It was from her superior and included in the *CC* the name of her superior's superior.

The response was long and painfully specific. Certain words leapt off the screen, accelerating her heartbeat and sending a lump to her throat: *academic integrity* and *student accountability* and *enabling behavior.* Her supervisor ended the whole thing with a classic admonishment, but one that Sue was startled to read with her own two eyes: *we need to have a meeting.* The icing on the whole crumbling cake was the reason for the meeting: Sue's *habitually poor judgment.*

The whole thing read like a dart to the heart. An accusation that said more about who Sue was as a person than a worker. The email could be a career-tipping consequence of her third strike in the office. But those last three words were the worst of it. The nails in the coffin on who Sue was. *How* she was.

Even so, as Sue closed down her computer and collected her knock-off purse from the space at her feet, all ready to head into her boss's back office and receive a final write-up or even a termination notice, she frowned and tugged the envelope from her pants' pocket.

She couldn't make Shepherd's pie without potatoes.

Chapter 4

Bea

Bea expected to wake up on the one-year anniversary of her sister's death and feel like the bad dream was over. She expected some kind of magic—closure or acceptance. Instead, she felt like it was happening all over again. Like any minute she'd get that dreadful phone call and schlep up to Westboro Heights and sit awkwardly at the security station where she had to explain to a bored sentinel *why* she was there. And worse, to learn that the perfect stranger already *knew*. That's how those things worked in Westboro Heights. The right people knew. And it made everything all the more real.

And yet, despite the fresh wave of pain, that very morning, she collected her mother. They stopped at a florist, purchased a lovely bouquet, then made the trip up to Westboro Mortuary where Sophia was laid to rest among her dead in-laws. Bea could manage that. She could do that. She had to, anyway.

After a tearful hour staring at Sophia's side of the marble slab she'd one day share with Greg, Bea dutifully drove her mother back to her rowhouse just outside the city.

But once they arrived, the engine idling in the early summer heat, her mother didn't budge.

"Have you been back there?" Dolores asked, her expression slack as she stared ahead emptily.

Bea knew what she was talking about. Yet, she asked, "Huh?"

Dolores turned to her and waited.

"No." Bea dropped her chin to her chest.

Out of the corner of her eye, Bea could spy Dolores nod. "Well, thank you for driving me," her mother replied, then unbuckled herself and left the car, wobbling up the stoop and disappearing inside the place where Bea and Sophia grew up; a happy home filled with happy memories.

Even when some family members prodded her to move, Dolores had no interest. To some, she was *too comfortable. Too content!* To Bea and Sophia, however, their mother was happy, the happy widow of a pensioner at home on her old-timey Philadelphia block with her window box flowers and three-step stoop and the newspaper slapping on the concrete at five o'clock every morning.

A deep sigh collected in Bea's chest, and she pushed it out hard. Lunch would be nice right about then. Maybe on a patio. She picked up her phone and considered who to call. Her coworkers? She wasn't in the mood for work talk. Her neighbor? She wasn't in the mood for small talk.

Since they were old enough to go out for lunch together, at a café where the cappuccino was pricey and the salads too green, Sophia had always been Bea's first choice. And, she liked to think, Bea had been Sophia's.

Was it a mistake? Putting all her eggs in one basket? Was it a dire mistake with dire consequences? It felt like that right about then, as Bea scrolled through her hollow list of contacts. It felt like a very stupid thing.

Then again, Diane *had* reached out... and about a get-together that was far more elaborate than a simple lunch date. But even so, Diane hated the city. And besides, she was probably out to lunch with the Ladies Auxiliary or wives of the Knights of Columbus (it wouldn't bother Diane to be the only one who wasn't technically a wife).

Sue should have been free. But Sue lived clear across the greater Philadelphia area. And more likely than not she was at Joe's beck and call on the weekends.

The morbid side of Bea briefly contemplated grabbing a turkey sandwich to go, driving back up to Westboro, and setting a picnic in front of that marble stone— the stone belonging to the Angelos couple, one still around and the other gone and in her place nothing more than a stone.

It occurred to Bea that headstones were like the other bookend of a marriage. One being the engagement ring, shiny and new, the other being that thick slab pointing up from the earth, beckoning future cemetery walkers to come click their tongues over the wife who died too young.

Bea quashed the anger rising up inside, the anger that there was no one to have lunch with.

It was one of the most hollow feelings in her life— having nowhere to be and no one to share it with.

Briefly weighing her options, Bea realized that she could *still* technically go have lunch on a patio somewhere. She could *still* stick her feet out from the shade of the bistro umbrella and warm them in the sun as she sipped an iced tea and escaped in one of her romance books (Bea's favorite and only guilty pleasure). She could *still* scroll through her phone, pretending to plan a stay-cation, perhaps, or maybe put together an online shopping cart and then promptly exit out of the browser when she remembered that she *still* hadn't paid that month's mortgage.

Ultimately, the only real option was to swing into a greasy drive-through on the way home.

There would be no phone call. No giggly, gossipy bistro sandwich to munch into as she listened to Sophia drone on about what it was like to be on the other side of the parent-teacher conference.

All there was for Bea now was the end of another school year and two lonely months, the time without the promise of courting periodic text messages from other mourners who were checking in on her. This summer, destitute and empty, would be all Bea's own. Her first since she was a baby and too young to recall having such an expansive, useless thing to herself.

And then, just as she'd punched the plastic straw through the jagged little hole at the center of her Diet Coke lid, her phone buzzed in the second cupholder.

Bea swooped it up and half-expected to see an auto-mated reminder to pay her cell phone bill or perhaps a text-memo from her new, fresh, hip principal who preferred pep assemblies to standardized tests. Either one would be welcome. She'd take any distraction.

Then again, it could be another promotional email promising fifteen percent off all swimsuits—the one sort of deal Bea could easily resist on the simple grounds that she'd sworn off swimsuits five years back.

But, no, it was none of the above.

At first, in fact, Bea didn't even catch the name of the sender because she was so distracted by the image preview in the text notification.

It was a picture of a familiar house.

A white shore house. The one just south of the boardwalk. The one she hadn't been to in years.

She ignored Greg's name and the message that *it was time* (why did people always say that after someone died?). She ignored the mock-up of a real estate listing that he'd thrown together to woo her along in the *right direction*.

Bea squeezed her eyes shut, set the phone back into the cupholder, leaned back into her seat and forced herself to dredge out the memory.

———

IT WAS the last time she and Sophia took a trip down the shore together—Aunt Lil's funeral.

Sue would have attended, but she was pregnant and scared to travel. Turned out she'd lost the baby anyway.

Diane showed up with Craig and Brittany, which basically meant that Diane wasn't there, either.

Bea and Sophia were the only two who would sleep in the shore house since Dolores preferred to stick to the motel and stay out of her husband's family affairs. Greg kept Matt home, claiming that it wasn't a place or an event for a young kid. Bea had raised an eyebrow at Sophia, but Sophia was masterful. Bea didn't realize it then, but she knew how to spin things.

"He's right," she'd argued. "Research suggests that at Matt's age, it's just not appropriate. I think it's more meaningful if it's just you and me, Bea. You know?" She sounded like a robot version of Sophia. *Research suggests?* *Appropriate?* Who had her sister become by then? Bea brushed off the pretense and accepted Greg and Sophia's stance, still caught in the pleasure of a weekend away with her sister; still willing to ignore anything and everything just to be with her.

The trip was brief, lasting just a weekend and entirely devoid of the usual shore activities. They kept to the business at hand, and when Bea, on Sunday night, suggested they go out for drinks, Sophia declined, preferring instead to make some hard decisions then and there before they were out of time.

They disagreed on almost every detail. Sophia wanted to reno and rent out, per Greg's suggestion. Bea wanted it all to stay exactly the same. No changes. At all.

Still, a compromise was formed.

They would reno and keep it for future vacations on the specific grounds that Bea and Sophia actually *used* the house. Bea even recalled the clammy handshake she shared with her sister, marveling at how small and strong Sophia's hands were.

It would turn out, of course, that no such vacations ever took place. Bea had the distinct feeling Sophia wanted it that way, as if she was punishing Bea for not getting her way. Punishing her for something, at least.

So, it was ironic, then, that the only one who would ever return to their slice of heaven on earth was Sophia.

And when she did, there would be no Bea or Diane or Sue. There would be no sneaking up to Wildwood for a night. No games of Truth or Dare. No Summer Society.

That silly little club had dissolved years before. Back when Sophia was still perfect and Bea was still a good sister.

———

"Give me this summer, please," she said over the phone, two fingers pinching the bridge of her nose, holding off the headache. It was humiliating, talking to her brother-in-law like that. Had Sophia done it too? Begged for mercy every time there was something she wanted from him? Bea couldn't picture it.

For Sophia, there was probably a different route into Greg's wallet. Still, who knew what went on behind the closed doors of a marriage? And especially in that one—the perfect kind with the gorgeous housewife and Greek God of a husband.

The Angelos family didn't own any other property in Gull's Landing, of course. They didn't own property down the shore, period.

Greg's family did, however, have a second home in the Hamptons and one in Vegas. He and Sophia used both, relegating Aunt Lil's kitschy three-bedroom on the beach to last place in the Angelos family playbook. It didn't matter what the property was worth now. It didn't matter that property taxes in Gull's Landing outpaced those in Stone Harbor.

Then again, apparently it did.

Greg said something off of the receiver, though to whom Bea couldn't tell. His voice came back on. "Yeah, okay."

"Okay?" she replied, her fingers flying to her mouth. "You're sure?"

"Yeah, take the summer, Bea. But we revisit this in September, all right?"

She nodded urgently, thanking him up and down.

Who knew? Maybe she'd pull together a few thousand and get herself established so she could take over the taxes and utilities and upkeep and *poof*, no problem, Aunt Lil's *other favorite* niece would ride into the sunset on the shore with her teacher's salary in one hand and the keys to the shore house in the other.

But even if she didn't get the money, she could at least have one last summer. One chance to go through all of Aunt Lil's stuff. One chance to be there again and drink it in—the best times of her life.

The only problem was that there was more to that house than happy memories from her youth. Something else lived in there, still. Some*one*, even.

Bea was not ready to return to the haunted old shore house—the one with Aunt Lil's painted face resting peacefully in the parlor. The one where Sophia—

She *could* ask her mom to go with her.

No. She couldn't. For one, Dolores Russo had made it clear that they could burn the place to the ground, and she'd be happy as a clam. For two, Dolores didn't *go* anywhere. The trip up to Westboro was as far as she was able to travel.

So, there she was, without the money or the strength. The strength to return to the place where they used to have it all. The place that made Soph and Bea more than sisters—the place that made them friends.

And then, later, enemies.

Bea thanked Greg over and again, put the phone down, sank into her kitchen chair and drummed her fingertips on the kitchen table until a good idea came to her.

And in one stroke of luck, it did.

There were others she could ask to go with her. Others she could *trust*. Who would understand.

Bea grabbed her phone again and began to scroll

through her contacts only to realize there was no way she could talk about it.

She couldn't share the situation over the phone or in a text. A phone call, well—there was no possible way of conveying the scenario without crumbling into a mess of sobs. And a text? She wasn't a teenager, and this wasn't the homecoming dance.

The whole thing called for something more than a call or a text or a message on social media.

Maybe an email would be better. She opened her phone again and clicked on her email icon, only to realize that she did not have Diane's email address. And Sue's was a work email from the late nineties. What kind of a friendship did they even have anymore? The kind where they'd show up at funerals and wring their hands? The kind where they'd text each other about a vacation and so easily brush it off until—

Bea blanched at her own stupidity on that one. She'd had a perfect chance to get back together with her old friends. And she'd chucked it out to the ocean like a brittle seashell. But maybe Greg's pressure was the wave that was washing it back to shore.

A letter.

Yes. She'd write a letter.

One to Diane, and one to Sue. Bea *did* have their mailing addresses. That was the sort of tidbit of information someone like Bea Russo clung to. Not email addresses.

Pushing off the table, she strode to her makeshift office area on the bar and slid her thick, spiral bound address book from its slot behind the standing file. Bea kept her address book meticulously updated, and when she turned to the D section, there it was, plain as day.

Diane De Luca-Bettancourt. Lynnecliff, PA (the hyphen was Bea's annotation).

And then, when she flipped to M:

Susan Merkle-Bleckert. West Mifflin, PA (again, with the hyphen).

Content to have a good plan, she slipped two blank sheets of stationery from their sleeve in the back of the address book and a pen from her cup and scrawled on the first page:

Dear Diane—

A million openings came to mind. Everything she taught her language arts students to use in their friendly letter lessons. Everything she taught them *not* to use, too. Clichés. Hooks. Silly things that would turn the reader off or make the writer sound like a loon.

Bea chewed on her lower lip and thought for a moment, even tugged the first page back to mark it up with a little outline.

But when she returned to actually write the darn thing, she felt lost. What could she possibly say?

Dear Diane… sorry I didn't want to go down the shore last fall, but I do now…

No. Dumb.

Dear Diane… I'm writing Sue, as well. I need your help desperately…

Humiliating. Wrong.

Dear Diane… How have you been? I've been…

Psh.

Dear Diane… Will you escort me to Aunt Lil's shore house because I'm scared to go in there, and then can you give up your entire summer to stay there with me so I can cling to the one thing that I have to remember my dead sister by???

She crumpled both pages and chucked them toward

the close-lidded trash can and then fell into a heap on top of the bar.

Her eyes closed, Bea hummed to herself until a new idea came to mind.

She sat up straight and grabbed her box of mish-mashed greeting cards, shuffling through until she found them, her hands shaking: a collection of postcards, curated over the years from any vacation she'd ever taken—a couple from New York and D.C., one from Florida. One from Vegas when she'd once joined Sophia for a weekend there years back. Most of them, however, were marked across the upper corner with *Gull's Landing* in easy, casual script. The whole lot of them now felt dated and silly, but still...

They would have to do. It would be weird and maybe even creepy, but they would have to do.

A postcard was the best way—the *only* way—to say *nothing* and *everything* all at once.

And after that, she'd pack.

And she'd go there—to Gull's Landing... where there was *nothing* and *everything*.

Chapter 5

Diane

S ummer had arrived. At least in Diane's world, where summer started when Philly got that late burst of winter again, complete with slushy rain that washed up against her house and shook its finger at her for not working out once in the past six weeks.

For a long while there, she'd been good. Really good. Diane would normally start her summer-ready regime on New Year's Day and stick to it right up until the family trip to Playa del Carmen. That's where Craig would take his two girls. They'd fly down first class (a treat, even for the De Lucas), force Brittany to use her pocket English-Spanish dictionary until they found the private shuttle that swept them down the humid streets to their timeshare.

Once there, Diane was typically about ten pounds lighter than she was the December earlier, so she felt free to indulge in daily daiquiris and greasy Mexican appetizers all day, every day as she lounged like a queen under a cabana (as opposed to the beach that spread out on just the other side of the infinity pool—the mother and daughter were less interested in how pristine the sand was and how clear the water looked. Poolside menus and fast service trumped anything else).

Craig, never much for the water, spent his mornings golfing and afternoons at the resort spa or restaurant. If they happened to bump into each other and everyone was in a good mood, they'd eat together or take in the live music as a family. More often, the afternoons slipped away to sleepy evenings and soon enough the next day had begun, all suntan lotion and Banana Monkeys until they were on a plane back home, sun-scorched and at each other's throats for whatever squabble had erupted on the second-to-last day.

As good as those vacations could be, nothing Craig ever gave Diane could match the summers of her youth, and she hated that fact.

"Hey," she said into the phone.

"I'm heading in for a custody hearing," Craig replied. She could picture him glancing down at his leather-strapped watch, a neat briefcase weighing his arm back down as he strode through the metal detector and met up with some client—usually a woman scorned, though sometimes it was a man unable to let his wife go. That was Craig's world: custody battles for the parents and asset division for everyone else. Despite it all, he never claimed he didn't believe in marriage. He'd never grown cold to the institution and instead often argued that it was simply hard for the right two people to find each other in such a great big world. The fact that he and Diane got their own shiny new divorce didn't apparently weigh into his worldview.

Or maybe it did.

"Quick question," she replied. "Remember last year when you invited me to Cabo?"

"Right before Sophia—" he started but was either cut off by the security at the courthouse or his own inability to finish the sentence, Diane didn't know which.

"Yeah," she answered. "Right before that. Well, are you interested in making another go of it?"

That was how things went between Diane and Craig. They could take a vacation together if they wanted. Easy.

"Ah," he answered, his voice dropping lower. "I can't. I wish I could, but…"

"But what?" Diane's heartbeat doubled. She frowned.

"It's not a good time, Di. I'm sorry, but… it's not a good time."

Without another word, the line went dead.

———

IT WAS TUESDAY, and Diane didn't need to check her calendar to know that she was due for Tacos and margs with the girls at Viva la Salsa.

Diane, despite her loud voice and deep laugh and garish affect, was a private woman when it came to some things. So, when, two drinks into happy hour, her girl-friends eventually poked around about Craig and their bizarre relationship (such was a weekly interrogation), she didn't share what happened.

Not with them.

And later that night after a round of post-margarita fish tacos and two tall glasses of water, when she called Brittany on the drive home… she couldn't say anything either.

That was her agreement with Craig. It was their pact: anything to do with their relationship (or lack thereof) was none of Brittany's business. As far as she knew, her parents had a friendly, healthy relationship from which they would always offer their daughter level-headed advice and unconditional support.

Anyways, there was nothing *to* tell. Since the divorce, Diane and Craig were just that: two people in a friendly, healthy relationship.

So why, then, was Diane forcing down this new bubbling jealousy? Why did she desperately want to drive up to Craig's house in Briar Creek, pound on his door and demand to know *why* he couldn't join her for Cabo?

Because she knew. That's why. In her woman's heart, she knew exactly why.

But then, when she did turn up at his house, well past nine o'clock that very same Tuesday, all vim and vigor and wild dark tangles of hair against the night sky, her impression fell to pieces.

He answered the door clad in a white t-shirt and boxers, his face drawn as he ushered her inside. Diane saw his wrist was bare—no watch. He'd probably been in bed when she knocked. No one was there, other than Craig. The house was dim, and the kitchen table devoid of any little extras—no half-full bottle of wine or remnants of an elaborate meal (Craig loved to cook—another reason they made for a bad match).

She could have asked *Why no Cabo?*

Or *Who is she?*

Or *What happens next?*

But instead, she tucked herself into the crook of his sofa, the same one from their marriage, and held his hand. And listened.

———

SHE SPENT THE NIGHT. Slept in the guest room upstairs and trudged down for coffee the next morning. In some ways, Craig's secret felt like another death in the family. In some ways, it felt worse. It was the sort of thing that bled out over their lives, coating Diane in dread.

Cabo was out, and that was fine. It was the least of her worries now. And, in truth, she wasn't sure she had many others. At least, not on the surface.

After a small bowl of oatmeal and some quiet small talk, she left him. Diane hated to; under the circumstances, it felt like their divorce all over again. Each promised the other that things would be okay. Not to worry.

Still, as she dragged herself back to her own home, new questions entered her mind. Questions she'd never once had to answer in her whole entire life.

With a heavy sigh, Diane pulled her car in front of her mailbox, collected the thin stack she'd missed from the day before, then eased into the garage and slapped them down on the passenger seat before burying her head in her hands and screaming into her palms.

Everything was *perfect*.

And now it wasn't.

With no one in the world to turn to and share her turmoil, the only thing Diane could do was head inside, light a million candles, and sink into a hot soapy bathtub. She was due at the library in a couple of hours, and if she didn't get herself back in the right frame of mind, then there was no way she'd have the energy to give a tutorial on how to shade using colored pencils. Her coordination efforts for the Adult Coloring Club had recently turned to educational responsibilities, too.

Grabbing the mail and her purse and phone, Diane dragged herself from her vehicle, feeling all fifteen of those extra pounds she hadn't yet shrugged off.

Once inside, she dropped the mail and her purse on the side table and tapped a manicured nail on her phone screen, unwilling to let the drama with Craig settle into the cracks. She wasn't that sort of girl, Diane. She was a digger, a crap-stirrer, a problem-facer. *Not* a dweller or a mope.

Come over for dinner tonight. We can drink wine and talk.

She hit send and thought about Craig and what made him who he was and what he'd done... until the night before. As she passed from the hallway, her hip knocked into the side table, sending the letters skittering to the hardwood floor like oversized confetti.

She threw up her hands, then bent over and collected them, one by one. Two ads, one thick request for further help from a Catholic charity Diane had once donated to over five years back. The water bill. *Great.* And, a postcard.

Initially, she started to toss the postcard with the other junk. Who sent postcards anymore—other than clever marketing reps from car dealerships?

But the scene on the front of it caught her eye. The photograph was a familiar setting: a sandy beach in the foreground and behind that a stretch of boardwalk above which sat a row of business fronts. A beachwear boutique, a malt shop, and a dated-looking arcade. The whole front of the postcard, in fact, had an aged affect, as if it was fashioned to look like a memento of '90s nostalgia.

Diane knew the boutique and the malt shop, and she definitely knew that arcade. She remembered sticking to the Whack-a-Mole for one whole summer, convinced she was destined to break a hundred redemption tickets and snag a four-foot high teddy bear. She remembered sneaking behind the Skee-Ball lanes and kissing boys.

As if her memories from the photograph weren't enough to solidify her interest, the relaxed script across the corner was: *Gull's Landing.*

Diane flipped it over, half-expecting more ad copy. That's how the world worked anymore, if the wrong person got ahold of some of your interests in life, you could be sure they'd send a commercial your way, wherever and whenever.

But it wasn't an ad.

Nor was it a happy message from someone on vacation in Diane's old stomping grounds. No *Wish you were here!* or *Miss you, Mom! Be home soon!* like Brittany once sent when she went away for camp.

Instead, it read like a secret note, the kind Diane would pass in class back in middle school. Scrawled across the white space on the back was a date and a time and brief instructions to pack well. No mention of why or where. But then, along the right where the return address should go, the sender simply added:

The Summer Society.

And Diane knew exactly what to do.

Chapter 6

Sue

Sue didn't lose her job at the Center. She was, however, transferred. Instead of logging student data and overseeing the testing office, she recorded textbooks to tape. This job suited her in a couple of ways—she had a nice voice and enjoyed reading, after all.

However, now she didn't get to work *with* anyone. Some days, when she showed up at the building and stuffed her purse into a cubby in the employee lounge then went to get her assignment and the old-fashioned black tape recorder, she felt like her new position was a glorified time-out. A punishment. It probably was.

There, in the quiet back room with stacks of cassette tapes and thousands of hardbound pages for company, she'd peek up at the little window that hung too high on the wall and try to remind herself what season it was.

The initial benefit was that her isolation allowed her more freedom to sneak out her phone and send text messages to her husband or even her mother. Sometimes, she'd have a whole day's worth of texts with her sister-in-law, who'd recently taken an interest in Sue.

Being an only child had set Sue up to handle loneliness better than most. It had also set her up for a deep-rooted longing for meaningful relationships, however.

When it became apparent that her childhood friendships were over and done (no thanks to Sophia's untimely death), Sue mainly turned to Joe. Her renewed energy for their marriage was met with much the same. They rediscovered each other, enjoying weekly date nights and weekend outings.

One night over dinner, she offered her pinky finger and made him promise that they'd stick to their new normal.

And he did promise.

And it was perfect.

So, come the following morning, when the façade crumbled beneath her feet like rotted-out floorboards, it was all the more painful.

They showered together, she got ready, she left for work. Upon arriving at the office, Sue realized she'd left her purse at home, and so she told her boss she'd clock in half an hour later. She couldn't sit in that room all day without her phone.

But when Sue returned home, she quickly learned how wrong she was. How *imperfect* her life really was.

The whole scene was something out of a soap opera, and Sue figured everything was over.

She'd been stupid. Oblivious, probably.

An hour later—after Sue formally called in sick, which she really was—she sat at the kitchen table, her back rigid, nostrils flared, heart pounding in her chest. Joe paced nearby, talking a mile a minute. Half of what he said were justifications and accusations and excuses.

The other half were desperate pleas for forgiveness. Sue wasn't sure where she fit in all of it.

"We've been so good lately," she managed tearfully, twisting a paper towel in the palm of her hands. "I don't understand."

"We were going to end it today, Sue," Joe reasoned, stopping and bracing his hands on his hips. "That's why she was here. We were going to end it."

His use of the word *we* stung like a Tetanus shot, sending a throb through her body. A fresh round of tears folded her face in on itself and she hated that she was that way. The crying type. She hated everything.

"Sue, please," Joe whispered, lowering himself to her now and grabbing her hands from her face. "Please, don't do this."

Her crying stopped suddenly. *Don't do what?* she wanted to ask. But she had a suspicion. This was their black moment. The darkest hour just before dawn. He thought she was leaving. She knew that she *should* leave him. But now she had it: the power. The leverage.

"You're done with her, then?" she asked, leveling her chin at Joe, pathetic Joe with his hairy arms and fatty shoulders.

He made the sign of the cross, and Sue wanted to vomit.

"Good," she spat back, finding her footing.

"So, we're okay?" He leaned away, his face softening.

Sue blinked and swallowed. "No, *Joe*. How can we be okay?"

A hardness took over his face. "I can't change the *past, Susan*," he replied. She hated when he called her Susan.

Her face crumpled again. She'd lost the upper hand.

Pitiful and wrecked, she merely nodded in response. "No, you can't."

He stood and began to pace again. "Whaddya want from me, anyway? Ever since—well, you know ever since *back then* you've been hard to live with. But now things are better, and I was going to end it, Sue, I was. I don't know what you want from me, Sue." At last, he fell into the chair at the end of the table. The one where he took his supper, when he was home to take it.

She rubbed the paper towel across her eyes and wondered why she'd stopped wearing makeup. She made it easy for him to look elsewhere. She couldn't recover from the death of her dreams, she'd slipped into a depression, and through it all she was her same, wimpy self. The little girl in her had turned into an uptight, nervous adult. Geeky 4H-participant with a brace face and glasses turned into a fearful introvert who counted calories and returned her library books on time. And Joe, the regional manager with a beer gut and a preference for *his mother's* Shepherd's pie, didn't ever live up to his potential either. He never finished his degree like he said. He never took the realtor course, either. He wasn't a book-guy, he said. He was a people-guy.

"I wanted a marriage from you, Joe," she whispered at last. "But it looks like I can't have it."

At that, he pushed his chair roughly behind him, and it fell to the floor as he swept dramatically toward her again, lowering onto one knee and grabbing her hands. "No, no, no, Sue, don't do this. I'll change. I swear. We'll get through it. She's a goner, Sue. It's just you and me, babe."

Sue had heard it all by then. And none of his pleas or excuses or rationalizing would change one thing: her total and utter humiliation.

She tore her hands from his, packed a bag, and went to her mother's house for the night.

Once there, she claimed their house was being fumigated. Joe was on a business trip. And she vowed to keep it all to herself until she made a decision. After all, what good would the truth do? That would just result in a mess. Sue might be weak-willed, but she had a strong mind. A quiet, thoughtful, *strong* mind.

The whole mess needed containment. So, she decided to keep it a secret. Her secret. Not for Joe. Not for their so-called marriage. But for her pride.

And she did. Even after she returned home the very next evening and his car wasn't in the driveway, she buried that secret deeper. And she buried it deeper and deeper, over the course of two weeks, during which they did a dance around the house—he apologizing each morning, promising he'd go back to church with her, promising he'd see a therapist; her keeping quiet and planning. Plotting. Preparing.

At the end of the two weeks, on a perfectly ordinary Tuesday in May when the weather was taunting her with hot days and rainy ones, she went to work.

Once there, tucked in the corner of her makeshift recording studio, she withdrew a blank envelope and a stubby pencil and charted a little plan for herself. A fresh start. But when she made a list of all the people she could turn to: the ones who, unlike her mother, wouldn't pass judgment... the ones who would welcome her with open arms and shake some life back into her... she almost came up empty.

Almost.

———

1974

Her mother had enrolled Susan in CCD at St. Mary of the Angels. She was a year behind since they'd bounced around for the past while, but that only mattered socially. The nuns were more focused on who took a second cookie during snack and anyways, Susan already knew the Lord's Prayer, Hail Mary, and even the Apostles' Creed, not to mention the supper blessing and her bedtime Rosary. So, at seven years old, she was swept directly into the First Communion Class, even though they were just one week away from the real deal.

Another blonde little girl there, Sophia, introduced herself to Susan, complimenting her chapel veil during the rehearsal.

"What are you going to repent for?" Sophia whispered as they kneeled quietly in the last pew and waited for the priest.

Scared she'd get in trouble, Susan just shrugged and squeezed her eyes shut.

"I'm repenting because I kissed Richie Warren on the playground."

Susan's eyes grew wide. She'd never even wanted a boy to kiss her, let alone gone out and pushed her lips on one of them. Sophia must have been a wild girl.

"Do you think I'm bad?" Sophia whispered louder.

Susan peeked around, waiting for a nun to come up behind and swat her on the rear for talking. The only way to hush the chatty girl was to answer, so she just shook her head and whispered, "No."

"So, how about you?" Sophia went on.

Susan began to sweat. Her heart raced in her chest, like it might tear through her skin and detach itself from her body. She was about to die in the back pew of St.

Mary's of the Angels without ever tasting the body and blood of Christ. Would she go to Purgatory? Or was that just if she hadn't been baptized?

"Shh," she hissed back, now more concerned for her salvation than her manners.

But Sophia didn't seem to mind. Instead of bristling or tattling, she murmured an apology.

It was only a week later, after the white-clad group of girls had completed their sacrament, that the two spoke again.

"I'm sorry about last week," Sophia said over doughnuts and apple juice in the Family Center next to the chapel.

Susan shifted her gaze toward her mother, who was chatting with a nice-looking couple who wore nice clothes.

The Communion class had broken up after mass, but now Susan found herself sitting on a metal chair across from Sophia and two other, older girls, both dark-haired.

"It's okay," Susan replied, before nibbling with focus on a cinnamon twist.

"I was nervous," Sophia went on, talking with a full mouth.

The girl to Sophia's left broke in. "Nervous about what?"

"About Penance," Sophia answered.

The second girl leaned forward, her dark hair falling over the second doughnut on her plate. The first was still in her hand. "What did you confess to, Soph?"

"I was going to confess about kissing Richie Warren, but I chickened out."

"It's not a sin to kiss a boy," the first dark-haired girl said, matter-of-factly.

"It is when you're eight years old," the second added, taking a big bite of her cruller.

Susan frowned. "I'm never going to kiss a boy," she admitted, tentatively inserting herself in such a grown-up conversation.

"Sure you will," Sophia said. "You just gotta find the right one, ya know?"

The other dark-haired girls giggled, but Sophia just waved them off and smiled conspiratorially at Susan. "This is my big sister, Bea and my cousin, Diane."

"Hi," the one with two doughnuts chimed in, sticking her hand out. "Nice to meet you; what's your name?"

"Susan Merkle," she answered, shaking the girl's hand.

"Nice to meet you, Susan Merkle," Bea said, smiling.

"Do your friends call you Susie or anything?" Diane added.

Susan swallowed and flicked a glance toward Sophia. Susan didn't have any friends. Not yet. Should she?

"I call her Sue," Sophia answered smartly, dabbing her mouth with a paper napkin and smiling at Susan.

"Oh yeah?" Diane asked, arching a dark eyebrow. "Since when?"

Susan wanted to melt into the floor. She kept her eyes down and tucked her lips between her teeth.

"Since we became friends last week," Sophia shot back. "Right, Sue?"

Her eyes flitted up, and she saw that the beautiful, boy-kissing blonde girl with chestnut skin and bright green eyes wasn't making fun of her. She wasn't laughing or playing. She was serious.

And just like that, on the same day as her very First Holy Communion, Susan—or Sue, she supposed—had also made her very first friend.

———

HER PHONE BUZZED in her pocket, and Sue realized she'd only managed to get one name down on her list.

She glanced at the door, then pulled her phone out, curious ever since her conversations with Joe's sister had run dry. Not many others sent her texts mid-morning. Not even her mother, who was more likely to message or call during lunch.

It was neither her sister-in-law nor her mother, however.

It was Joe.

She hadn't spoken directly to him in the past two weeks.

The text he sent had no message, it was just a picture.

Two tickets to San Diego, California.

Not once had Sue ever said she wanted to go to San Diego. But did she want to go? Well, sure. She'd love to get to the West Coast and see what all the hubbub was about. Still, she'd never said that. Not to Joe. So, where did he get the tickets? And why?

She had two choices: assume the worst and say no. Or ignore her nervous instincts for once in her life and say *yes*. Yes to a vacation, yes to her husband, and yes to… a different kind of fresh start.

Was that it? Was that what he was doing? Starting fresh? Was that what everyone always talked about when their lives were sliding downhill? *You need a fresh start! A new beginning! A second chance!*

Maybe. Maybe it was time for that in Sue's life. To give her marriage another go.

So, without a second thought, she replied.

Yes.

Yes, she would go to San Diego.

Then, she wrote a second one.

I'll take both.

A small grin formed on her mouth as she pictured Joe's dumb looking face at his meek wife's sudden turn. But she would. She would take both tickets, and she'd find someone to go to San Diego with her. Maybe a student worker. Maybe her mother.

Maybe... maybe she'd take both tickets—pluck them from Joe's sausage fingers—then spin on a heel and ask if he was coming *or what?* And she'd play *him* for once.

But in the throes of all that newfound rage and confidence and vim and vigor, she got a piece of mail. A piece of mail that shut her down and made her question what in the world she was going to do with two airplane tickets to San Diego and one dead marriage.

It was a postcard. A postcard with a photo of Gull's Landing and a date and a time in the very, very near future, signed *The Summer Society*... and Sue wondered what, exactly, was the difference between returning to the past and heading into the future. When it came to new beginnings, maybe there was no difference at all.

Chapter 7

Bea

Bea drove alone. What other choice was there? She drove alone all the way down to Gull's Landing, veering through tolls and coasting clear down to the little white house on the southern edge of the boardwalk—just yards from the beach, at the corner where the sun-worn boards met the white sand.

She parked her car in the space between the house and the last business on the south side of the boardwalk. Then, she sat for a moment, wondering if Diane and Sue got her postcards. Wondering if they'd call her or text her or write her off entirely for being a nutso. She wouldn't blame them.

Glancing up to her left, onto the boardwalk's end, Bea rolled her windows down and took a deep breath, inhaling the smells of the shore. The salt air curled across her and wrapped her in old memories, but her attention focused anew on a small group of teenagers meandering from the wooden planks down a sandy set of steps and onto the beach. Each with a surfboard crooked awkwardly in their grips.

At the helm of the rubber-clad group, walked a man in his own wetsuit with a head of thick, dusty blond hair and a face weathered by the sun but not quite wrinkled. Not *old*. Just… aged. Maybe like how Bea thought of herself.

Curious and desperate for a distraction from her silly call to action, she left her car and stepped around it, walking to the edge of Aunt Lil's back fence that sank in waves along the white mounds. From that angle, she could see where the group had originated. Surf's Up.

It was the same surf shop from her youth, but with a new name and look. Cleaner and simpler. Less junk cluttering the walkway in front. No sidewalk sale racks full of bright shirts—sizes S and XL only.

She lifted her hand over her eyes and found the group again, on the space of sand just beyond Aunt Lil's backyard. A little line of teenaged bodies in rented wetsuits. The instructor, assumedly, kneeling on his board in the sand and gesturing about.

Bea had a sudden itch to kick off her shoes and jog out there and join them.

Sophia had always wanted to learn to surf. Maybe she had at some point in time. Maybe she had come down the shore with Matt, even. Maybe they took lessons together. Bea could picture her sister doing that, but it hurt her heart to realize that Sophia might have had a life full of little secrets. She might have been surfing for the past decade, and Bea wouldn't necessarily know. It wasn't as if Sophia came back from every vacation and gave Bea a running tally of every last thing she did. It wasn't as though Sophia continued sitting down to a lockable diary past the age of sixteen.

Before tears stabbed her eyes, Bea shook the thought and let herself into the backyard, where she settled into a weathered Adirondack chair and watched the fledgling group of surfers.

Weedy sand and errant clumps of sea debris caught her eye as she felt the chair creak beneath her weight. Neither she nor Sophia had done anything with Lil's yard—there was no upkeep, nothing to make it seem to others that anyone was around to care. That fact made Bea feel suddenly sadder than before. At least, however, Greg had purchased and installed security cameras. Then again, Bea had no idea if those were still operational. Supervision on the place was minimal, and she'd always wondered when they'd return to the house and find it vandalized.

Perhaps that dose of fear had settled deep enough in her heart that it was part of the reason that she preferred to sit and watch the sandy-haired man (in surprisingly good shape for his age, though not without a bit of a paunch in the unforgiving wetsuit) as he methodically pushed his pupils out to the water, one by one, like baby sea turtles.

She sat there for the length of their lesson, watching as most of them wobbled up and down, sinking into the waves and coming up for air, choking and laughing with the rush of the tide.

The scene reminded her of her childhood. Splashing in the surf and getting caught in rip tides—always a frightening thing that had driven Aunt Lil to tattle to the lifeguard that the girls weren't taking the beach rules seriously enough.

Bea's heart panged at the memory. Maybe she should have said yes to Diane the year before. Maybe she should have called them sooner. More often.

But she hadn't. All she could muster were the two quick postcards. Silly, but still.

In Bea's car awaited a menagerie of little things to draw them back in time—it was her way of preparing. Just in case they *did* show up and wanted to play a hand of cards on the back porch or bake a cheesecake from scratch. Just in case The Summer Society hadn't been washed out to sea after all those years.

She stood from the chair and turned up the path to Lil's back door, where she pushed a little brass key into the keyhole. And she waited.

Images of what lay beyond the door buzzed in her brain. The scene of it. The haunted house that Aunt Lil's had become not only with the old woman's passing and subsequent wake, but with her niece's death as well. Greg told Bea and Dolores all he knew, but he'd also said he left everything in its place—or at least, as it was left by the authorities—taking only her purse and cell phone back home with him.

In her mind's eye, Bea imagined that Sophia had sneaked down there on a secret renovation project. She imagined that the interior would be outfitted in chic new furniture with perfectly kitschy elements of Lil and their girlhood. She imagined an innocent place setting—maybe a stale turkey on rye on the table. She imagined a still life painting of her perfect sister with her green eyes, innocently reaching for her purse, distracted, perhaps, by a good commercial on the TV or maybe a phone call, even. She imagined exactly what Greg described, at first, at least: a perfect accident. A beautiful death. Simple. Clean. Neat. Just like Sophia always was.

Bea's eyes flitted down to her hand on the doorknob, and her gut clenched.

Leaving the keys there, she slowly backed away, thinking better of the whole ridiculous plan. Maybe Greg was right. Selling was for the best. Money aside, maybe that's even what Bea would do if it was her call to make.

Frozen there, she waffled between properly calling Diane and Sue and explaining away her idiocy and then, on the far other end of reason, just leaving the shore and returning home without a word about the whole thing.

"Are you in the market?"

Bea whipped around to the voice behind her. She spotted him just on the other side of the fence, his feet bare. His wetsuit was now peeled away from his torso, hanging around his waist beneath a dry white t-shirt.

"Pardon?" she asked, frowning and taking a tentative step off the porch.

"This house. Are you looking to buy?" he offered an earnest expression—something between a smile and a grimace.

Bea shook her head. "I'm sorry, but you are—?"

"Brooks Morgan," he replied and jutted a hand across the low pickets. "I own Surf's Up." He nodded his head to the shop just yards off.

She blinked, glanced around, then tried for a tight smile in return, allowing her legs to carry her down Lil's crumbling flagstone path to the fence. She pressed a hand to her chest. "Beatrice Russo. This was my aunt's place. My sister and I own it. For now." After they shook, her hand hung in the air for a moment; she quickly tucked it back to herself. "Did you, uh, *know* my sister?"

"The blonde woman? Angelos... right? Sonia?"

Bea's mouth twitched. "Sophia."

The man went on, accepting at face value his error and sweeping her back into the conversation like it was no big deal, her presence there or his or the fact of Sophia's death, for that matter. "No, I never saw her. I never saw anyone come here. Not until the police showed up, of course. It was a big deal around the boardwalk, ya know." A shadow crossed his face and he nodded past her to the house. "When the news crews showed up, I poked around." His gaze flashed back to his business front. "Can't be too careful. I wanted to know if it was a break-in or something."

"You mean…" she began, referring vaguely to the discovery of her sister's body and this Brooks person's implication of foul play.

He pressed his mouth into a thin line. "I'm sorry about what happened."

Bea crossed her arms and nodded. "Thanks."

"So, you're not looking to buy it, then." He smirked, and, impossibly, she smiled.

"What? Did my brother-in-law promise you a commission or something?" It was meant as a joke, but her voice came out flat. She cleared her throat. "He's going to see about listing it, is what I meant," she added for clarity.

He shook his head. "I have a place a block up. I just like to keep tabs. For all of us here."

Bea smiled faintly. "Well, thanks for that, I suppose."

Nodding, he took a step back, and she began to study him a little harder. Familiarity took the place of her unease. He was a local, new maybe. Still, verified, by all accounts—his surf shop and troop of would-be surfers. The deep tan and sun-kissed, salty-looking waves on top of his head. The cool confidence of someone who'd been around long enough to have a low tolerance for Shoobies.

"Brooks," she said at last, running the name through her lips, the last sound clicking on the back of her tongue. "I've never met anyone named Brooks."

He dipped his chin to her. "I've never met anyone named Beatrice."

"Call me Bea," she said spontaneously. She couldn't recall the last time she told someone to call her Bea. "I'll be here for a little while. I'm wrapping up my sister's affairs."

"You said you both owned this place. It was your aunt's?"

She stalled, piqued by his acute attentiveness. "Right. Yes. But like I said, we're selling now."

"You haven't been here much?"

Bea shook her head. "Not really. No one has been here in years. Well, except for—"

Brooks took another step away, closer to the board-walk and farther from Bea and the shore house and the odd interchange that had taken shape between them. "That's too bad," he said. "I gotta go. Come around if you need anything, all right?"

"Oh," she frowned and bit her lower lip, raising her voice to add, "Sure. Thanks, Brooks."

"See ya, Bea!" he called as he jogged up the steps and vanished inside and out of sight.

Bea decided then and there that she *was* staying.

And as for Diane and Sue? Well, now they had no choice. She'd called a meeting of The Summer Society. And the other girls *had no choice.* They were the founding members, too. They had to come. It was mandatory.

Especially when Bea turned back to the house and

froze. If her friends didn't show up soon, she'd be sleeping in the Adirondack chair.

Because without them, there was still no way she could step a foot inside. Not even with a handsome surfing shopkeeper nearby.

Chapter 8

Bea, 2009

"I can't go in there." Bea paced the street side of the shore house; Sophia and Diane watched her.

"What're you talking about, Bea? You've been in there the whole weekend." Diane's voice was devoid of compassion, as per usual.

"I know, but she's *in* there, now."

In her final will and testament, Aunt Lil had requested an in-home vigil. With Uncle Sammy long gone, there'd been no one to talk any sense into her, and so, there she was. In her front parlor. The space that, in life, Lil called the sitting room. How fitting.

"Is it an open casket?" Diane asked, huddling against the chill of the late fall breeze. Brittany and Craig had already gone in, and Bea could feel her friend's desperation to return to them. To get away from her, the insecure victim of her aunt's death.

"Yes," Sophia answered, stepping into the street and stubbing out her cigarette before bending to collect it.

Sophia didn't smoke, but one of the cousins had offered it up, and she'd taken it, resting the thin paper tube elegantly between her fingers like a movie star until its ember crawled up far enough that she could douse it. "Aunt Lil wanted a show."

Diane laughed. "She would, wouldn't she?"

Bea had stopped pacing and now held the corner of the white picket fence that wrapped around to the front of the house. The wood was long in need of a paint job, and Bea suddenly felt a rush of emotion envelope her. First, she had to plan the funeral, now she had to attend the funeral, next she'd have to clean up, and then... who knew what was next for the property? Would they have to sell? Did Lil have some arcane clause about turning her house into a boardwalk museum? Or maybe everything would fall into an estate sale, and Bea would be forced to witness strangers picking through what ought to have been her and her sister's inheritance. It was all too daunting.

"Did she plan her own death, too?" Diane asked. "Or maybe predict it?"

Sophia snorted. "Diane, now's not the time."

"No, no. I mean it. With her cards. Was she still reading them?"

Bea swallowed. "Yeah. She was. I don't know if she read her own death, though. She was getting a little loony towards the end."

"Yeah," Sophia agreed. "In her last wishes, she even detailed what she wanted to wear for her wake."

Diane held a hand over gaping mouth. "Tell me she's in a bathing suit."

Bea couldn't help it. A smile drew across her lips.

By the time she worked up the courage to go inside and join the few other mourners—Lil had far outlived most of her girlfriends—Diane had already reunited with Craig and Brittany. Sophia, for her part, put on the hostess act, seeing to it that everyone had a beverage and that the fruit and cheese platters weren't too mucky.

The sudden absence of her two friends forced Bea to collect the strength to stand at the casket. There, she studied the woman whom she'd grown up with. For all the time that had passed, Aunt Lil looked exactly the same. Perhaps that was an effect of the mortician's careful work... or that Aunt Lil had dallied with the mortician some years earlier—after Sam's passing of course. Maybe he wasn't normally so good with bringing a person back to life. Maybe he was gripped by the loss of his sometimes partner, too.

Aunt Lil's bleached-out hair outlined her face like cotton candy—sweet and light and nearly pink it was so processed. A bright shade of blue coated her eyelids and peachy blush warmed the hollow skin that stretched from her black painted lashes (falsies, perhaps?) down to her coral-frosted lips. The colors glowed against deep wrinkles, and despite the formal occasion, ol' Lil's leathery cleavage protruded from a lacy white robe—her favorite swimsuit cover. For such a thin, small woman, a great deal of handiwork must have gone into fixing Lil up to look like a living doll version of herself, and the sight was at once jarring and comforting, as though Lil was looking down from above and laughing at her corpse as it lay there, stuffed and primed and propped just so.

Bea signed the cross and clutched a heavy Rosary against her chest as her throat grew tight.

Then she fled through the house and out to the backyard, where she stood at the edge of the beach.

She stayed there for a long while, watching as a few people walked the beach. Summer, of course, was over.

The crowds of tourists had thinned considerably, and Bea wondered what it was like to be a local in such a place. She had a sense. Spending so many summers and meeting so many locals had afforded her bits of insight. She considered herself a part-time townie, like something out of the movies. Dangerously straddling the line that separated an appreciation for the summer business and a resentment for the Shoobies' intrusion on their natural habitat.

Bea would much rather straddle the line and be an almost-local than a tourist. The tourists were rotten, by and large.

"You okay?"

It was Sophia's voice behind her, soft and sweet, playing foil to the sounds of waves crashing in the distance.

Bea nodded and turned around. "Are you?"

A frown materialized on her little sister's mouth, but before she could answer, Bea scoffed. "What am I saying? Of course, you are." She smiled through furrowed eyebrows at Sophia and took her sister's hands in her own. "You've got your boys. You'll be okay, right?"

Sophia opened and shut her mouth without a word, working at something. "Bea," she started after several moments and half a dozen blinks.

Bea lifted a brow. "Yeah?" Their hands broke away, and Sophia hugged herself.

"You think I have it good, don't you?"

Balking, Bea coughed into her fist. "What do you mean? You do have it good. You have a beautiful life, and a full one. Greg. Matt. Come on. It's nothing like mine. I'm going home to a stack of papers to grade and a dishwasher full of cups and plates to put away. If I'm lucky, maybe there will be a voicemail from the guy I went out with two weeks ago. That's asking a lot, though." She laughed, trying for self-deprecation. Deep down, Bea's life was so empty that she *depended* on her sister to have the one that she'd built up in her mind. The one that Sophia flashed to the world like a two-carat diamond—significant yet tasteful.

Sophia glanced down and nodded. "My life isn't perfect, Bea." It came out as low as a whisper, but Bea heard every syllable.

"Why not? Because of Aunt Lil?" Bea wasn't delusional. Of course no one's life was perfect, but Sophia would have to be dense to claim hers wasn't as close as possible. It was. It *had* to be.

Frowning deeper, Sophia shook her head. "Why do you do that?"

"Do what?" Bea shot back.

"Paint me as some… some damn princess or something?"

The bad language came out of nowhere, and Bea glanced beyond her sister. "Soph, whoa. What's the problem?"

"You need me to be this goddess or something, Bea. You hold me up on pedestal, and you refuse to let me down, you know that? I can feel it, you know. I have felt it forever."

Bea started to shake her head, but Sophia went on.

"I'm not perfect, just like you aren't. Okay? I have bad days, you know. I'm not some Type-A mom who has it all together."

At that, Bea replied, "Yes, *you are*, Soph. Come on. You have your little planner and you get your roots touched up on time, and your house is clean, and you cook healthy food. You do have it together, Soph. What's so wrong with that? It's a *good* thing, you know." It wasn't an accusation. It was the truth. A complimentary one, at that. And Bea meant every word. But she didn't know why her sister took it as a slight. "Sophia, it's a *good* thing. I wish I had half the life you have. I'm being serious. Soph, I am proud of you." It killed Bea to see that somewhere, somehow along the way, she'd gone wrong. Her praise had turned to something else. And the guilt that had settled deep in her stomach started to boil back to life.

"You just can't let me be normal, you know that, Bea? You refuse to let me just be—"

"Everything okay, girls?" Diane appeared at the back door.

The two nodded vigorously and strode back up to the house, each with her arms wrapped about herself as the temperature nosedived with the setting sun.

The rest of the weekend, after the Mass and the burial and the goodbyes to family and friends—locals and out-of-towners alike—Bea couldn't shake her conversation with Sophia. The incompleteness of it, dangling in her chest like a threat. But each time she broached the matter in an effort to rehash and make nice, prodding Sophia gently about her world and the elements that made it up, Sophia batted her down, assuring Bea that she was right. Her life was good. She was silly to pretend otherwise and silly to be so defensive. So sensitive. Besides, they had other things to worry about, like the plan for the shore house and Lil's belongings.

But before they parted ways Monday morning, Bea stopped her little sister as she folded herself into her car. "Soph, I'm sorry for our fight. I'm sorry I said you were so perfect, okay?"

In response, Sophia plastered a smile across her lips

—full, pink lips that pretended to smoke a cigarette for a cousin she hadn't seen in ages... lips that spoke kind words to the funeral guests and gratitude to the priest and comfort to the mortician who broke down during the burial and sobbed quietly as he crumbled a handful of sand onto the casket.

"Bea, you were right. I am as perfect as they come. Really, I am. I promise. You have *nothing* to worry about."

Chapter 9

Diane

She slammed her car door and cried out, "Take my head off why don'tcha!" A missile of a car sped away up the road that divided the beachfront properties and the boardwalk from the rest of Gull's Landing. It felt a little like being home, there, at Lil's house, the cramped street-side parking and crazy drivers just paces from the inviting Atlantic.

Diane had spent the whole drive thinking back on the last time she was down the shore. The old bat's funeral. The in-home wake. Brittany begging her to get a shore house, and Craig reminding them that they had timeshares across Mexico that sat waiting.

Diane's thoughts eventually veered ahead in time toward Sophia's funeral, and she couldn't escape the facts surrounding her cousin's death and how the shore house sat there on the beach, complicit in the tragedy.

At that point on the drive, her foot grew a little heavier on the gas. Her hand itched with the temptation to call up Bea or Sue and ask what in the world they were going to do. Was it all a prank? A practical joke among old friends? Some trick to see if Diane still remembered?

But she kept her assumptions in check, staying the course all the way until she pulled to a stop in front of the white house with its washed-out picket fence and sun-beaten broadside.

The whole property appeared to have been left behind. Diane had been under the impression that Bea and Sophia were renovating it and maybe renting it out as an Airbnb, but it looked like no one had been there in ages, despite the fact that someone had definitely been there just a year before.

She popped her trunk and grabbed the brown Trader Joe's bags—one with an oversized bottle of organic champagne and orange juice and the other with snack foods. The cryptic invitation gave no specifics, and Diane refused to show up unprepared. If she arrived and neither Bea nor Sue were around, she fully intended to break into the shore house and camp out for a couple of days. Who knew? Maybe it was a hoax, and she'd turn it all around and even invite her *other* friends. Maybe the Book Club gals would be up for a weekend down the shore? They could join her as long as they left Jane Austen at home.

Her eyes glanced off the front of the house and landed on the silver sedan in the single parking spot to the left, squashed up against the railing of the boardwalk.

Bea's face appeared at the side of the car, suspicious then pleased. "Diane?" she called, waving like a nut. "You came!"

Diane grinned and strode with a purpose, her hand

thrusting the bags high up in the air, victoriously. "Thank God you're here. I was a little worried that someone decided to lure me out here and hold me hostage or murder me or something." She winced at the bad joke, but Bea hugged her anyway. Hard.

Then she squeezed Diane's shoulders and repeated herself. "You *came*."

"I had no choice, hun," she replied, moved at the poor thing's surprise.

"What do you mean?" Bea asked.

"I mean *us*. Old times. Our *pact*."

Bea took the bags and laughed. "Yeah, well, that's what I was going for, I guess. I can't believe you even remember."

"How could I forget? And besides, it was originally *my* idea that we take this trip. I knew it was only a matter of time before you hijacked it and played it off as your own." Diane laughed, and Bea did, too, as she pulled two duffle bags from her trunk and waved Diane around the back.

"I didn't hijack anything. I just—we'll talk about it inside."

"Well, I do hope you'll explain why you sent a weird postcard like some sort of serial killer with an MO." Diane joked again—and cringed again. It's like she was suddenly that sort of person. The sort who was always making lame jokes about getting killed in some back alley. Maybe that's what happened on the heels of someone's death—maybe you kept bumping into the wrong thing to say like you couldn't possibly avoid it.

Bea hesitated, falling a step behind her. "Was it *that* weird?"

"What, you mean the postcard? Yeah. It was weird as hell. But I figured it out. I'm here, aren't I?" Diane smiled at her friend and shifted her bags in her hands. "Do you remember when we made it?" she asked as they trekked along the top of the beach. "The pact."

"Sure, I do. We had that creepy old Ouija board in the basement. Aunt Lil's friend was over and told us all we were tempting the devil," Bea answered over her shoulder, raising her voice above the gulls and boat motors.

"Well, we were," Diane pointed out. "That was the night Sue admitted that she made her Barbies kiss," she added, laughing as she slogged awkwardly through the sand to the back door.

"I really thought she was going to have a heart attack or something," Bea added through laughter.

Diane examined her friend. Bea looked like crap. Her roots were wires, her skin white and fleshy. But she was lighter on her feet than the year before. Excited, even. Diane replied, "That was the first time I ever played Truth or Dare, come to think of it. I know this because I remember that I always wanted to play growing up, but I never found an in, not until I convinced you three to come to the dark side."

"It didn't take much convincing. We loved the thrill. But I remember being a little scared, too. I felt like we had no choice. I figured we had to fess up to the most awful thing we'd ever done simply because of the rules of the game."

"Right," Diane replied. "You and Sue were rule followers. And I was a rule breaker. Soph, too."

Bea frowned. "Sophia wasn't a rule breaker. She was Little-Miss-Perfect. Don't you *remember*?"

"She confessed to stealing your ma's bra and stuffing it with tissue. Don't *you* remember?" Diane asked, laughing all over again. But she watched out of the corner of her eye as Bea lifted her chin away and stared off.

"That wasn't so bad. What was your confession again?" Bea asked. They'd stopped in the backyard of the house, and Bea propped her bag up against a dry-rotted patio table as it leaned under the back window.

Diane frowned, thinking. "I don't even remember my own. Sue's stood out because it was so cheesy. And Sophia's I recall because I did the same damn thing. I guess I had too many Truth-worthy things to even remember my own big one." She racked her brain for a minute, then set her bags on the ground and snapped her fingers. "Yes, I *do* remember! I remember because I was totally proud of it. I let Jimmy Walton touch my bra strap behind the Rectory before CCD one day."

"Just the strap?" Bea dipped her chin and crossed her arms, and Diane threw her head back, cackling at the ridiculous memories and how easily they could be called into clarity. The weirdness of being young was a poignant thing, apparently.

"Hey, I was *thirteen*, for cryin' out loud! Whaddya want from me?"

"Then why were you wearing a bra if you were only *thirteen*! I thought you didn't get your boobs until freshman year!" Bea had doubled over laughing, now, but Diane just propped her hands on her hips and arched an eyebrow at her friend.

"Same reason as Sophia, and she was only *ten*," she answered, waiting for Bea to unlock the door and let them in. But she did no such thing. Instead, she took a step back and quietly stared up at the house, squinting at the second-floor windows.

Diane cleared her throat. "So, is there a reason we're still standing out here in the heat? I'm sweating like a dog, Bea." She fanned herself and tugged her shirt away from her now full-sized bosom, pulling air down and freeing the heat.

Her friend's face turned solemn and she held up a key. "Here. I can't do it."

"Oh." The word fell out of Diane's mouth. She let go of her top. "Yeah. Sure."

Bea trudged to a metal chair that had been repainted so many times that anywhere the paint had chipped looked like a rainbow-colored gash.

Diane examined the key for a moment, then turned and lowered herself into the chair next to her friend. "You haven't been in yet?"

Bea shook her head.

"Didn't you come last summer? With Greg?" Diane swallowed, edgy that the conversation had turned sharply south.

Again, Bea shook her head.

Dipping her chin down, Diane tried a different track. "Is Sue coming?" Sue was always better at those sorts of things. Sentimental things.

Bea looked up and shrugged, slapping her hands on her thighs. "I have no idea. I really didn't expect *either* of you to come."

"Well, we made a pact, right?" Diane asked through a half-smile.

Bea grinned. "That was a long time ago. I don't know what I was thinking sending the lame postcards."

"Hey, it worked on me, didn't it?"

"We were thirteen when we made that promise. It was a joke. It was just for fun. I mean, we were playing the stupid Ouija thing."

"It *was* fun," Diane reminded her. "Maybe that's why

it stuck, you know? Just because Sue had a coronary over the—"

"Shh," Bea interrupted.

Diane closed her mouth and listened. Seagulls squawked over the water, and waves roared ashore. People screamed and laughed in the distance, and there was not one singular sound Diane could make out against the busy beach traffic on the Jersey Shore. At least, nothing important.

"What?" she hissed at Bea.

Bea's eyes rolled right then left and she twisted her head around the backyard, her gaze never settling.

Then, Diane heard it, too. "Oh, there it is!" she said. A clattering dong. She squinted out to the ocean. "It's just a bell buoy."

But Bea shook her head. "It's coming from—" her words fell away as her head turned to Aunt Lil's house.

Diane swallowed and followed Bea's gaze. "Maybe she's got her wind chimes in there."

A shudder passed between them, and Diane felt a throb of excitement. "We've got to investigate. Come on. Follow me." She held her hand to Bea, who took it, and before either of them knew what she was doing, Diane had ripped the Band-Aid off.

They were on the threshold, the key stuck in the lock as the wooden door creaked open. And there it was again. The rhythmic striking, like a death knell.

Chapter 10

Bea

There was no need to flip a switch. The windows faced east, and the sun hadn't climbed too high yet. Light poured in, soaking the kitchen that stood at the back of the house.

Everything was opposite from what Bea expected.

If Sophia had come back to renovate the place as a sweet surprise, she didn't get that far. The place was exactly as it had been a decade before. And for that matter, it was exactly as it had been five decades before.

Aunt Lil could rise from the dead, come back, and she'd never even realize she'd been gone for longer than the time it took to ride the tram car up the boardwalk.

Diane appeared to inspect the place slowly, with fascination, but momentum tugged Bea through the hall and into the front room.

The faint dong clanged again, sharper, and this time, Bea's head snapped to the front door.

It wasn't the bell buoys. It wasn't the spirit of Aunt

Lil, her gaudy necklaces jangling and echoing across the shore like Marley's ghost.

It was the doorbell.

Diane and Bea stopped on the shag carpet together and giggled with relief.

"Whew!" Diane crossed to the door, leaning into the round window. "Ah ha!" she declared, smirking back at Bea and sliding the deadbolt.

Bea glanced around the room, drinking in the corduroy sofa and yellowed accent pillows as Diane opened the door and cheered.

"Susan Merkle! How the hell are ya!"

Bea grinned as nervous Sue stepped over the threshold with a neat suitcase in one hand and her leather purse held in place over her abdomen with the other. "Hi, girls," she said at last, bracing as Diane wrapped her in a hearty bear hug.

"Sue." Bea strode to them and wrapped the two in a hug. It felt good.

She pushed down the emotions of being there, in that house again together. One short of their group.

"I'm so glad you made it," Bea said once the embrace melted into an awkward semi-circle as they stood facing the rest of the house.

"Well, I was a little scared, to be honest," Sue replied.

Bea squeezed her shoulder. "I know. I'm sorry. I was in a weird place when I sent the note." She looked back at Diane. "Still am, I guess."

Sue replied with a soft look. "How are you, Bea?"

Bea blinked and sucked in a deep breath, glancing about her surroundings and returning her gaze to her two friends, the only two people left on earth willing to tolerate her, probably. She let out the breath and smiled. "Better now. Better every day."

"So," Diane clapped her hands and rubbed them together before studying the foyer, "What's the plan here? How long are we staying? What are we doing? I'm not the kind of gal who scrapes popcorn off of ceilings, but I can paint. Is that the idea? You're putting us to work for a week? Is that why you called us back?"

Bea shook her head and frowned. "No, no. Well, I mean, maybe we can do some projects if you want. Mostly, I just wanted to spend the summer together. Like old times." She bit her lower lip, holding off on the whole truth for a bit.

Sue's face wrinkled. "Oh, Bea. I'm sorry, but I can't stay long."

"What do you mean you can't stay long?" Diane asked, pushing her hands onto her waist and digging her heels into the carpet. "It's *summer*. You work at a *school*."

"I'm... well, I have plane tickets. I'm flying out to California this weekend. Joe surprised me with a vacation. But I can stay here for a couple of days."

Bea and Diane exchanged a look.

"Well, it's great you're here, anyway," Bea replied. "A couple of days is enough for me. Sounds like a great vacation for the two of you." She flicked a glance to Diane who frowned.

"I think both of you are holding back on me," Diane spat out, her hands on her hips and legs apart in a power stance. "And I intend to get to the bottom of it. A few days? A week? I'll be here until I have the whole truth and nothing but the truth, so help me God. Even if I have to stay until Labor Day. I'm not budging."

And with that, Bea knew Diane De Luca was hiding something, too.

———

THEY'D LEFT their bags at the foot of the stairs, none of them ready to ascend to the bedrooms quite yet. At least, Bea wasn't ready. And Sue was still her nervous self.

Diane dug around the kitchen, rinsing three of Aunt Lil's crystal goblets while Sue wiped the kitchen table and Bea twisted open the orange juice lid. When the table was clean and the goblets dry, she set about uncorking the champagne, immune to the loud pop as Diane and Sue shrieked at the noise.

"So, how's life, ladies?" Diane asked, pulling food from her bags and arranging it on the table. A tub of hummus. A bag of pita triangles. A packet of ginger snaps. Lastly, a book. On it, a bare-chested man posing ridiculously in front of a nearly bare-chested woman. "Oh, Bea. Here." She tossed the book to Bea. "I got you something for your collection."

Bea flushed, though more in warm appreciation that Diane knew her so well and less from embarrassment. Grinning as she read the back cover, she shook her head. "I knew I invited you for a reason."

Diane laughed, but Sue redirected the conversation back to Diane's question. "Well, I'm working the summer session once we—once I get back from San Diego. Otherwise, nothing new for me. Same old, same old. For the most part."

Bea nodded along, her eyes now on the first page of chapter one. "School's out for me. I have another year before I can retire with all my points. Six more would be better." It was a mundane conversation, and that was okay with Bea. She needed some normalcy. To gripe about work and bemoan the five pounds she continued to gain and lose and gain and lose in an endless cycle.

"What in the world do you do all summer?" Diane asked her.

"I could say the same thing about you," Bea kicked back playfully, then she slapped her new book on the palm of her hand. "At least I read."

Diane answered, "Hey, I have two part-time jobs and head up about a gazillion clubs. I don't even *have* a summer break."

"So, how is it that you can stay the whole summer?" Sue asked innocently.

"Well, I just told the shelter *and* the library that I'd be back in September."

"You didn't, Diane." Bea furrowed her eyebrows, but Diane grinned mischievously.

"I'm kidding, but let's get real, here. Your message was entirely vague. You're lucky we didn't show up with all our worldly possessions, ready to move into this place."

Bea considered this, and what dawned on her was how much Diane and even perhaps Sue needed the escape. They needed the invitation. Maybe even more than she did.

"I wouldn't move here," Sue chirped after a sip of her drink. "But I am here for you, whatever it is you need. Maybe we'll make a new tradition. We can kick off every summer here, kind of like old times." Sue's eyes lit up at her own small, sweet idea.

Diane opened her mouth to reply, but Bea let out a long sigh.

"Well, that's just it—" Bea's voice quaked as she began.

Diane reached across the table and grabbed her hand. "Are you in trouble, Bea?"

Bea shook her head and licked her lips. "No. But this

place is." She lifted her chin and looked from Diane to Sue, swallowing. "Greg won't pay the utilities anymore. Or the taxes. He wants to sell, but I asked him for a little more time, you know?"

A quiet pooled across the table, and Bea wasn't sure what her friends were thinking.

When, after a moment, neither replied, she added, "That's why I sent the postcards."

"You mean you need money?" Diane answered at last, leaning back in her seat and crossing her arms over her ample chest. Her mimosa sat abandoned on the table in front of her.

Bea flushed bright red. "No. No, no, no. Don't worry about that. Don't be ridiculous. I just thought that we could have one more go, you know? One more summer together. The last meeting of The Summer Society." She glanced down at her hands and swallowed and frowned. "It's cheesy. I know. I—"

Diane's body relaxed and she settled into her chair, apparently satisfied. "It's perfect."

Sue frowned deeply.

"I thought," Bea went on, her ability to be honest trapped in her heart. "I thought we could pull together somehow. I thought we could go back to the good old days. Maybe take a look at Lil's things. All that."

"So, you're keeping the house, right?" Sue asked. "Do you need to do paperwork or something? Greg will let you take over on the bills, right? He can't just… *sell* it, right?"

Before Bea could answer, Diane shook her hair off the back of her shoulders and leaned forward. "Listen, Bea. Even if Greg wants to pull out, you don't have to. We've got history here. Don't let him bully you into selling for a fast buck. Keep the place. We'll all do better.

We'll come here more often. We'll go back to the good old days like you said, okay? We'll help you clean it up, okay?"

The kindness in Diane's offer distracted Bea momentarily.

But Sue shook her head. "You said this place is in trouble," she pointed out, her face a fretful landscape.

Bea sniffled and took the last swig of her drink, before setting it down carefully and clapping her hands together. "All I want to do is be here together with you both. And maybe I'll take you up on your offer, Diane. I really would love to go through Lil's things. Save what we can. We'll make it the best summer possible. A memorial for Soph. A finale. The Summer Society's last hurrah." She glanced up pathetically at her friends, hoping her point landed with more precision than she was able to muster.

"Wait," Diane interjected. "You mean you're *not* going to keep this place?" She held her arms out, red-painted fingers wiggling across the musty air of the house.

Bea lifted her shoulders and let them fall. "I can't afford to."

"So, you *do* need money," Sue replied, pouting.

Swallowing against the tears that started crawling up her throat, Bea shook her head. "No, no. We'll just sell. Seriously, that's the plan. It's what Sophia would want, anyway. She'd want us to finally renovate and sell. We never did, you know? And she was such a fresh-start type of person. And Greg is willing to help with that as long as we get out ahead."

"No," Sue answered, her voice shaking and louder than usual.

Bea and Diane exchanged a look.

"What do you mean?" Diane asked.

Shifting in her seat, Bea thought about the last few years. How her relationship with Sophia grew to a breaking point. She thought about how Sophia kept pushing her to go out and meet people. *You need a life!* she'd told Bea. But Bea didn't want a life. She wanted no such thing. She wanted things to be how they used to be. She wanted to shake off the guilt and she wanted Sophia's perfect existence to sustain her. To keep her going. She wanted her sister to keep living her perfect life. *Bea* wanted to die first, eventually... years off when Matt had gotten married to a nice girl who appreciated his recluse of an aunt and might help foot the nursing home bill. Or maybe Greg's vast estate could cover it in the end. Who knew? But now, she wasn't even "related" to Greg anymore. And now, she didn't have a chance to work on the aunt-nephew relationship with Matt that she seemed so terrible at.

But now, Bea was left wanting what Sophia *would have wanted*—that God-awful phrase. And she would want to take down the Christmas lights. Scrub the toilets. Clap the dust off her hands and drive home.

"That's not what Sophia would want," Sue answered, unwittingly playing into Bea's private thoughts.

On the brink of losing her nerve and interest in the whole thing, Bea pressed the heel of her hand to her head. "What would Sophia want, Sue?"

"She'd want you to keep the house." It was Diane who answered, but Sue was nodding vigorously. They were teaming up on Bea who blinked away a fresh tear then dried her cheek with the back of her hand.

"Sophia would want me to be a better sister," she whispered at last.

Sue stared at Bea. "What does that even mean?"

Diane lifted an eyebrow and then echoed Sue, "What are we missing here, Bea?"

Bea's face crumbled. "Sophia could have had a perfect life. You know?"

"Sophia *did* have a perfect life, Bea," Diane argued, leaning forward and reaching her hand across and pressing it on the top of the table. "She was always perfect. Just like you said. *Little Miss Perfect*. Way up until the end. And you, my dear," Diane went on, dropping her chin, "were the perfect sister."

Swallowing a sob, Bea looked up and searched her friend's expression then looked at Sue, who was nodding.

They didn't know. They *didn't know*.

And neither did Sophia.

Chapter 11

Sue

"I refuse," she declared after they'd eaten the last of the hummus, taken a walk to the boardwalk market for a *real* dinner, then strolled the beach for a good hour. "I absolutely refuse."

"We can't just stay down here the whole week," Diane argued, waving her hands to indicate the first floor of Aunt Lil's house.

They'd arrived at the agreement that they would simply treat the next few days as a reunion. And with that came ascending to the second floor eventually, at least, in Diane's pointed opinion. Diane with the supposed bad back and nosey nature.

"Oh yes we can," Bea added. Sue let out a breath. If Bea was on her side, then the matter was settled. "We will sleep on the couches. I'm not ready to go up there tonight."

"What if you're not ready tomorrow?" Diane asked. "Why don't you just let me go up? If I see anything, I'll

come down and tell you about it. *Calmly*, too. I promise."
She signed the cross and held up two fingers for good
measure.

"Tomorrow," Bea said firmly. "We'll go upstairs
tomorrow. In the morning. After coffee and when we
have lots of daylight and caffeine courage."

So, it was settled. Thankfully. They kept to the downstairs bath, where they slipped into loose shirts and left
their pajama pants in their overnight bags. Lil had plenty
of blankets and crochet pillows, and it was too hot for
layers anyway.

At the market, Diane had bought wine, but Sue stuck
to water. The mimosa had already given her a headache
that morning.

Bea passed around bowls of popcorn. All they
needed was an episode of *The Price is Right*, and it would
be exactly like old times.

"Truth or Dare," Diane said, setting her crystal
goblet—the same one from that morning, rinsed anew
and now glowing deep red—on the side table and taking
her glasses off.

"No." Sue shook her head. "Come on, Diane, we're
too old."

"Too old?" Diane shrieked. "Maybe *you* are, but not
me. Don't you remember? Bea and I were just talking
about that night. You know the one."

Sue frowned. "No, I don't. What night?"

"The one where you asked the Ouija Board if we
were all going to Hell?"

A deep flush crept up her neck, but she couldn't help
but giggle. "That was the same night we made our club.
Remember?"

"How could we forget," Bea added. "We did the
blood brothers thing."

"Oh my gosh," Sue gasped, "I almost forgot about that. Did you know that I told my mom about that?"

Bea clicked her tongue. "You didn't."

"You *would*," Diane joined in, leaning forward and reaching for her glass.

"Yeah. I told her years later, though. When I was older. She said I might have gotten AIDS. I was freaked out forever after that." Even now, Sue's stomach churned at the thought. As a young woman, fearful of catching this or that or struggling alone on some scary medical road, she always thought that getting married was a safety net from the bad things in the world. The diseases and the loneliness, alike. If you were married, someone could drive you to your chemotherapy treatments. If you were married, someone would check the fuse box in a power outage. If you were married, you'd surely never get an STD. That turned out to be a lie, after all. Marriage wasn't protection—it was a false sense of security. Fortunately for Sue, however, she turned out to be immune from the worst of it. That's what her miscarriage did. Losing her tube and sense of purpose had put all bedroom things on hold.

No wonder her marriage was a sham. She'd taken a part in that.

"I can't believe you stayed our friend." Diane grinned.

"I actually thought about that, too," Bea admitted, smiling sympathetically at Sue. "When the news came out about all that, I distinctly remember thinking *we were so stupid!*"

"We didn't know any better," Diane reasoned. "We did crazy things, and we didn't have anyone to tell us to knock it off."

"We didn't do very crazy things," Sue reasoned,

frowning. "Just typical teenager things. That's why we made the pact, though, remember?" Sue asked, shaking her inner thoughts and rejoining the present moment.

Bea took a sip of her wine. "Of course. We were scared our secrets would get out."

Diane lifted an eyebrow. "No one ever knew that Sue's Barbies kissed."

Bea smiled. "No one ever knew that you let Jimmy Walton touch your bra strap... *and* that you and Soph *padded* your bras!"

Sue rolled her eyes then allowed herself a small smile. "Bea, what was your Truth that night? I can't remember."

"It was stupid," Bea answered, retreating to her corner of the sofa and pulling her popcorn bowl to her chest.

"Come on, Russo," Diane taunted. "Out with it. We haven't dissolved yet. We're still The Summer Society. Your secret is safe here." Diane cackled to herself, and Sue grinned.

"Come on, Bea," she added, curious. "What was your big confession?"

"No, it was *dumb*," Bea replied. "I don't even remember it."

"Oh wait a second," Sue said, her eyes lighting up. "I remember yours! Because I was mad that I hadn't thought to use it first!"

"So, what was it?" Diane asked.

Sue's smile stretched across her face, and it felt like all her troubles were dripping away, down the drain. The innocence of their younger years was so close at hand that she could almost pretend she had never even met Joe, that schmuck.

Before Sue could answer Diane, Bea waved her off. "I'd never kissed a guy."

"That was it? You were only *thirteen*," Diane ribbed her.

"Well, you and Sophia had," Sue remarked, smirking mischievously.

"It's no big deal," Bea said. "Seriously."

"Well, not when you're thirteen, that's true," Diane replied. "So, come on. Let's play. Bea, you go first. Truth? Or dare?"

Chapter 12

Diane, 1980

At the time, none of them knew just how good life really was. Well, they knew it, but they didn't talk about it.

After all, when you were fourteen years old, life was a misery, right?

It was for Diane De Luca. Frizzy hair and no butt weren't exactly the sort of combo a teen girl strived for.

All four of 'em were laying out on the beach, as far away from Aunt Lil and her old cronies as they could get without being submerged in the Atlantic Ocean. Each girl on her towel, they sat in a jagged circle around a red Coleman soda cooler, which was the only thing keeping Diane from melting like an ice cream cone out in that heat.

"I'll pick Dare instead," Bea whined.

They all knew that was a crock, but Diane was the only one who wouldn't tolerate Bea and her goody-two-shoes act. "No. We all did Truth, and you will, too."

"Then why even give me the stupid *choice*?" Bea complained again. Diane was about to slap her upside the head, really and truly. She was.

"Right now is the Truth round. We can do the Dare round next."

Diane could have sworn she heard Sue whimper like a baby animal, and it was exactly why she wasn't about to let her very best friend in the world wimp out. Diane had standards for Bea, and she stuck to them. Unlike Sophia, who let Sue be a total dork.

"Um... okay, fine," Bea replied, letting out a sigh. "When I was eight, I swiped a cookie from the pantry before dinner. There. Done."

"I don't even buy it," Sophia piped up, rolling her big green twelve-year-old eyes. "My sister hasn't broken a rule in her life. Mark my words. She's got a better one. Come on Bea. What is something true that you never ever told a soul? Not even *me*?"

Diane eyed Bea, catching a hitch in her breath and watching as Bea shifted in her seat and put on a look like she was racking her brain, willing to play along, finally. Sophia's begging had worked. Better than Diane's hard drive. Leaning back into her bean bag chair, Diane folded her arms over her chest. "Aw, who cares, anyway? I dare all of ya to shut up so we can do something more in-ter-esting."

"No, no. She's about to say her Truth," Sophia replied, holding up her hand for silence.

Diane watched as Bea sniffed and shrugged, then opened her mouth to answer.

"You three have to swear on your lives not to tell *any*one," Bea said, her eyes narrowing on each of them.

"This oughtta be good," Diane replied, leaning forward again and signing the cross. "I swear."

"No, I mean it, Diane. You gotta keep your trap shut on this. It's humiliating, truly." Bea glanced around the beach, her face wrinkled with worry.

"Did you kill somebody?" Diane asked, half-joking. Only half. But still, what was so bad that they had to swear on their lives?"

"No, I didn't kill anybody," Bea shot back. "Don't be stupid."

"Then what is it?" Sue rejoined the conversation, her curiosity getting the best of her, as usual.

Diane studied Bea, who licked her lips then chewed on the lower one before glancing to her sister. "Soph, remember last summer when you wanted to kiss Mikey Molino?"

A laugh bubbled up from Diane's chest and she pointed a finger at Sophia. "I remember that! You were only eleven. I said no way. Too young." Diane shared this as a point of pride. She had been, for once, the mature one in the group during that particular day in the arcade.

Sophia pretended to gag herself, and Diane broke into a belly laugh. "Bea," Diane pointed out, "you were the one who told her to kiss him!"

Bea's face turned redder than a cooked lobster.

Sophia stabbed her finger at her sister. "You said you'd kissed a boy when you were eleven, remember, Bea?"

"Yeah, I remember. That's where I'm going with this. That's why I said you have to swear on your lives that you'll never tell anyone any of this."

"Hey," Sue nagged, "you can't tell anyone my secret, either."

"And I don't want *my* secret to get out," Soph globbed on.

Diane pushed air through her lips and shook her head. "Okay, okay. Here's the deal. We'll make a pact, all right?"

"What's a *pack*?" Sue asked.

Diane rolled her eyes. "A *pact. T.* With a T at the end. Gee whiz. We'll make a pact to keep each other's secrets forever. I mean, it would make me feel better, too. I gotta say. What if someone finds out that I let Jimmy Walton touch my bra strap? They could throw me out of CCD for good. My mother would send me to boarding school lickety-split. Then where would I go?"

"You could always come here, Diane." Bea leaned into her and nudged Diane with her shoulder, offering a half smile. "If you ever got kicked out of anything, you could just come here. Send a letter or something, let us know you're here, and we'll come meet you."

Diane wasn't actually worried she'd be kicked out. Where did it say you couldn't let a boy touch your bra strap? Especially if you didn't even have any boobs yet and the whole piece of underwear was just for looks? But she liked where her friend was heading with this, because in truth—there was a decent chance that Diane would be kicked out of somewhere at some point and she'd need a place where she could run away to. Really and truly.

Mainly, though, she was dying to hear Bea's confession. Especially if it was something Bea's own sister didn't even know about. If only Diane and Bea were alone somewhere, and she could be the first to hear it. Then she'd definitely have one up on ol' Soph.

A thought popped in her head. Something she'd read in one of her mom's magazines. She sat upright then grabbed her purse, digging inside. Coming up empty, she looked around the beach. Then saw it: a shard of seashell. "Here, look." Without a moment's hesitation, Diane took the sharp point of peach-colored armor and sliced it across the tip of her thumb, hardly even wincing. She handed the shell to Bea. "Blood oath. We each do it, and then we have to swear."

"Sounds like something a weirdo cult would do." Sophia folded her arms and gave Diane a skeptical look.

"Psh, it's not a cult thing. It's a…" Diane searched her brain for the right word. She wasn't book smart like Bea or Soph. "We're not a cult, okay? We're just a club. Like the Boy Scouts or something."

"We could make our own Girl Scouts club!" Sue chimed in. "I'm in Girl Scouts. I can teach you everything about it—"

But Bea held up her hand. "Girl Scout girls don't make their Barbies kiss."

Sue's face reddened and she slunk back, but Diane saw Soph lean over and whisper something into her ear, and she relaxed.

Diane couldn't help but smile at their bond and glanced at Bea. "We're a club. A secret one that makes blood pacts."

"What should we call ourselves?" Sophia asked.

Diane thought about it. "Girls of the Shore."

"But we don't live here," Sue protested.

"True," Sophia added. "But we meet here every summer."

"Summer is when we shine," Bea said.

"Okay, so… The Summer Club?" Diane pitched.

"What about The Summer Scouts?" Sue tried.

All four of them shook their heads. "No," Bea said. "Something more sophisticated. I mean—" she held her thumb up and nicked the shell across it, pain briefly crossing her face "—if we're taking a blood oath, it has to be sort of serious. You know?"

"I got it," Sophia said, her eyes bright. "I totally have it."

"What? Spit it out, Soph," Diane said.

Sophia answered, her chest puffed out and a sly smile on her mouth, "We'll be The Summer Society."

"I love it!" Sue cheered, clapping like a little kid.

Bea reached over the cooler and gave her sister a high-five.

"I like it, too," Diane agreed. "And if any of us is ever in trouble," she went on, "we'll meet back here. On the beach."

"But people would see us out here," Sue whined. "Can't we have a more private meeting spot?"

"Like a clubhouse?" Sophia asked.

"Okay, then we meet upstairs at Aunt Lil's. In our bedroom," Bea offered.

The other three nodded. Diane added, "We meet in our room on the second floor. We can call it The Summer Society Room."

"And we'll keep each other's secrets," Bea added as Sophia and then Sue pricked each other's fingers, squeezing their eyes shut and shrieking with pain and laughter.

All four pushed their thumbs together over the cooler and smiled at each other.

Diane leaned back and rubbed the miniature wound along the pink fabric of her striped beach towel. "All right, Bea, gehead. Tell us your secret."

Bea let out a long slow breath, then replied, apparently satisfied that she could spill her guts without judgment. Or at least, without anyone tattling on her. "When Soph asked if she could kiss Mikey Molino, I could tell she really wanted to do it. But I knew she wouldn't do it if it was, like, a weird thing to do. So, I told her that when I was eleven, I kissed a boy, too."

"That's *it*?" Diane asked, her left eyebrow reaching so high on her head she felt it might disappear into her hair line and turn to frizz.

Sophia chimed in. "You *lied* to me, Bea? To get me to kiss a boy?"

Diane looked at Bea, who sulked. "I wasn't trying to *get you* to kiss a boy, Soph. I just knew you wanted to. And I wanted you to be happy."

"I don't get it," Sue complained. "What's the big deal?"

Even Sue figured Bea was pulling a fast one. Diane snorted.

"Yeah, Bea. What's so wrong with that?"

It was Sophia who answered, hurt flashing in her eyes. "You *lied* to me?"

Bea replied, "I knew you wanted to kiss him, and I figured it was no big deal, Soph. Didn't you want to kiss him?"

Diane cut in. "Of course she did. It was all she talked about the whole summer until she dumped the poor jerk. That's a rotten confession. Nothing you could get in trouble over. That's for sure. What a crock."

Sophia grinned and loosened up. "I have to say. It was a great kiss. Now that I think about it, I sort of regret dumping him."

"Maybe he's still around?" Sue tried helpfully. "He's a local, after all."

But Diane was confused. Part of Bea's revelation was left unfinished. "What did you lie about, Bea?"

"Kissing a boy when I was eleven," Bea replied, her

face a sheet of humiliation, though Diane couldn't understand why.

"Oh, who cares? Eleven *is* too young. I didn't kiss Jimmy until my birthday." She threw her shoulders back and eyed the others.

Sue gasped. "You mean your party? When you played—"

"Seven Minutes in Heaven," Diane answered proudly. "That's right. It was our first kiss. *With* tongue." Diane ought to get extra points for fessing up to two great secrets.

"So, that must have been Bea's first kiss, too," Soph pointed out. "With that boy you liked, Stevie. When you two went into the closet."

Bea wiggled on her towel and looked down.

"Okay, so what? She fibbed so that you could live out your biggest fantasy guilt free," Diane said to Soph, taking up for Bea even though it was the lamest Truth she'd ever heard in her life.

"No, it wasn't my first kiss," Bea answered, glancing up guiltily. "He wouldn't kiss me. When we got in there, I sort of closed my eyes and leaned in, and then I heard him say *'Yeah right, there's no way I'm touching you'* and then we just stood around in there for a while. Six minutes and forty-nine seconds, to be exact."

Tears appeared in Bea's eyes, and Diane had the sudden urge to hunt down that pimple-faced loser and kick the crap out of him. She even started to stand up.

"I'll go drag him back here and we can all take a turn punching his lights out," Diane said, enraged on her best friend's behalf.

"What a jerk!" Sophia shouted. "We should trash Stevie's locker when school starts back up."

"Just write him a letter," Sue added uselessly. "Tell him that he hurt your feelings."

Bea shook her head. "It's fine. Really." Then, she laughed through her tears. "I don't know why I'm crying. That wasn't even my full confession."

"There's more?" Diane asked, lowering onto the towel and sitting closer to Bea now as she slung her arm around her shoulders.

"Yeah. After that, I never tried it again."

"What? You mean you never played that icky game?" Sue asked.

"No." Bea shook her head. "I've never kissed a boy. I probably never will."

Chapter 13

Bea

"It's the truth. I swear on my life," Bea answered, throwing her head back and laughing with wild abandonment. It felt good to be back with her friends, like old times. Even if they had regressed to the ridiculous games they played as kids.

"You mean to tell me," Diane replied, holding her wine glass in the hand that was pointing a red-manicured fingernail at Bea, "that you found yourself in the presidential suite of Caesars Palace with a millionaire, a bottle of Dom Pérignon, and a tray of chocolate-covered strawberries and you just... *left?*"

Tears streamed out of her eyes—laughing tears, the good kind. The best kind, Bea realized. She nodded her head and finally recovered from the fit of hysterics. "Yes," she gasped, then took a swig of her own drink. "I left."

"*Why?*" Diane asked, her eyes wide and mouth

agape. "I mean, if it were an *Indecent Proposal* situation, and you were, like, *married*, I'd get it... but, *why?*"

Bea took a deep breath and drew her shoulders up to her ears then let them slump back. "It was too much. You know? I think the moment I knew I couldn't stay was when he dragged a strawberry off that damn shiny plate and held it out in front of my mouth."

"What did you do?" Sue asked, enthralled. "I mean... how did you leave? Did you say you'd be back?"

Shaking her head, Bea replied, "I said I had forgotten I had an appointment." Her mouth broke open again and she fell forward on another wave of laughter.

Sue—aghast, no doubt—clicked her tongue. "At least you made it out alive."

Diane wasn't amused, though. "Bea Victoria Russo. It was the middle of the night. What in the hell did he say when you told him you had an *appointment?*"

Bea composed herself again and answered through a new stream of laughing tears, "He offered for me to take his chauffeur."

"Oh, that is weird," Sue replied. "That means you made a good decision, Bea."

Bea waved her off. "It wasn't weird. It was *Vegas*. You know? And to answer *your* question, Diane, I'm just not the type. You know that. It didn't suit me." She pulled herself together for good.

"Do you mean the millionaire didn't suit you? Or the Dom?" Diane cackled to herself.

"She means the hotel-room-with-a-stranger part, I'm sure," Sue answered, bristling with her goblet of water.

"Sue's right. I guess I'm a wimp. What can I say? I couldn't commit."

Diane set her drink down and pulled her afghan up

around her. "Champagne with a rich stranger doesn't sound like a situation that warrants commitment." She gave Bea a look, and they sat at a sort of impasse for a moment.

"Commitment or not—I mean it was moving in the opposite direction, it wasn't a place I wanted to be. And he wasn't a man I wanted to be there with. Maybe you'd have made a different choice, Diane," Bea dipped her chin and resituated her gaze on Diane, who balked.

"Are you calling me a gold digger?"

"Ladies, come on," Sue interjected, but Bea's hand flew up.

"No. I'm not calling anyone a gold digger. I'm saying that you and I have different tastes."

"I wasn't aware you had any taste at all!" Diane cried, laughing derisively.

"Diane," Sue pled, but again Bea brushed her off.

She was game for a little back-and-forth. It would do them all good. "I do have taste. Fine taste, in fact."

"So fine that you refuse to date at all? Come on, Bea. What's the deal with that? You're over the hill. You're single. Never married. You don't even own a cat."

"Yes, I do," Bea protested. "I do have a cat. She's at my mother's right now. Light of my life, that little furball."

"Oh, no. That's even *worse*. You're single, never married, and you *do* own a cat. Tell me it's just one."

"Don't you have a cat, Diane?" Sue chirped.

"Well, that's not the point," Diane returned. "The point is, this game is about getting down to it. And you just gave us this beautiful story about Sin City and *Phantom of the Opera* and a chance meeting in the lobby and one night of bliss and then—" Diane snapped her fingers "—*poof*, you leave."

"Like I said, it was over-the-top. I was uncomfortable!" Bea replied, hiding behind her wine glass. "It's not like he was a *Craig*," she added at last.

"What's that supposed to mean?" Diane shot back. "A *Craig*?"

"Craig is *nice*. He's a good guy. He's down-to-earth. Accessible. All that. You know what I mean." She closed her eyes and took a long sip of her drink before setting it back on the coffee table and trading for a bottled water she'd found in her trunk. No point in going to bed dehydrated. It would make the next morning that much more painful.

"I don't want to talk about Craig, okay?" Diane settled deeper in her corner of the sofa, wiggling her toes back under the blanket and retreating like a scared animal.

Bea and Sue exchanged a look. "Is it your turn to go?" Bea asked, leveling her gaze on her old best friend.

Diane jutted her chin out. "Sue can go next. I'm taking a break from the game."

"Okay," Bea replied. "Sue, Truth or Dare?"

"Truth," Sue answered through a yawn.

"Truth. Okay. Go for it." Bea leaned back and waited for a dorky Sue story.

"Can we change how this works? Can you just ask me a yes or no question? Like we used to play sometimes?" Sue asked.

"We always played it this way. You have to come up with the Truth. No questions. Remember?" Bea answered.

"I actually have a question for Sue," Diane broke in, recovering somewhat from her strange pouting.

"Yes, great. Ask away," Sue replied, gaining momentum despite passing on the wine.

Bea stared hard at Diane, but Diane ignored her and instead swirled the remaining ounce of red fluid in her goblet before downing it with one swig and curling the glass back into herself. "Why didn't you ever have kids?"

A turbulent silence skittered across the living room.

"What?" Sue sounded like she was choking on the word as it fell from her mouth, mottled and coughy. She cleared her throat and repeated herself. "What?"

Bea slapped a hand down on the sofa. "I think we've had enough."

"No," Diane protested. "She can talk about this. She *should* talk about this."

"Diane, we *know* why she didn't have kids." Bea gave Sue an apologetic look.

"No, we don't. We know she had a miscarriage. Hell, we all had miscarriages."

"I didn't have a miscarriage," Bea replied.

"Us marrieds did. Soph did. I did. *Sue* did. But why didn't you try for another? Or adopt? Or foster? Did you get a dog instead?"

"*Diane*," Bea hissed. "Shut *up*."

"Okay, okay," Diane said, easing up. "I'm sorry." She shook her head, then reached over to the love seat where Sue sat alone. Diane grabbed Sue's knee over the blanket. "I just wanted to know because when we were kids… that's *all* you talked about, Sue. All you seemed to want was to have a little family. One boy and one girl. I can even recall the names you had picked out. Katharine and Dean. After Katharine Hepburn and Dean Martin. Remember?"

Sue didn't cry or whine or pout. She sat quietly for a moment, then, finally, a small smile grew over her mouth. "I've never talked about it," she replied, her eyes glancing off Diane and over to Bea.

"Talked about the miscarriage?" Bea asked gently.

"No," Sue answered. "The truth."

Chapter 14

Sue, 1982

"No thanks," Sue replied to Aunt Lil. "My mother wouldn't want me to."

"What she don't know, won't hurt her," Diane pointed out, flopping onto the sofa. "Gehead, Sue. It's just for fun."

"Oh no," Aunt Lil answered. "If Sue doesn't want a reading, then I'm not going to read her cards. It's a bad omen."

"A bad omen?" Sue asked, gulping.

"You don't read for someone who isn't interested. It's bad juju, I swear, sweetheart. Anyway, I've got a date tonight, lovies."

"A date?" Sophia joined Sue at the fold-out table. "Whaddya mean a *date*, Aunt Lil?"

Uncle Sammy had died the summer before, but at the time, he and Lil were on the outs. Still, devout Catholics to the core, they'd never have divorced. That was another reason Sue felt a little funny about those freaky tarot cards. Uncle Sammy was the picture of health until his marriage went south.

"I mean a *date*. You know," she cleared her cigarette smoke with a wave of her hand, and some of the ash fell from the butt to the carpet. Sue watched it settle into the shaggy fibers and wondered if Lil's floor was covered with invisible little accidental burns. Miniscule sears from falling ash. Then again, maybe there were no accidents when you were a tarot card reader.

"I know what a *date* is," Sophia scoffed. "I mean with *who?*"

"Oh, just a nice man. Don't you girls worry your little selves. You have fun with *The Price is Right* and your snacks, and I'll see ya later."

She grabbed the nearest girl—who just so happened to be Sue—and pulled her in for a frosted pink kiss on the cheek and sang out *Toodaloo!* before clacking in her heels to the front door, her lacey white swim cover-up flapping against her skinny backside as she left into the night.

Sue never knew what to make of Aunt Lil. She wasn't the sort of mother-figure that made a nervous girl feel safe, and yet she was the sort who... well... made Sue grow up a little. Like mothers sometimes ought to.

"Let me read your cards," Sophia said, tugging Sue's wrist to the folding table.

Sue shook her head and pulled back. "No, no, no. You don't even know what you're doing."

Sophia let her go and replied, "Okay. Then, Diane, come'ere. Lemme read your cards."

Diane peeled herself from the sofa and plopped into the chair, but something burned inside of Sue. A wild hare or an impulse to break free for one night of her life.

She was a good Catholic girl. She didn't believe in

tarot or black magic or any of that. So, who cared if she played along with her girlfriends for once? It'd be good for her, and it wouldn't compromise her values or beliefs. Bea and Diane would stop teasing her for being too proper all the time. Maybe she'd even have fun.

Did she want to have fun?

Sue tugged on Diane's arm. "No, let me. I wanna do it after all."

"You do?" Sophia, Diane, and Bea all asked at the same time.

"Yeah," Sue replied. "Read my cards. It's not like any of this stuff is real anyway."

Diane stood from the chair and waved Sue down, and she and Bea crowded in behind as Sophia shuffled the deck like she was about to deal a round of Blackjack.

"Ahem." Diane coughed into her fist behind Sue's shoulder. "Do you even know how to read these, Soph?" she asked, her voice scornful.

Across the table, Sophia shrugged and slid the cards into a tidy stack. "Bea and I have watched Aunt Lil do this since we were in diapers."

Sue reminded herself it was all a gag, and kept her gaze on Sophia, who took a deep breath and closed her eyes before pulling and positioning two cards just so.

"Okay," Sophia laced her fingers and flexed her hands over the table then looked down and read the words from the bottom of each image. "The Empress and The Tower."

Bea giggled behind them, and Diane joined her. Soon, they were all laughing and Sophia had slotted the cards back in their pile and stowed them in the little wooden organizer.

"I don't know what the heck I'm doing. Forget this."

Soph stood, "I say we watch *The Price is Right* and eat licorice."

"I vote popcorn and a walk on the beach," Diane replied.

"Let's call a meeting, otherwise we'll never come to an agreement," Bea said. It was their thing—to pull out The Summer Society like a trick. They'd call a meeting, hash things out, then adjourn the meeting. Democratic and reasonable as ever, so long as there wasn't a split vote, in which case they'd move to a tie-breaker scenario where they flipped a coin, if possible.

"Let's start with our options. We could stay in or we could go out. Raise your hand if you want to stay in."

Only Diane didn't, and she was therefore overruled.

"Okay, snacks. Licorice or popcorn?" Bea asked.

"Hey, the world is our oyster, right? Why can't we have both?" Diane asked.

And just like that, they were girls again. Good girls who didn't dabble in silly things like fortune-telling or twilight beach walks or all those sorts of habits that could get them into *real* trouble. The kind of trouble they couldn't get out of. The kind of trouble that even a secret society couldn't protect them from.

Chapter 15

Bea

"You think you lost the baby because of Aunt Lil's tarot cards?" Bea asked Sue, skeptical. Sue was the sort to fall for conspiracy theories and wild notions. It made sense that she might have read something more into what was always meant to be a silly game.

Sue frowned. "No. I don't think that whole thing *made* me lose the baby. But I think it was the beginning, you know?"

"Beginning of what?" Diane asked, her tone more somber now, compassionate, even.

"Of me trying to be something I wasn't."

"Just because you let Sophia deal a couple of cards? I wouldn't say that's a great example of forsaking your morals, Sue," Bea reasoned, wrapping a second blanket around her shoulders and hunkering deeper on her end of the sofa. It was getting late, and they really ought to grab a little shut-eye.

Sue let out a long sigh. "What I mean is that I gave

in. Just because Sophia was pretty and cool and nice… I figured she was a good role model, too. You know? A leader, I guess. A good friend."

Bea froze. "What are you saying?"

She felt Diane's body tense on the other end of the sofa.

Sue, however, went on, oblivious to her accusation. "I mean I trusted her. You know? And that was the one thing I can sort of point a finger to. That first time I let my guard down and said *yes* instead of *no* for once."

"Sophia *was* trustworthy," Bea shot back. "You could always trust her. It was a stupid card game."

"Sophia wasn't a leader, though," Diane added, her gaze narrowed on Bea, a warning. She shifted her gaze to Sue, and Bea felt her heart sink to her stomach.

"Right," Sue agreed. "You two were the leaders. I followed Sophia because she was hip and gorgeous, but I didn't know she was just following you two the whole time. It never occurred to me."

"You're being ridiculous," Bea spat. "Both of you." Her eyes flashed from Sue to Diane and then back to Sue. "The cards? Come on. We were always around those cards. That was Aunt Lil, not Soph. I even read them once, remember? And what did that have to do with your miscarriage, anyway? Nothing, that's what. If you're saying that you made other bad decisions because you followed Sophia who was following us, then you're accusing us of making bad decisions, too." She crossed her arms and huffed. "And you're admitting you're nothing more than a follower."

Sue shrank back. "Sorry, Bea. I'm not accusing *anyone* of *anything*." She blinked. "I *am* a follower."

"All she's saying, Bea, is that Sophia wasn't necessarily the girl Sue thought she was. She wasn't so perfect, you know?"

Bea desperately wanted to get up and run away—out to the backyard and down onto the beach. She wanted to stand in the lapping water and scream across the ocean.

But she didn't. "You know, Sue? You're right."

"I am?" Sue asked, her face at its breaking point with worry lines and raised brows.

"If Sophia ever did a bad thing, it was because of me. But don't throw her under the bus when she's not here to defend herself, okay?"

"Okay, Bea," Sue managed. "Sorry. Okay?"

Bea watched her friends look at each other, but she was done with the conversation. Done rehashing the past and their stupid childhood antics. Maybe it was all a bad idea. Maybe she should have dragged her mom—kicking and screaming—from her little rowhouse all the way down the shore to help her pick up some things before Greg took over.

"I'm sorry, too," Bea replied. "I flew off the handle. I just—"

"It's okay, Bea. We understand," Diane said, grabbing her hand across the sofa. "Sophia *was* pretty damn perfect, if you ask me."

"Me, too," Sue added weakly. "Sorry I said anything about it."

Bea softened. "Oh, Sue," she replied, "Don't apologize. I'm sensitive, I guess."

"We weren't being sensitive enough," Diane said. "Soph was great, Bea. She really was. Sue's trying to talk through her life, that's all. Right, Sue?"

Sue nodded. "I'm sorry. That was stupid of me to blame Sophia. She's not why I lowered my standards."

Bea swallowed and pulled her blanket tighter.

"Sophia had high standards for all of us you know. And for herself."

"Yes, she did," Sue replied.

Diane nodded her head. "Yep. She really did."

Bea turned to Sue. "It's my fault we got to this point in the convo." She chewed on her lower lip. "Our fault, actually. We're the ones who were pushing it. The miscarriage thing. For what it's worth——" she flicked a glance to Diane, whose face was impassive, open "—— Diane made a good point. We were both concerned. But you don't have to talk about your miscarriage. We're here if you do want to, though. We're here for you, now, Sue. I wish we were back then, too."

"I should have reached out more than I did," Sue answered, her voice deeper. "I figured I didn't need you. I didn't need *us*, you know?"

"How are things, anyway?" Diane asked. "I mean with Joe? Did you just agree to let the dream die? Sorry —I mean, did you just decide it wasn't in the cards?"

Bea and Sue laughed, but Diane frowned. "Sorry. Wrong thing to say, I guess."

Sue shook her head. "When it happened—the miscarriage, I mean—I sort of... shut down."

"How so?" Diane asked.

"I figured it wasn't, like you said, meant to be. And by then, I was sort of disgusted with myself. My body. And Joe, too."

"Why Joe?" Bea felt she was prodding. Pushing too far. "I'm sorry," she added. "I'm prying."

"Hey, my secret's safe with you girls, right? We made a pact, didn't we?" Sadness washed from Sue's face and for a split second, Bea thought she glimpsed the sweet little girl Sophia had taken to. The one they coveted like a little pet—first at CCD and then at school. And then every single summer until they were young women. The innocent one. The good one.

"We're The Summer Society, right?" Bea replied. "Swear on our lives."

Diane held up two fingers. "Summer Society's honor."

A goofy grin spread across Sue's face, and she covered it with a musty pillow. Bea even saw tendrils of dust puff out in the air of the low lamplight. She cringed at their little setting, there in the orangey-yellow living room—smoke-encrusted and dated as an old penny. But she kept quiet, and they listened as Sue spilled everything.

From how she closed up shop south of her collar-bone all the way until she finally caught Joe in the act. *Decades* after she started suspecting he was stepping out.

Through it all, all of Sue's mournful admissions and soupy, self-deprecating tangents... something occurred to Bea.

Sue might have been barren—or not, who was to say? Miscarriages were more common than cracked eggs in the market. Sue might have been fooled into a shoddy marriage with a loser who didn't know the difference between a hole in the wall and, well...

But Sue, despite all her fears in the world and all her nerves and her superstitions, had gone out there and done it. She dated someone. She married him. She forged a career and worked hard. She tried to have a baby and live her dreams. She dared to live.

And all the while—for ages—Bea sat in her boring condo in her boring suburb and drove to and from the same classroom for thirty-some-odd years and her only reprieve... the only times she followed any wisp of a dream, were when she got together with Sophia. When she rode on her sister's coattails to wild Vegas adventures or weekend spa retreats. It was all on her younger sister's good grace and sympathies that Bea had had any life at all. Sure, it meant quality time with the most important person in Bea's life. But, what about *Bea*? When was she going to become the heroine? The main character in her own story? When would she stop playing foil to the pretty, perfect Italian blonde with impossible green eyes and white teeth and a great laugh?

As she sat there, listening to Sue recount the icky moment she pulled up to her house and found out that everything she'd built her life on was crumbling and instead of falling back into that same old bed... Sue snatched her soon-to-be-ex-husband's plane tickets and chose to fight back. In a small way, sure. But still, she wasn't sitting there at that house, complacent and victimized.

She was doing something. Anything. And Bea needed to do something, too.

For Sophia's memory or despite her death... it didn't matter. Bea needed to do *something*.

"We can't let it go," she whispered, cutting Sue off just as she finished declaring that she might end up a hobo on some beach in California, but that was okay by her if it meant that she was finally free.

"You mean Sue?" Diane asked.

"I have to go to San Diego, Bea," Sue started to reply, "I already made up my mind. Come with if you want—" but Bea threw up a hand and twirled it around in a circle.

"No, I mean this place."

"I don't understand," Sue replied.

"One summer isn't enough. Especially if you're going to California and Diane has to get back to her social life. How will we get together? When? And where? What if Sue meets another jerk? Or Diane burns through all the men on her dating app?"

Diane smirked at Bea and lifted an eyebrow. "There's a chance I could..."

"What if I retire early? What will we do? Where will we go?"

"You're going to buy Greg out?"

"There's nothing to buy. He doesn't own it. I told you. He just pays utilities. Taxes. That sort of thing. We can make it work. Girls, come on. We can do it together. Don't you think?" Bea glanced from Diane to Sue and back again, her eyes wild and her head starting to throb with a dull ache from the wine. If she could keep Aunt Lil's then she was doing something with herself. With her *future*. Even if it meant that she was, after all, holding on to the past.

"It's a bigger financial commitment than you probably realize," Sue pointed out, seemingly more comfortable in her own skin now that she'd poured her heart out. "And anyway, I have a better chance of going back to Joe than I do of finding another husband, so you don't need to worry about that."

"Don't you dare say that," Diane warned, her voice acid. "Over our dead body will you give that loser another chance. And if you're serious, then Bea's right. We'll have to have an emergency locale for you. A refuge." Bea suspected Diane was partially joking, but the reality was, she wasn't.

Sue *was* a follower. She needed her friends to stand and be leaders.

"It can't be that much money. I mean, if we winterize and talk to the county assessor and maybe petition to bring the tax down, it'll be what? A couple thousand? A few thousand? Each year?"

"Do you have an extra few thousand dollars floating around, Bea?" Sue asked. "I don't. I might be penniless if I follow through with the divorce. And what if we do stay here? We'll need more money in the summer months, if we're actually here—using the water and electricity and all. It takes money to keep a vacation home. Especially one in Gull's Landing. We don't have extra money, Bea. At least I don't. And you don't, either, from the sounds of it."

Sue stared at Bea and then, together, completely involuntarily, they both turned their heads and looked at Diane. Princess Di, as Craig called her when they started dating—Bea remembered this fact because she could distinctly recall thinking that *yes*. That's exactly what Diane became when she met Craig Bettancourt, Esquire.

A princess.

Chapter 16

Diane, 1985

"He's staring at you, Soph," Diane pointed out, leaning back on her elbows and throwing her head at the trio of boys crossing in front.

"Gee whiz, Diane," Bea hissed. "Keep it down, would ya?"

Diane lifted a brow at Soph, and they both rolled their eyes, but Diane saw her cousin's gaze land back on the tall dark-haired one in the middle. A total looker. A cocky one, too, if Diane's intuition proved true. She almost regretted encouraging the whole thing.

The boys stopped at the far end of where the girls had set up camp with their red cooler and pink-striped towels (both on loan from Aunt Lil).

One boy, a skinny blond, chucked a frisbee down the shore. The redhead complained good-naturedly and jogged off to fetch it, and Diane couldn't help but laugh.

"Hey ladies." The blond boy pushed his hand through his loose tangles, and Diane exchanged a look with Bea. The blond was nothing to sneeze at, but he seemed younger. Goofy.

"Hey boys," she answered on behalf of the group.

"You're not from here," the dark-haired one pointed out, hands on his hips like a cop or something. His eyes seemed to narrow on Sophia, and Diane could have sworn she was puckering her lips. They grew an inch under his stare.

Still, it was Diane with the guts to keep the conversation flowing. She wrapped her towel around her chubby stomach and sat up, raking her fingers through her frizz and praying to God that it wasn't half as bad as it felt.

"You don't know that," Diane spat back.

"Sure I do," he answered as the redhead returned with the frisbee. "You're Shoobies."

"What's a Shoobie?" Sue piped up, her sunburnt face squinting in the sun. Diane wanted to knock her with an umbrella. She was making them all look like a bunch of nerds.

"Look," Diane cut in before the boys could answer. "We got a house here." Diane drew her finger like a sword up to the white house behind them.

"You don't live there," the blond boy replied. "We'd know you."

"Oh, yeah?" Diane asked. "How?"

"We're local, that's how." The redhead said it with a pride that Diane figured she'd never know. Living in Philly, even in Briar Creek, just didn't have the same glamor, apparently.

But that didn't stop her from putting on airs. "Yeah, well, if you're so local, then why don't you tell us what there is to do around here anyway."

The boys snickered, and Diane glanced down at her girlfriends, grinning.

They had been dying for this exact sort of interaction for the past five years. An in with the locals. Cute ones. *Boy* ones.

The others pushed the redhead toward Diane, and she could see that his body was aflame with freckles. When he came closer, she saw that his red hair was less red and more auburn. And even with the freckles, he wasn't pasty. Not like typical redheads. And his body wasn't that skinny. Not like the other boys. He was sort of even muscly. For a teenager. A sly smile curled his lips and he gave Diane the eye.

Really.

He *gave* her the *eye*.

It was the first time in Diane's entire life that a boy had given her the eye (Jimmy Walton sure as hell never even looked north of her shoulders), and when he did, she knew it was over for good.

"We have fun," he answered, and she could have sworn he'd taken another step closer to her.

She lifted an eyebrow and resisted the urge to tug at her obnoxious hair again. "Oh, yeah? How?" she answered.

The others had grown silent, watching them, apparently, and waiting for the tension to burst.

The boy shrugged. "We surf. Water ski. Sometimes we hang around the boardwalk or check out the arcade." His gaze shifted up behind her. "Not so much anymore, though," he added, his chest puffing out half an inch.

Diane knew the arcade all too well. It was for kids. They weren't kids anymore. Was this muscly, tawny-skinned redhead a kid?

Hell, no. That much she could tell.

"Cool," she answered. "What about at night? You can't surf or ski at night, can you?"

She felt her girlfriends hiss on their beach towels below her. Bea and Sue hated being out at night. It gave them the creeps. But it gave Diane a thrill. And she knew Soph agreed, which put Bea in quite the pickle.

"We don't hang out with Shoobies at night," the boy replied.

Diane frowned. "Well we don't hang out with *townies* any time of the day *or* night," she shot back.

He shrugged and held up his hands. The air pressure seemed to lift and a salty breeze washed between them. The sounds of gulls squawking and his friends buzzing behind him and Bea and Sue's pleas that she sit back down were all drowned out by the throbbing of blood as it coursed through her veins and rushed to her head.

Glowing with adrenaline, she narrowed her gaze on the redhead. "And we don't talk to strangers, either."

She turned in the sand and began to rejoin the girls, when he grabbed her wrist and twirled her like a dancer.

"I'm Craig," he said, and pulled her right hand into his. "Let's not be strangers anymore."

At that, his friends went wild, clapping and oohing, and even the girls gasped from their towels, but Diane was too far gone to notice or care.

She held his hand and replied, "Diane. Some people call me Di." It was a fib. Diane always wished someone would nickname her Di like Sophia had nicknamed Beatrice *Bea* and Susan *Sue*.

Now was her chance.

"Like the queen?" he replied.

Laughing, she shook her head. "You mean the princess? Princess Di?"

"Princess, queen—what difference does it make? As long as I can be your Prince Charming."

"THAT WAS the cheesiest pick-up line I ever heard in my life," Bea whispered as they stood outside the ice cream parlor. The boys were inside, ordering and treating the girls all thanks to the moment on the sand. Craig and Diane's introduction had turned into a strip of hot glue, melding the opposite-sex groups into each other.

"I don't think I've ever even heard a real pick-up line ever used," Sue mentioned. "It was like something out of a movie."

Diane flushed with delight. "He's cute, right?" She was asking, but she didn't need an answer.

The girls nodded along, and soon enough the guys were back with four extra cones between them, Craig handing his to Diane as they took up together on a stroll down the boardwalk. With plenty of daylight left and even more summer, anything was possible.

Ahead of them, Diane watched as the dark-haired boy—Doug something or other—sidled up next to Sophia.

This wasn't as thrilling or entertaining as the beach scene with Craig and Diane spinning with control toward a sweet scene out of a sappy Valentine's TV special. Sophia *always* drew stares and offers of dates. Boys were *always* sidling up next to her wherever they were—be it along a sidewalk in downtown Philly *or* the boardwalk.

Even so, Diane kept her eye on the pair, realizing that this time was different. Sophia returned Doug's interest, laughing and grinning at him happily.

Not a single one of the girls had ever had a serious, long-term boyfriend. Not one of them. Flings? Sure.

Crushes? Always. Never a real-life romance. Not in the fall, winter, spring, *or* summer.

But here they were, two of them paired off already and one of them falling fast in love.

Diane and Craig talked about nothing and every-thing that day. From her big, loud Italian family to his big, loud Spanish-Irish clan. *His* word, not hers. She was pretty sure she'd never heard the word clan, and she liked it. She liked him and his confidence and his quirky good looks and quirky good words.

Their witty banter from the beach had turned soft, and she quickly learned that Craig was a total sweet-heart. He had family in Philly, downtown. He spent lots of time there. He spent lots of time everywhere, actually. His family traveled to Mexico about every single year and across the States, too.

He confessed, unabashedly, that he believed in true love and he was actively searching for it, but he never saw a tourist as interesting and beautiful as Diane.

That was when the record scratched for her, and she figured it was all a scam. Really and truly, how could this boy say as much when he'd seen Sophia? Or any number of weirdo tourists who probably passed for "interesting" in the eyes of a townie?

Inwardly, she waffled about whether to call him out. But Diane only degraded herself privately or to her friends. She knew better than to reveal her hand to a potential love connection. It was highly preferable to be interesting rather than boring, after all. So, instead of brushing off the compliment or asking if he was blind, she simply answered, "Thanks."

And really, truly… that was it. The beginning. Some might have called it the beginning of the end. But Diane called it the beginning of forever. And deep in her heart, in the spot where she stored her true feelings, protected within her loud, flamboyant armor, she decided that she was going to have that boy. She was going to be his princess or his queen or whatever name he wanted to call her. Maybe one day, she hoped privately, away from her friends and in her quiet moments alone and her private moments with the Spanish-Irish clansman named Craig, he'd call her his wife.

It became her little personal secret: that the frizzy-haired, abrasive Italian girl wasn't all hard. She had a soft spot. And she'd found love. She wouldn't confess it to her girlfriends, at least not for another several months.

But anyway, in two months' time, Diane wasn't the only one with a summer secret.

Chapter 17

Sue

The next morning, after they tabled the money conversation, Sue awoke before the others. She crept quietly to the kitchen and fiddled with the old coffee maker—some oversized contraption from the early nineties, no doubt.

After figuring it out, she ducked back into the living room and grabbed her bag and dressed quickly in the downstairs bath as Bea and Diane snored together on the big sofa. How they'd fit, she had no clue. No way did they sleep well.

Then, after waiting a beat to see if either one arose, she poured herself a mug and slipped out to the backyard.

The sun hadn't had the chance to warm up either, apparently, so Sue cradled her steaming coffee under her chin and walked to the beach, thinking hard about what she'd told her friends. All her marital secrets and then some. Guilt nearly swallowed her whole.

As a girl, she'd learned to keep the problems of her marriage private. It was her mother's advice. And Dear Abby's, too.

As a woman, Sue came to believe that advice, choosing to apply it in broad strokes across everything. Even when deep down she knew that certain things ought to be fair game. Certain things she ought to have taken to a therapist or a close friend. She never did, of course.

Now, here she was, a middle-aged woman with a lifetime of disappointment and she still felt like a bad wife for revealing Joe's dalliances.

The trip to San Diego began to feel like something else—something other than a fresh start or an escape or even a vacation. It began to feel like a way to run from her problems rather than a way to overcome them.

She began to wonder if she ought to stick around the shore, after all. Maybe she'd mail the tickets back to Joe. She could include a goofy postcard, even. And on the back, she could tell him it was over.

I'm through with your cheating rear end!

Send the papers to 1480 Boardwalk Drive, Gull's Landing, New Jersey!

That's where you can find me!

Honestly, though, she didn't want him to find her at all ever again. She liked this new phase—this age of exploration she felt she was sliding into. Like that book *How Stella Got Her Groove Back*. Or the one—what was it called? *Eat, Pray, Love.* Yes. That was Sue now.

A woman on a journey.

But if she went to San Diego, it would be alone. And maybe alone wasn't a good way to be in her current condition. After all, she spent every day of her life alone.

Maybe the journey she needed wasn't a cross-continental one. Maybe it was more like a mission. An expedition snuggled inside of her friend's expedition—Bea's. Maybe... Sue *should* stick around. If not for her, then for her friend.

Then again, if Sue wanted to stay in Gull's Landing, she would have to help Bea save Aunt Lil's old shore house. A monumental task, probably. And an unnecessary one, possibly.

Did they really *have* to have a vacation home to continue The Summer Society? They could use Bea's condo. Or Diane's house. Or even a second floor with two queen beds in Hotel Del.

Then again, it sure would make things easy to stay in place. And it would make Bea happy.

And in her heart of hearts, Sue believed it's what her best friend in the whole wide world, Soph, would have wanted.

Ironically, however, if there was anything that was an obstacle to prevent Sue from sticking it out there on the boardwalk and in the old house on the beach, it was *her*. Sophia.

Sue was scared to go upstairs. Scared to take up that haunted space. Scared to see the truth.

Even more than that, though, Sue was scared to be around when Bea learned the truth.

———

1985

The summer when Diane and Craig hit it off was the summer Sue first considered the fact that there might be something more powerful than friendship.

That something?

The scariest word in the English language. In fact, Sue Merkle preferred not to think of it as one word but instead three letters.

S. E. X.

It was more palatable that way. She could swallow the letters and not feel a smidge of guilt that she was going straight to hell for even uttering such a dirty thing. For even *thinking* about it.

Sue was one-hundred percent positive that *none* of them were having S. E. X. She wasn't, for one. She knew Soph wasn't and wouldn't. They'd made their own pact on that one. And as for the older two, Sue figured Bea to be quite like her. A little daunted. A little too Catholic.

Then there was Diane. Wild Diane with her fast-talking boardwalk boyfriend. One night, when the girls stayed up late in the living room, secretly sipping Aunt Lil's wine and giggling into the wee hours of the morning, Bea asked Diane point blank if she was sleeping with Craig.

Sue hated that phrase. *Sleeping with* someone. It was deceptive. It reminded her of her favorite re-runs of *I Love Lucy* and how married couples didn't always necessarily *sleep* together, so if they were *sleeping together*, then why did that have to mean the S. E. X. word?

Diane caught them all off guard when she signed the cross and said, "Not on my mother's life. Sure, we fool around. But I'm saving myself. Just like you."

That night was the first time in the history of their friendship that Diane De Luca got her feelings hurt. Sue could feel it in the musty, smokey air of ol' Lil's living room.

"Sorry," Bea replied. "I just figured since we can't peel you two off of each other."

Diane huffed. "I might eat too much and swear too much and drink and smoke, but I know better than to seal my casket."

Sue was confused. "What's that supposed to mean?"

"If my mother finds out I'm *doing it*, then I'm as good as dead. Plus it's in the Ten Commandments, ya nerds. Thou shalt not… *do it*."

It ended the discussion, and Sue felt a little softer toward Diane after that.

But just because none of them were *doing it* (another awful way to talk in circles around the whole icky thing), didn't mean that that very concept wasn't driving every single decision all of them made that year. All of them except Sue, of course.

Still, she figured that S. E. X. or no S. E. X., Diane probably would have counted that summer as her best trip down the shore to date. She was a new woman. Happy and a little less bossy than usual. A little more distracted and tamed, in some ways.

As for everyone else? Well, for Sue, it was headed towards the usual type of summer, where she had to fight to go home at a reasonable hour and fight to stay in Gull's Landing instead of heading to Wildwood for a night. Everything was going as planned until that one particular night when Sue almost died on the beach.

It all happened the night of the wiener roast.

Initially, Sue observed the whole thing unfold from a distance, but that's what Sue was good at. Watching. Keeping an eye on the others. They didn't realize it, but without her in the backdrop, even Bea—the leader—couldn't protect them.

Especially when the problem was inside of their clique.

And the thing of it? Well, the thing of it was that this *problem*—this little moment that really shouldn't have been much of a big deal at all—became a really big deal. Sue knew as much. She saw that over the next decade, as they graduated high school and some of them moved on to college and got married and had kids, it ate away at their clique more than anything else.

More than time.

More than distance.

More than Sue's own personal tragedy ever would, because that—a late-term miscarriage—might have been a little of the sticky stuff. It might have been the thing to reel them all back in and situate them squarely on those threadbare old beach towels they re-used over and over again from Aunt Lil's linen closet.

And the funny thing was? It wasn't Diane's fault. It wasn't even Bea's. Not in Sue's opinion. It wasn't Soph's, either.

It was *his*.

That's why, when Sue met Joe and had her reservations, she batted them away. Because in 1985, she came to learn what she could expect. Where she could set the bar.

She could set it as high as her best friend. Or as high as Diane. Unfortunately, at the tender age of seventeen and even despite her keen observations of the event in question, she set it with Soph.

When she should have set it with Diane.

There they sat, on the sand just down from Lil's backyard. The girls had dragged the chairs together while the boys collected primal stuff to create a small fire —rocks to frame it out and beach wood for burning.

Aunt Lil, all too pleased that the girls were making love connections on her very property, supplied hot dogs, s'mores fixings, and even the red cooler—that time chock full of ice and soda.

Looking back now, Sue might even throw a bit of the blame on Lil. But not much, because what did she know? She figured they were still kids. She figured the girls were playing spin-the-bottle and getting their first kisses, then and there. At the ripe ages of seventeen and eighteen, respectively.

Well, that much could have been true for Susan Merkle, anyway. It would have been better if it were. She didn't have her first kiss until the following summer in the alley out back of Freddie's Footlongs (why were hot dogs such a prominent thing in her formative years?) when the dishwasher pushed up against her, hot breath and body odor wafting across the wet, stinky pavement, and asked if she wanted to kiss him.

She did, actually.

And so they kissed, all teeth and tongue and alleyway shouts from the next diner down. Sue ought to have regretted it. She ought to have kicked herself for not having her first kiss in Gull's Landing like a cute, fun, hip girl. But that's how it went when you were a girl like Sue. Never the right moment. Never the right choice.

"Truth or Dare," Diane started, as they held hot-dog-laden wires out across the flame.

"Aw, come on, Diane. We're too old," Bea complained. Sue agreed.

"I'll play," Sophia said, giggling as Doug tickled her.

Sophia was the only one not in her own seat, which was perfectly empty by the way. Instead, she draped herself across Doug Hurley's lap. Sue kept an eye on his hand, twitching each time it rubbed its way across Sophia's stomach.

Doug Hurley made Sue want to hurl. She never

shared that with anyone since the others seemed to like him well enough. Especially Soph, of course.

"Truth," Sophia added. Her eyes glowed greener above the sparks, and Sue caught Doug slip a finger beneath the hem of her shirt. Sue gagged.

Luckily, the game took precedence, and Sophia slid off his lap and sat in the sand between his legs. That chair was still available.

Maddening, really.

"Have you ever been in love?"

All heads turned to Bea, who'd taken it upon herself to ask the question. Bea sat in the seat next to Sophia's empty one and across the fire from Sue.

Bea was staring at the fire, entranced, it looked like. Didn't even turn her attention to Sophia or Doug or Diane, Diane being the one who really ought to have had the turn to ask.

The fire crackled and a roar of waves crashed on the beach, and Sue wished she liked the blond guy or that the blond guy liked her—Jeffy was his name. She wished she had bigger boobs and a cuter swimsuit, and all the wishes she usually had in private grew heightened in that very moment. She shifted on her chair and turned her hot dog then drew it back and set about sliding it into the bun. But her focus was acutely on Sophia's answer.

It would tell Sue everything. That Sophia, with her perfect hair and clear skin and kind heart, had really, truly bad taste. Sue was no expert in all things romance. But she could spot a bad egg from a mile away. And Sue was Sophia's best friend. Other than Doug Hurley and a few random boys from school, there was no other candidate.

That really was the moment of truth.

When Sue would think about that night later, she'd wonder why she still stuck by her best friend afterwards. Why she didn't snap her fingers and cry out, *"Ah ha! I can even pick 'em better than you, and I don't even pick 'em!"*

Sophia's eyes closed for a moment longer than a blink. Sue took a bite of her dog then looked at Bea. Bea was looking at Doug. Doug leaned forward and his fingers slithered like claws around Sophia's torso, pulling her back protectively.

What happened next was unclear. Sue couldn't tell if the nudge was purposeful or flirtatious or accidental or aggressive. It was too dark. She was too dumb in the ways of summer love.

Then, when Sophia leaned deeper into his lap and nodded her head like her life depended on it, Sue sucked in a breath. Too much air, too quickly.

And right there, in the middle of The Summer Society's last game ever of Truth or Dare, Sue Merkle started choking on her hot dog.

And she'd never forget. It wasn't that jerk Doug-Makes-Me-Wanna-Hurley who came to the rescue.

No sirree.

It was Craig.

The guy manning the 'smores station clear on the other side of the fire. He jumped through the flames and hauled Sue up in one heaving, hulking shake and *pop*, out flew a chunk of meat and bun, squarely onto the wide arm of Doug's chair, landing with a *splat*.

She remembered that after Craig saved her life, it wasn't appreciation that first revived her heart. It wasn't gratitude and warm-hearted cheer.

It was humiliation.

"Ew," Doug said. Bea and Jeffy and Diane were

surrounding Sue, patting her and rubbing her and tending to her. And her very best friend in the world came last to the huddle around poor little chokey Sue. She cooed along and smoothed Sue's hair.

But that's not what stood out to Sue. What stood out to her was when Doug doubled down in the near distance by saying, "Can somebody get some bleach before I upchuck?"

And awfully, miserably, Bea turned to Doug Hurley and—this part Sue could picture clear as day—she leaned down and took her bare hand and swiped the glob off.

But that's not what Sue *saw*.

She *saw* Doug, his eyes fixated on Bea's bosom. She saw his sneering face go dark, and she saw that everything was wrong with that night.

Later, after her embarrassment washed away and she saw the whole event for what it was, Sue liked to think that it was that brief, heroic moment that Diane decided Craig was the one and that Sophia decided that Doug Hurley was nothing more than a boardwalk playboy brat.

The former could have been true, but the latter proved *false*. Sophia never considered Doug Hurley to be a boardwalk playboy brat.

Another month would pass until their relationship ended with a great, dramatic finality.

It happened right after Sophia recovered from a week-long summer flu, newly healthy but still a bit mournful for some reason. Probably because she had to miss out on the last seven days of Aunt Lil's pancakes and Mack's greasy pizza.

Or maybe because their vacation was coming to a close. When Sue and Bea and even Diane all admitted

EnvisionWare

Library

Date: 7/6/2023

Time: 1:51:34 PM

Name: EVANS, MARGARET A

Fines/Fees Owed: $0.00

Total Checked Out: 3

Checked Out

Title: Lies and other acts of love
Barcode: 204091012429020
Due Date: 7/27/2023,23:59

Title: The summer society
Barcode: 204091012613230
Due Date: 7/27/2023,23:59

Title: The summer guests
Barcode: 204091011967692
Due Date: 7/27/2023,23:59

that they were happy to get home and get back to normal, Sophia protested that she'd never be normal again.

Not after she'd suffered the greatest heartache a woman in love *could* suffer.

Chapter 18

Bea

Surprisingly, Bea did not wake up with a hangover. She wasn't groggy or anxious. She sprung to life as if it was 1978 and Aunt Lil had bacon on the griddle and pancakes bubbling on the stove.

When she slipped off the sofa, tucking the blanket around snoring Diane, she saw Sue's spot on the love seat sat empty and took off towards the kitchen to find her.

And then it all made sense.

Sue had bacon on the griddle and pancakes bubbling on the stove. Instead of a cigarette dangling between two knobby knuckles, she held a coffee mug.

"Now I remember why I invited you," Bea joked, striding to the griddle and taking up the tongs to help.

Sue grinned. "Hey, I'm happy to be the cook all summer. That means I just stay down here, and I don't have to go up there." She lifted her chin towards the second floor, but something else caught Bea's attention.

"All summer? Aren't you flying to California this weekend?"

Sue flipped a pancake onto a waiting plate and shook her head. "I don't know, honestly. I…" She poured another circle of batter into the cast iron pan then looked up and met Bea's gaze. "I don't know if I want to leave yet."

Bea smiled and pulled Sue in for a side hug. "San Diego would be a nice escape for you, Sue."

"But I don't want to be alone. And you need me, Bea. I think Diane might need us, too."

Bea broke off the edge of a crispy slice of bacon and popped it in her mouth. "Yeah, well. We need each other. We have for a while now, I suspect."

"Is Diane awake?"

Bea shook her head. "No." She clacked the tongs then removed the bacon from the griddle and arranged it on the paper towel Sue had set out. "What will you do with the tickets?"

"I'm not sure. Maybe I'll overnight them to Joe. He can take his friend." She wiggled her eyebrows, and Bea's mouth fell open.

"Who are you and what have you done with Susan Bleckert?"

"It's Merkle now. Sue Merkle."

Bea's smile fell away when Sue didn't look up from the pan. She wondered how she could have let her friend suffer for so long. She wondered, too, how Sue could allow *herself* to suffer. Mainly, though, Bea worried that it wasn't over. If there was one thing she found to be true in life, it's that people didn't change. People couldn't run from their demons or their ghosts or whatever it was that held them in shackles. They stayed in place. Until they didn't have the choice anymore.

"Morning." Diane entered the kitchen, her hair matted in impressive angles against the side of her head, her makeup smeared like a clown.

Bea grinned at her. "You're a sight to behold."

"I could say the same about you two," Diane replied, pointing a red-tipped finger and twirling it around at Bea and Sue who exchanged a look.

Without the added complications of fake lashes and a blow-out, neither Bea nor Sue looked much different from when they went to bed. A little more crumpled, perhaps, but not different.

"Please. You look like you spent the night draped across Bernie's bar top," Bea shot back, laughing as she swiveled around with the plate of bacon. "Here. Make yourself useful."

"Bernie's," Diane replied, her voice floating. "Now that's a blast from the past. I remember singing karaoke there with Craig. That had to be the very last summer we were around here, you know that? Before he shipped off to college."

"Before we all left, yeah, I remember," Sue added, carrying a tower of pancakes to the table as Bea brought the syrup and butter.

Bea couldn't recall the last time she had a stack of hotcakes and a side of bacon. It was decadent and sinful, and it was exactly the right way to start a summer vacation. Especially the sort of summer vacation that wasn't *quite* a vacation.

"Now *that's* a view," Diane proclaimed through a mouthful of pancakes just a moment after they sat down.

"I know. We took it for granted," Bea began, turning to take in the ocean. "Oh my God." Her hands flew to her wiry ponytail and she cinched it tight then rubbed the pads of her pinkies quickly on her undereye bags. "Oh my God, what is *he* doing here?"

It wasn't the ocean Diane was admiring, after all.

"You *know* him?" Diane pressed.

Behind them, walking through the gate in a fresh white tee, half-zipped wetsuit and bare feet, with a shiny-coated golden retriever jogging at his side, was none other than Brooks Morgan.

"Kind of," Bea whispered.

She pushed back in her chair and walked to the screen door in time for him to wave.

"Good morning, Bea!"

"*Ooh*," Diane hissed in the background, and Bea snapped her fingers behind her back to shush her friend.

"Brooks, hi! Good morning." She stood at the screen door as he waited on the other side.

If she opened it, he would see her greasy hair and smell the fact that she hadn't showered yet and had been stuck on a damp old couch all night.

"Aren't you going to open the door?" Sue said, and Bea sensed her standing and coming to the rescue.

Bea tried for a casual laugh. "Oh, right. Sorry! It's, um, early, isn't?"

"Not that early," Brooks answered, holding his watch up. "But no, no. No need to open up. Darla's Frisbee flew into your yard this morning." He waved a hand into the middle distance, and Bea's shoulders dropped. Relief.

"Oh, no problem."

"Care for some coffee?" Diane rasped from her seat at the table, not three yards away. Bea looked back and saw her friend through this stranger's eyes. He'd think they hired a boardwalk prostitute to join them for breakfast if he took one look at her, and she prayed he'd turn down the request.

"Well, we're almost out, but I mean we could set another—" she started awkwardly.

He held up his hand. "No worries, girls. Maybe another morning. I've got to open shop in a bit. You ladies have a great day."

He whistled for his dog, Darla, who'd found her Frisbee, and they left together, jogging out onto the sun-kissed beach.

Bea wilted back into her seat, a line of sweat forming on her forehead and up along her spine. "Does the AC work in this place?"

"It wouldn't matter even if it did. You've got the *hots*, woman," Diane declared, gulping her coffee and grinning like a fool. "Why on *earth* did you shoo him away like that?"

"Diane, *look* at me," Bea protested. "Hell, look at *you*. Look at all of us! We don't want to scare him off, do we?"

"He didn't seem afraid," Sue offered coyly.

"Oh, what do *you* know?" Bea spat back, pushing a soaked square of pancake around her plate. She'd lost her appetite. Too much going on. Too many emotions to juggle.

"So who is he?" Diane asked.

"He owns the surf shop next door. That's all. I met him before you showed up last night. He was teaching a group of kids, and he swung in to ask about the house."

"Oh?" Sue dabbed her mouth with a paper towel. "What did he want to know about the house?"

A silence filled the table. The answer was obvious.

Bea shrugged. "He wanted to know if it was on the market. That's all."

"Was he here last year?" Diane asked, her voice losing its edge and slipping down an octave.

Nodding, Bea kept her reply brief. "Yes. I think he's been here a few years. He saw the media vans and all the hubbub. He said he sort of keeps an eye on things. Because of his business, and whatnot."

"Whatnot." Diane grunted then blew out a sigh. "I wonder what it was like here. Didn't you just itch to drive down? When it happened?"

"No," Bea answered firmly. "Not even a little bit. Not at all."

"I can understand that," Sue said. "When I got your invitation, I thought it might have been a prank. You know, from the same types of kids who torture cats on Halloween or something. The only reason I even *considered* coming was because of Joe and the fact that I had a few days to kill."

"Wow," Diane answered. "That's a dark assumption."

Sue shrugged, and Bea pressed her fingers into her temples, massaging.

"You know," Diane went on. "I almost drove down here myself. Back then, in the fall when I was thinking of taking a vacation."

Bea frowned at her. "Without me?"

"You wouldn't come, remember?"

"And you *wanted* to be here? That soon?" Bea took another drink of coffee, this time sipping slowly and meaningfully as if to channel the caffeine directly to the source of her growing headache.

"I mean, I felt that pull, you know? Call of the void, almost. And it's not like it was some dramatic thing, not after all. Not after the investigation, right?" Diane asked.

Bea set her mug down and stared at it.

Sue added, "We never did learn what happened,

Bea. Maybe I wouldn't be so scared if it was something innocent."

"You *do* know what happened," Bea shot back. "My mother *told* you. She told everyone, and it *was* innocent." She shook her head and pressed her fork down on the center of her uneaten pancakes, squishing them until they were mush.

"She said it was heart failure," Diane answered softly.

Bea replied, "It *was* heart failure, *Diane.*"

"Heart failure caused by *what?* Sophia was the image of health, Bea," Diane pressed, and Bea wanted to reach across the table and smack her in the face.

Sue cleared her throat, and the noise propelled Bea to shoot up from her seat and carry her dishes to the sink, where she set them without scraping and then poured a second mug of coffee.

The others kept quiet at the table, but she knew they were looking at each other, gossiping about her with their eyes.

After a long swig, she took a deep breath and returned. "This is hard to talk about. No matter how she died, it would be hard to talk about." Bea lowered back to the table.

Diane and Sue offered sympathetic looks which helped to still Bea's pulse.

She swallowed then lifted her hands from her lap and dropped them again. "Sophia wasn't the picture of health she appeared to be." It felt good—that initial burst of a confession.

"Did she—?" Sue began.

Diane frowned and cocked her head. "Was it—?"

Bea squeezed her eyes shut. A single tear spilled from

one, but that was it. She'd gotten through the hardest part.

Diane pressed her hand on the table in front of Bea. "You know, I had a girlfriend whose husband died of cardiomyopathy. He looked totally normal. He was fit and handsome. The last few years, though, he went downhill. But you wouldn't have expected it to be a heart issue, you know? I mean look at me." Diane gestured to her torso and then pinched the hanging skin of her jowls. "I'm a walking commercial for heart disease." She shook her head. "But not him."

"Was it that, Bea? Cardiomyopathy?" Sue asked gently.

Bea's mouth set in a line. In all her life, when she'd been on the edges of someone else's tragedy—a coworker's ailing grandmother or a student's suddenly deceased parent—the cause of death was always among the first pieces of information that went out.

She had brain cancer. Terrible tragedy.

Or,

Fatal car accident. No seatbelts. Followed by a clicking of the tongue.

So then why, for Sophia, was Greg circumspect? And even more than that, why didn't Dolores push the issue?

Why did Bea have to fight to get every tidbit of information—why did she have to drag Greg down to the coroner's office and all but force him to get answers?

If only Soph was more like Bea. If only she hadn't married, then Dolores and Bea would have been the first to know why Sophia left her family and came to Gull's Landing and then, promptly and without any explanation, *died*. Maybe, if she hadn't married, then Soph wouldn't have died to begin with. Or maybe if she'd married someone else.

But *why. Why, why, why* didn't Sophia *say* anything to her sister? Why didn't she tell her?

And finally *why* didn't Bea see it?

"No." Bea let out a sigh. "It wasn't cardiomyopathy." The disease criss-crossed her tongue like a joke. If *only* it was cardiomyopathy. That would have been leagues more tolerable.

She closed her eyes and felt the skin on her forehead twitch as images of Sophia—glamorous and loving Soph —spun through, and when she opened them again, she was looking through a glaze of sadness. "She was struggling a little, but Greg said she seemed better. He said she was getting better every day."

"What is this mystery disease, Bea?" Diane asked gently. "You have to have known *something*. Why are you holding back?"

Bea couldn't take the prodding any longer. She was about to burst out with the truth, but revealing it would mean accepting it, and accepting would mean that it *was* true."

"Did they push for an autopsy?" Sue asked.

Bea took a deep breath. "Yes."

But she knew that they didn't even need one.

Chapter 19

Bea, 1985

"I think I'm in love with Doug."

They were sitting together on the sand. Just Bea and Soph. Diane and Sue had dragged the cooler back to Aunt Lil's to refill it with soda. The boys hadn't come around yet.

Bea frowned at her little sister. "Really?"

"Yeah," Sophia answered, her tone defensive. "So what?"

"He's—well, he's cute, sure. But he's a local. It would be, like, a long-distance thing. And besides, Soph, you're smarter than him." Bea passed the suntan lotion, matter of fact about the whole thing, but still surprised that Sophia's feelings ran as deep as they did. To Bea, Doug Hurley was a summer fling. Nothing more, nothing less. He was gorgeous, no doubt—not cute, but verifiably gorgeous. Even so, Sophia was out of his league.

"You mean to tell me that if Doug wanted to be your

boyfriend, you'd pass?" Sophia squirted lotion on her arm and started rubbing.

When she put it like that, it was different. If Soph was a ten, Bea was a six—on a good day. Their own mother had even said as much. Quite literally. *"Sophia is Bo Derek. Bea, you're... that one gal from the barbershop your father used to go to. The one with beautiful dark hair and a strong body and—"*

It was all she needed to say. Sophia was a sex symbol from the movies and Bea was her dead father's no-name hairdresser from downtown Philly.

"You really love him? You've been seeing him for like a month, Soph."

"Yeah, Bea, gee whiz. What's your hang-up? Aren't you happy for me?" She worked the lotion up her shoulders and across her collarbones. Bea frowned.

"Of course I'm happy for you, but none of us know what you see in Doug. He's a playboy, Soph."

"You're just jealous, Bea. And if Diane and Sue agree, then they're jealous, too."

"What are we jealous about?" Diane's voice came from behind them, and Bea whipped her head around. She did *not* want the conversation to explode.

"Nothing, never mind," she said, giving Soph the eye.

Her sister was good enough to settle it then and there. "Here." Sophia tossed the bottle up to Diane. "You're jealous of my tan. Get rubbing."

And like *that*, the tension dissolved into nothing.

Bea looked at Sophia with renewed fondness, and when Doug and Craig and Jeffy appeared on the boardwalk and called down to the girls, she made a personal vow to trust her sister.

But she broke that vow.
Just hours later.

Chapter 20

Diane

"Sure, we got together for drinks, what? Five years ago? She looked great." Diane handed the last dish to Sue, who worked the towel in and out and set it in the drying rack.

Once Bea left the kitchen to get ready for the day, Sue and Diane opened up a review of every time any one of them had come into contact with Sophia in the past ten years.

Bea still clung to her silence, unready, apparently, to *go there*.

Vague and concerning, it was a surprise that Bea didn't want—or need—to share more information. Surely Sophia, Bea's very best friend in the world, would have revealed everything. Hell, if Diane had to guess, she'd have assumed Bea would have accompanied her sister to every single doctor's appointment and been so numb to it all that it would just fall out of her mouth like a pharmacy receipt, long, boring, and sterile.

Instead of tromping up the stairs and getting down to work with sorting through the bedrooms and bath and poking around to see if Soph had happened to leave anything behind on her private excursion, Bea had suggested they hit the boardwalk first, for a quick walk. Maybe fresh air would inspire her to open up.

Before that, however, they washed up the morning's dishes and took turns in the downstairs bath to make themselves presentable. Especially on the off-chance they ran into anyone they knew, like, for example, the charming beach man and his lovable Darla—the pair who turned Bea into a blubbering mess.

"Who looked great?"

Diane turned around at the question and gasped.

"Who looked great five years ago?" Bea repeated, her mouth a pink smudge at the center of what looked to be a disguise. She wore a floppy sun hat above oversized black sunglasses. Her thin, athletic build was sheathed in a gauzy white swim cover-up, and the resemblance stopped Diane's heart for a beat or two.

"My God, Bea. I thought you were—"

"Sophia," Sue whispered beside her.

"Oh." Bea pulled her sunglasses down, and exhaustion appeared above her pink lip gloss. A tentative smile, though, crept across her mouth. "Really? No one ever said we looked alike."

"With that get-up, you really do."

"I've got dark hair," Bea argued, pulling a strand around her neck as proof.

"I know you have dark hair. Or *had*. Don't think we can't see those roots, Bea Russo," she joked.

Bea's smile turned to a wince. "Sophia definitely kept her roots up."

"When you're blonde, it's not much of a hassle," Sue

offered. "Anyway, I always thought you two looked alike. Not twins, of course. But you always looked like sisters. Your olive skin and green eyes and great eyebrows. And your height, of course."

Diane watched as Bea's face softened. "Sophia had a better body. She had a *waist*. And delicate hands, you know? Do you remember that? She had such feminine hands. Like yours, Sue."

"She was soft; you were hard. That's what always made you and me a good match," Diane added, her hands on her hips. "We were the strong ones. And Sue, you and Sophia were the sweet ones."

Sue smiled gratefully.

Bea nodded. "I guess we were a good group."

"Still are." Diane clapped her hands and announced it was her turn to freshen up before disappearing down the hall.

———

"So who were you talking about? Were you talking about Sophia? You said someone looked great." They were locking up the house and heading out for their walk when Bea tried again to wedge her way into the topic at hand. Her insecurity broke Diane's heart.

Sue glanced at Diane, searching for help.

Diane replied, "We were talking about Sophia, yes. I got drinks with her about five years ago. I figured you knew. I, mean, we even invited you, Bea."

"I don't remember that," Bea murmured, pointing down the beach and guiding them past the first set of steps up to the boardwalk. "Let's go to the second landing."

"You don't want your lover boy to see you?" Diane ribbed her friend, but Bea didn't laugh.

"I don't even know him. He just came by yesterday. I told you. He's a local busybody or something."

"Maybe we'll ask *him* what happened to poor ol' Soph." Diane regretted saying it the moment the words slipped from her mouth, but it was too late.

"Nothing *happened* to Soph," Bea spat. "I told you. She had a bad heart. Weak. There were complications, but this isn't some soap opera. No one broke into the house and killed her. There's no *mystery* to solve."

"If that's true, then tell us something, Bea," Diane replied, stalling at the top of the steps, a surrey nearly sending them all sailing back down to the sand.

"Tell you what, Diane?"

"Why was she here? *Alone*? Were you going to meet her? Was Greg? What in the world was she doing here *alone*?"

"I think she was going to start renovating," Bea replied. "Let's walk, come on. It'll do us good."

"If she was going to renovate, why didn't she call you and bring you down here?" Diane was ready to have it out. She couldn't stand the unknowns anymore. Sure, she could appreciate Bea's heartache. But to taunt them with it—well, that was just cruel and unusual, and it absolutely pointed to a soap opera death.

"Geez, Diane, I don't know. Why didn't she call *you*? Sounds like you two were closer anyway."

Diane and Sue stopped walking. Bea slowed ahead of them, then turned, her expression masked by her disguise.

Another surrey rolled past, and Diane and Sue dodged it in tandem. "What's that supposed to me?" Diane cried out. "You two were best friends. You said you had lunch at least once a month. You two had *each other*. All the time."

Diane strode with purpose to Bea. "Do you think I was sneaking in behind your back to spend time with Soph?"

"No," Bea answered, unfolding her arms and pulling her sunglasses down. "I'm sorry it came out like that. No. I don't think that. I just... you said I couldn't go to the lunch, but you never asked me *to* go."

"Sophia said she invited you, but you were busy." As the words lined up in the air, Diane saw the picture.

And she saw that Bea saw it, too.

"I'm sorry, Bea," she whispered, taking her hand. "I —I didn't realize. I just, well, trusted her." They stared at each other silently. Seabirds squawked in the distance. "Do you want to talk about it, Bea?"

Traffic on the boardwalk was growing denser by the moment. Shrieks of laughter trilled across the air, and Diane glanced down the way toward Pelican Pier, its carnival rides whirring in the air above the boardwalk.

Bea turned and followed her gaze, distracted (or at least, pretending to be). "Remember the Ferris wheel?"

Diane smiled, accepting that this whole vacation, or whatever it was, was going to be less of a vacation and more of a therapy session. She could handle that. She could give one week—or one month, even—to help an old friend. "Of course, I remember the Ferris wheel. I think that was the last ride I ever went on."

———

1985

"Listen, I like thrills, but I don't like tossing my cookies." Diane drew a hard line when it came to the Gravitron, or at least, Gull's Landing's version of the Gravitron. She'd heard horror stories from nearby Morey's Pier and how the Gravitron was nothing short of a puke-machine.

"Okay, fine. How about the Ferris wheel?" Craig asked, looping his arm around her waist in that way she loved. With Craig, Diane didn't think about the jelly roll that was her midsection. Well, she *did*, but she came to accept it. Like he had. He anchored his hand on the side of her ribs, right beneath her chest in that perfect spot that wasn't too fat but wasn't indecent, either.

"All right, you convinced me," she answered and then snapped her fingers at the girls and pointed across the Pier.

"I'm getting a little tired, Diane." Bea yawned for effect, and Sue mirrored her.

"Me too," Sophia answered. But Doug tickled her sides and whispered into her ear until she shrieked through giggles, "*No*, Doug, you cannot come tuck me in."

"Gag me, why don't you." Diane mimed sticking her middle finger down her throat. Yes, it was a relief to see that Sophia was finally starting to feel better after her week-long sickness. But the return to this puke-inducing courtship was enough to send Diane over the edge. When it came to summer romance, she didn't want to be like them. Sophia and Doug. They were an act. A crock. Really, truly. She just wanted to spend time with Craig and have a little fun. It helped that he was a sincere sweetheart of a guy.

Why did Sophia have to be one of those girls? The

kind that hooked herself to a pretty boy and held on for dear life?

Diane flicked a glance to Bea and saw the worry wrinkles. That's what she called them. When her best friend was in distress and it played out across her face like a movie projection on the big screen.

"Hey, you know what, Bea? You and Sue can go back. I'll hang with Soph."

"Oh, come on. We're all adults here," Doug moaned. "Everybody can do what they want, am I right?" He winked at Craig, and Diane saw Bea's face twist harder.

"If the girls want to stick together, then I guess that's what they want. Right, Doug?" Craig asked.

She beamed at her boyfriend and mouthed a thank-you. He squeezed her side.

"I've got an idea," Sophia said, her eyes clearing for a moment. Just before they'd all met back at the Tilt o' Wheel, Diane and Soph had slipped a few sips of whatever in the world was in Doug's flask. Soph had taken a few extra, and it showed on her face. Diane kept the secret for her, but her glassy eyes belied their private indulgence.

"Actually, *I've* got an idea," Diane broke in. "Let's all do one more ride, then us girls will turn in for the night. A compromise, okay?"

Bea gave Diane a grateful look and they started off for the Ferris wheel, Sophia wrapped in Doug's grip ahead of them.

"Talk about tossing your cookies," Craig whispered to Diane. "I think Sophia should sit this one out."

"It's just a Ferris wheel. As long as she stays in her seat, she'll be okay," Diane assured him, touched by his concern.

Once the six of them arrived at the line and waited

their turn to get on, Sophia seemed to grow even more goofy and bizarrely drowsy. Her eyes kept sliding closed, her mouth falling open. Doug, for his part, played the hero, tucking her hair behind her ears and whispering into her ear, propping her up like a puppet.

Bea leaned into Diane when they neared the front of the line. "She says she's in love with this guy."

Diane frowned. "She's not in love. She's in lust. I've been there a million times. I know the difference. But right this minute, I'd say it's neither. I'd say she's out of her mind."

"We can't let them out of our sight, okay?" Bea pled.

At that, Diane turned to Craig, facing him and keeping her voice low. "Listen, is Doug—can we *trust* him?"

Craig shrugged. "Doug's harmless. He's just excited to finally *meet* someone. You know?"

"What do you mean?" Bea pressed.

"Doug's girlfriend just broke up with him like a month before summer started. He was really broken up, you know? When we met you girls, ka*pow*, you know? He was like, over it. It's been a good summer for him. For me, too." Craig leaned over and kissed Diane square on the cheek.

She lifted an eyebrow at Bea. "See? It'll be all right. We'll keep an eye on them and then call it a night."

Bea agreed, and the carnie waved their group in, one pair at a time.

Diane and Craig slid into their own little bucket of heaven. Soph and Doug into theirs, and Bea and Sue into the third one to lift off. Soon enough all six were in the air together and separately, huddled inside their own worlds.

Thoughts of Sophia and Doug and Bea's angst over

their slobbery relationship drifted off to sea as Diane curled herself into Craig, weightless and quiet as they crept into the sky above Gull's Landing.

As their passenger car crested the peak, Diane turned to Craig. "The summer's going to be over soon, you know."

"Yeah, I know."

"Isn't that—well, I mean… it's sort of a big deal, I guess."

"It's just a summer," he replied, laughing. "We'll have another one."

"We will?" she asked, studying him through the lights of the Pier.

Craig pulled her tighter to him and kissed the top of her head. It was the funny thing about their relationship. He seemed to kiss her everywhere. Not just on the lips. But on the cheeks and the top of her head. The back of her hands and the tops of her shoulders. Sweet kisses that sent electricity through her body. "We'll have lots of summers together. I promise," he whispered.

Diane let out a sigh of contentment and rested her head against him, breathing in the salty ocean air and wishing she never had to leave. Or, if she did, that she could take him with her.

"What if you go to college and meet someone else?" She couldn't help it. It was the question that nagged her brain to a breaking point.

"I could ask the same thing about you, you know," he answered.

"Yeah, well, I'm no sorority girl, you know."

"I don't want a sorority girl. I want you, Di." His voice was lower now, more serious.

"I wish I could go to Penn State. It would make everything perfect, wouldn't it?"

She sniffed and looked down at her hands. As it was, just enrolling at her local college, Diane would have to work through school. Sure, she wasn't in dire straits. She'd figure it out and be fine. But Craig was big-time. Diane couldn't keep up. She knew she couldn't.

"Why can't you?" he asked.

She pushed air through her lips. "Duh, Craig. I can't afford that. Neither can my folks. Not for four years, anyway. I got in at the community college, and that'll be okay. It's not like I have any grand plans to be a lawyer or a doctor. Right?"

"Then what are your plans, Di?" he asked. She met his gaze, and for the first time since they started dating—which, to be fair, wasn't that long of a spell—she saw something in his expression that she hadn't seen before. An expectation. A standard. Like he could make her whatever she wanted to be, with the snap of his fingers.

Suddenly, in that moment, every ice cream cone he paid for, every burger he bought her, the seashell necklace he turned up with—it meant something.

"Hang on. How can *you* afford to go to Penn State? You told me your folks work on the boardwalk."

She thought about what he'd told her earlier in the summer. His family vacations and his world travels.

"Don't tell me your job at the marina is covering college," she said.

He nodded. "Sure it is. That plus financial aid and a few scholarships. I work hard. So do my folks. We don't come from much, maybe. But we get things done, you know?"

She didn't know. But she did trust him.

———

DIANE ALWAYS WOULD TRUST CRAIG—THROUGH the two years she'd struggled at community college, to the summer he proposed and told her he'd pay her way at Penn State, all the way up to their wedding day and the birth of Brittany and even during their bizarrely amicable divorce. The one they filed for out of some misguided acceptance that they had, indeed, married too young.

Diane, Sue, and Bea had walked clear up to Pelican Pier, grabbing a shaved ice for fun and settling onto a picnic table just outside the park and on the other end of the boardwalk, almost two miles from Aunt Lil's.

"Did I ever tell you about Craig's father?" Diane asked Sue and Bea. She knew she hadn't. It was one of those intra-marital secrets. The sort that you desperately wanted to leverage as juicy gossip with your girlfriends but that you didn't dare unless you were okay with being a rotten person on a fast track to hell.

After Sophia's death and Bea's obvious mental strife and then everything that Craig shared with her, though, hell didn't scare her so much. Besides, Mr. Bettancourt was out of the picture by now, and telling Diane and Sue this little nugget might soften them to what Diane would have to tell them later on.

Plus, she *needed* to get it out of her brain and her heart. The little truth—now so removed from Diane's own daily life and so seemingly irrelevant to the rest of her world— was something that Diane needed her friends to know, even if it wasn't her truth to share and even if it was a rotten thing to do. You see, sometimes, in order to be a happy person, you had to make a pit stop at being a rotten person.

It was a strange thing, but something Diane swore by. Less along the lines of *if you don't have anything nice to say, come sit by me* and more along the lines of *if I can't share this with someone then my guts might explode and what good will that do anybody?*

"Didn't Mr. Bettancourt work here?" Sue asked. "I remember thinking he might be able to get us one of those huge teddy bears." She smiled and dug into her Seabreeze Slush. Diane wondered how Sue kept so innocent and sweet despite her heartbreaking life. All that happened around her didn't ever seem to penetrate the bubble of naivete and goodness, or at least, Sue carried on through that heartbreak. Diane would do well to be more like Sue. Anyone would.

"Yeah, he did. He worked all over this place." Diane jutted her chin toward Pelican Pier. "He was in middle management, but near the end he made his way up and even did a stint as Pier supervisor."

"His mom, too, right?" Bea asked. Her demeanor had shifted. The brisk walk and cool treat had calmed her. Settled her, it seemed. "Didn't Mrs. Bettancourt work in the timeshare office?"

Diane nodded. "Well, anyway—and please, this is a private matter..." she hesitated long enough for her friends to promise their discretion. "Okay, so anyway, a few years back, his dad got caught writing bad checks."

Sue's hand flew to her mouth, but Diane went on.

"There was this whole big investigation and it came out that they were in debt up to their noses. Mr. Bettancourt was incarcerated for a little while. Mrs. Bettancourt got off with a slap on the wrist."

Bea gasped. "Get out of town!"

Diane shook her head sadly. And she was sad about the whole thing. Back when it first happened and still now.

"Didn't you two have a good relationship with them?" Sue asked.

"Yeah, we did. As far as mothers-in-law go, Barb was great. Generous, sweet as honey. She treated me like a daughter. Still would, if she were around."

Sue's mouth fell open, and her eyes grew wide. "Did she die?"

"No, no," Diane answered. "She's alive and kicking. They moved to Jamaica, actually. They wanted Craig to go, but he said no. She sends emails with blurry pictures of their little house on the water. For going bankrupt and being cast as wannabe white-collar criminals, they're doing okay."

"Wow," Sue replied, in awe. "It goes to show. Second chances aren't too hard to come by."

"Oh, I think they are," Bea argued.

"Not necessarily." Diane slurped down the last of her Waterlicious and cleaned her hands along a too-small paper napkin. "Sure, they had to do their time, and they'll have to pay reparations forever, but they're happy as a pair of clams. True love was probably part of the equation."

As she said it all, wrapping up the story and rounding back to the unconventional happily-ever-after, Diane realized that it wasn't gossip she needed. It was validation. It was the clearing of her conscience and the affirmation that no one was perfect, but even the imperfect could be happy.

"True love," Bea breathed the words and rested her chin in her hand. "And the second chance, kind, too. Wow. Who'd have thunk it, really? Craig had the most nuclear, steady family of anyone. What a trip. *Literally*."

"I don't know," Sue replied. "Who really wants to move somewhere to start over, though? How can you live a normal life in a place like Jamaica? It's a vacation, not a long-term solution." It was Sue who made this point, which caught Diane a little off guard. She didn't typically carry such haughty opinions. She was a go-along-to-get-along type of gal.

Still, it was a valid point.

"Not me, that's true," Diane agreed. "I like my life perfectly fine out in the burbs. I just need a vacation once or twice a year, and I'm a happy girl."

"You mean you're happy to be single?" Sue asked.

Diane frowned. "Well, no. I'd much rather have a man. And I don't think there's anything wrong about that, by the way. But what I meant was that I agree with you. I couldn't hack it in Jamaica. I'd miss Book Club and the Humane Society and the library geezers with their sharpened colored pencils. I mean, hell, I don't think I could really hack it *here*, in Gull's Landing, much longer than a couple of months."

"I could," Bea said, her gaze fixed on the water.

Diane followed it out to see Jet Skis zigzagging across the water. A big ship, out in the distance, trudged its way across their view, turning into a postcard you'd find in a water sports shop on the boardwalk. Or an advertisement. *Cruise on over to Gull's Landing, where it's always five o'clock.* Diane smiled inwardly. There was something about their place on the boardwalk, that much was true.

"Really?" Sue asked Bea. "You don't strike me as the type who would retire on the beach."

Diane happened to agree with Sue. "Honestly, if anyone is the sort to run away from the city and come here or move down to Florida and buy a little ranch-style with a lanai, it's *me*."

"I've spent my entire adult life in the suburbs. All I

do is work, go home, sleep. Work, go home, sleep. A decade of something different would do me good."

"Would you want to live in Aunt Lil's?" Diane asked. "Sell your house? Quit your job?"

"I can't retire yet," Bea answered. "And if I did retire early, then I'd be screwed. I still have student loans from when I went back and got my Master's, if you can believe that. Plus, I took out a second mortgage on my house in order to add the second bathroom. And there's my car payment. My finances are a freakin' mess."

"Oh," Diane replied, swallowing. "I get that. I understand."

"Really?" Sue asked.

"What do you mean, *really*?" Diane spat back, laughing at her. "Of course I understand financial strain."

"But how? Craig pays your way, right? The alimony you were telling us about back at Sophia's funeral," Sue asked innocently, but digging around someone else's finances—even a best friend's—was never an innocent thing. Not even if Diane was the one who first invited the scrutiny.

"What alimony?" Bea asked.

Diane threw up her hands. "I open my mouth in a moment of grief and look what I get for it. *No*," she narrowed her gaze on Sue. "I mean, well, *yes*, he has paid my way. We had a very nice lifestyle together. But now that we aren't together anymore, I'm on a budget. A strict one, too."

"Strict as in a five-thousand-dollar allowance every month? No mortgage, no car payment?" Sue lifted an eyebrow, and Diane gawked at the woman's nerve. Really *gawked*.

"Susan Merkle, what has become of you? Where in

the hell are your manners?" she snapped back, but it was half-hearted. Deep down, she was proud of her pipsqueak friend's sudden uprising.

"Is that true, Diane?" Bea asked.

"No," Diane shot back. "Not the five-thousand-dollar allowance, at least. I mean, yes, we have a nice agreement. But nothing like what Sue's saying."

"Diane, could you loan Bea the money? Help cover her for a year until she can get something together? Maybe you could even charge interest!" Sue lit up with the grand idea—a solution to the world's problems. Their world, at least.

Diane swallowed and frowned. Sue's social ineptitude took the place of her unusual boldness, and the conversation splintered.

Bea rushed to decline any offer of a handout, tsking Sue and declaring that she did *not* need help, and all she wanted to do was spend the summer together, yadda yadda yadda.

But truth be told, if Diane *could* help, she *would* help.

And even truer than that, if ol' Craig *could* help, he *would* help, too.

And in that crumpled moment of awkwardness, a lightbulb flickered inside of Diane. Her true feelings about it all. Her true feelings from the past decades... but she squashed them down, extinguishing the growing glow by hitting the kill switch.

Instead of being cool and calm and careful, Diane did the only thing she seemed to know how to do when she was in the company of her girlfriends.

She spilled the beans.

Chapter 21

Sue

"You mean *bankrupt* bankrupt?" Sue asked, bewildered. Just a year before, Diane was sitting in Mrs. Russo's cramped kitchen, bragging about the Michael Kors watch Craig had gifted her for her birthday. She'd driven up to the gravesite in her brand-new Mercedes.

At the time, Sue ate it up like a fool.

Now there she was, a different setting—salt spraying across the boardwalk, damp settling into her lower back and staying there—and a different year and she was gawking all over again. For a different reason.

Diane heaved a sigh. "It's a mess," she said through her hands as they rubbed up and down her face. Sue wondered how many facials Craig had paid for. She wondered if those plump lips were kept in good shape by injections, like the women in Sue's magazines—of course Diane's weren't botched like that tacky column that Sue couldn't help but pore over as she snickered to herself over the foibles of *poor, maligned celebs and their plastic surgeries gone wrong!*

She wondered a lot of new things about Diane that she had never thought to wonder about before.

Sue and Bea looked at each other, then Sue leaned into the picnic table. "Is he okay?

Diane's face fell. "No. Well, yes. It's such a ridiculous problem to have. I mean who cares if a rich person goes bankrupt, right? It's like they almost deserve it. Work hard, make money, spend it, be happy—the American dream, right? But if you work a little *too* hard. If you make a little *too much* money, and if you *look* like you're spending that money... well, God forbid, right? I mean there's no winner. Even if Craig was giving half his paycheck to charity, people would look at him and think he didn't deserve a cent."

"What do you mean?" Bea asked. "What exactly happened?"

Sue's heart ached. She'd never been in Diane's position—and she would never ever *be* in Diane's position—but Craig was a good guy. And Diane was a good woman. Neither one deserved to lose it all.

Did they?

Diane's eyes fluttered open and shut and she pushed the backs of her hands across them. "It's stupid, really. He got careless. Over time. First with his folks. When his dad had the money trouble, Craig flew to the rescue. He took the case on pro bono, obviously. Spent all his time trying to get them out of trouble. His old clients lost trust and respect. New clients were duds, I guess. And the whole time—the last five years, he says—he didn't change his spending habits."

"And what were those?" Sue asked tentatively. She

didn't mean it to be judgmental or nosey, but Bea flashed a look at her.

Still, Diane answered. "Exactly what you're thinking, I'm sure. Of course, my house has been paid off for years. But he had a big mortgage on his, I guess, plus his name is on mine. We don't cover anything for Britt, but Craig didn't change his dollar amounts when it came to birthdays and Christmas. And he did the same for me. I know... I know," Diane interrupted herself, "we're weird. But that's how it goes. We get together. We go out and eat and catch shows. And Craig pitches in for the half-marathon as a sponsor, and he maxes out his tax credits, and he keeps donating to the Briar Creek Booster Club, too. He shares his money where he can and as much as he can. Too much, I think. It's important to him. He always wanted to give back to Briar Creek. It was the only way he felt he could ever truly make it his home."

"So, what's going to happen?" Sue asked.

"I don't know. I asked if he'd just move into his parents' old place here. I was under the assumption that he kept it after Bob and Barb moved. But they already took it. The bank, I mean. So, Gull's Landing is out. And," Diane squeezed her eyes shut tight, "unless I can buy it out, they'll take my place, too." She melted to the table. "Geez, I haven't even really processed any of this bull crap," she hissed with her head on the sun-washed wooden tabletop.

"Oh, Diane," Sue fretted. "Wow. You must be so stressed."

Bea wrapped her arm around Diane's shoulders and pulled her in. "The good news is that you're here, right? You can spend all summer here, if you need to, Diane."

"I can't, though. I mean, I'll stay awhile, sure, but I

have to get back to work. I can't afford not to, at this point." She crumpled forward again. "Oh my God, I've never had to say that once in my *life*, what is *wrong* with me?"

Diane shook her head and clenched her fists. "I'm just so damn angry about it. I've been keeping it all in, too. I'm about to burst. Thank God we didn't put our names on Britt's mortgage. That's the only thing I'm grateful for."

"Are you mad at him?" Sue asked. Images of Joe— loser Joe who wouldn't know what to do with a dollar if he found it on the street— flashed through her mind. He'd be totally lost without her. She'd been the financial head in their household. And Sue would never have let even a single cent go unaccounted for. That's why, when the affair came to light, part of Sue wanted to laugh.

Because she knew with near certainty, that as for the other woman, well, Joe wasn't spending a single dime on her. At least Sue had that. And at least, once their divorce went through—if she could convince herself that her marriage really had failed and if she could convince their priest to grant an annulment—that she'd be okay. She could buy her own vacation to San Diego whenever the heck she wanted. She wouldn't even have to use his tickets. She could throw them in the trash. But Sue wouldn't do that, of course.

After all, if she was the sort of person who *could* throw away two perfectly good airline tickets in the trash, then she wasn't the sort of person who ever *would* do such a thing to begin with. Even so, the thought of using them now felt silly. Maybe she could get a refund and rebook. Maybe she *should* mail them back to him with a little note that said *Cheers to the end! Now get out of my house!*

"No," Diane replied to her. "I'm not. That's the craziest thing in the world, but I'm not mad at him."

Bea leaned an elbow onto the table, flashed a look at Sue then stared hard at Diane. "Diane, I don't understand something."

"What?" Diane asked, her eyebrow etched high above her eye.

"I don't understand why in the world you two got a divorce to begin with."

Sue's eyes grew wide. It was her self-same question. The one she wondered every single time Craig Bettancourt entered her mind after Diane had broken the news to them years back—in a phone call.

Diane let out a low laugh. "You know what?" she asked in response.

Sue and Bea waited.

"I don't understand it either."

Chapter 22

Bea

They were heading back to Aunt Lil's, the sun beating down on the boardwalk as they moved through the growing crowd.

With Sue's confession about Joe and then Diane's confession about Craig... it seemed to Bea that she alone had been the only one to resist the pull of coming clean.

But what was there to admit?

She'd led a dull life. That of a hanger-on to her sister. Such was becoming more and more clear.

Then again, there was the one thing. The event that spurred her to let potential relationships die after date three because she was so damn afraid. The event that shot Bea down the lane that she never did bounce out of all her life.

The night that changed the course of history—Bea's *and* Sophia's.

The event that even Sophia didn't know about but

that broke her heart all the same. In fact, maybe it did more than break her heart.

Maybe, that last night in Gull's Landing back in 1985 was the beginning of the end and, in some butterfly-effect way, it had even killed Sophia. Bea shuddered.

They passed Licks on the Landing, the ice cream shop that had been around since the girls were old enough to carry their own cones. Then the Boardwalk Arcade. Beyond that, Mack's Pizzeria, its red and orange sign lit up despite the searing rays of sun.

With each step closer to the house, Bea went back and forth. To cough it up? Make her guilt known? Or tamp it down? It was no big deal, probably, and Diane and Sue would not only understand... they'd applaud her. Surely, they would.

But if Bea *did* tell them what she did, and what she got for it—then they'd take the conversation somewhere she didn't want to go. They'd turn it all against Soph, and nothing was Sophia's fault. Nothing whatsoever.

Bea desperately needed to keep Sophia perfect. Because if Sophia was not perfect, then what had been the point? What had Bea been protecting her from? What had Bea sacrificed her entire life for?

"Hey look," Diane broke into her thoughts. Bea followed her friend's finger. "They must have just rolled it out. A boardwalk sale!"

If there were two words that could snap any one of them out of a funk, they were "Boardwalk Sale".

Gull's Landing was famous for the tradition. Over the summer, every so often, the retail shops at the southern end of the boardwalk would put on a surprise sale. It went against every marketing strategy in the book, but it *worked*. Like a sidewalk sale on a Main Street of a small town, they'd push racks outside of their shops and prop up wooden signs with killer discounts.

Half off everything on the boardwalk!

Buy one get one free!

75% discount—this rack only!

The women floated toward the first shop like zombies, their hands dancing across plastic hangers and cheapie sunglasses in plastic buckets as other like-minded women crowded in around them.

Bea felt all of fifteen years old again, looking for the lowest price on something—anything—that could pass for cool.

Three shops down, Bea wandered into Clothing by Carly (a cheesy name for a boutique, truly), where she smoothed her hand down a white lace swim cover-up. It was a dead ringer for Aunt Lil's burial get-up, and Bea laughed inwardly, warmly, at the fact that she could still picture the woman, face up in the white silk tufted casket, her makeup heavy, and her cleavage on display, a gold Rosary draped artfully in her hand.

"I know you," the man behind the cash register said, his accent thick as though he fell straight out of the Bronx. Why he had landed in the middle of a women's apparel shop could be anyone's guess. That was the boardwalk—quirky and kitschy and full of surprises, after all.

Bea glanced around for someone else, whoever the man must have been talking to.

"No, no. *You*, yeah. Summers back when we were, what… twenty? Younger, probably."

She turned her head back to the cash register, and her gaze focused on him. He was the opposite of what she expected. Certainly no Carly. Much more *Carl*, really, and not a *Carly* kind of Carl, either. Not a women's apparel sort of guy.

His receding hairline was poorly disguised through an attempt to spike the top up and forward. A thick gold chain drew attention to a chubby neck, too tan and too thick. His shirt, beige and only half buttoned revealed a shaved chest. Bea's eyes flitted back to his face. A Romanesque handsomeness existed there, behind the tacky style. She squinted.

Despite her career as a teacher, and the requirement to learn upwards of a hundred names every school year, Bea had never been good with them—names, that was.

But his was waiting in the back of her brain like a dormant virus.

"Jeffy?"

"That's me," he hooked a thumb at his chest. "You're Bea."

Bea clenched her teeth and nodded.

"Right." he answered. Something glinted in the far corner of his smile. A gold tooth. "How you been doin'?"

Swallowing, Bea shook her head and stumbled through the lie. "Fine." She glanced around for the exit, suddenly discombobulated. "It was nice seeing you," she called weakly over her shoulder, then slipped into the sunshine and closed her eyes.

"Wait a sec." His voice followed her, and Bea's eyes shot open. She searched the racks for Diane or Sue and found them—at the next shop down.

"Sorry, I have to catch up with my friends," she murmured in his direction, avoiding him as well as she possibly could as he followed her outside.

"Bea," he said. "I'm sorry to hear about your sister."

She flipped around. "Sophia."

"I'm real sorry to hear it. What a sweet girl."

She took a deep breath. "Oh."

"Her passing," he went on. "You know, when I heard it happened here—just next door, *wow*! Man, I was shaken up. I didn't know yous girls were still comin' around. I'dda had you over for a drink or whatnot."

"That's all right." Bea turned back to her friends, about to call out to them until Diane spotted her first and waved. Bea turned back to Jeffy. "It was nice to run into you. I, um, I gotta go."

"Oh, sure. Sure. Maybe I can get your number and we—"

"Bea!" Diane called. "Buy a wetsuit and get a free fifteen-minute surfing lesson!"

Bea flushed and sliced her hand across her neck in a clear sign of stress.

Even from her distance, Diane put two and two together, said something to Sue, who was sorting through the rack of rubberwear, then strode over to Clothing by Carly.

"You must be Carly," Diane joked to Jeffy. "Great shop you got here." She then turned her attention to Bea. "What? Did you find something you want to try on?"

"No," Bea replied, wondering how to extract herself from the clutches of the imbecile running the shop. Her instinct was all wrong, though. She gave Diane the eye.

"Wait a minute. Jeffy?" Diane gasped. "Craig's old friend? Get outta here." She looked him up and down and then, in true Diane De Luca-Bettancourt fashion, added, "You look like pure crap."

Bea's head snapped to Diane and she glared.

But a low growling laugh tumbled from Jeffy's mouth. "Diane-Diane," the way he said it turned her name into a flashy casino on the Vegas strip. "You haven't changed one bit, have ya? How the hell are ya?"

Bea was impressed that he remembered their names so well. Though it was a janky start to a reunion, Bea was a little charmed. Jeffy was okay.

Diane put on a fake smile as her eyes slid to Bea and she cocked her head, addressing her friend as if Jeffy were invisible. "Craig and Jeffy, remember? Their friendship lasted until our wedding." She turned her head back to him. "Doing just fine. And you? *Carly's*, eh? Is that supposed to be you, or—"

Bea racked her brain. She was *in* Diane's wedding, for the love of God. Why couldn't she remember Jeffy being there?

"My sister's joint. I'm babysitting while they're on a girls' trip. My sister and her girlfriends, I mean. I live in Wildwood now. Don't worry—" he winked "—I'm hardly ever around here anymore."

Breathing a sigh of relief, Bea rested a hand on Diane's shoulder. "Good to see you, Jeffy. We have to be going."

"Aw, where you gotta be? Come on, I'm bored as hell over here. Well, I'm not entirely bored, not with this sale they sprung on me. But we could grab a slice and talk about the good ol' days…" he wiggled his eyebrows. "Say, whatever happened, anyway? You never came back."

Diane shrugged. "We grew up, I guess. Good luck with Wildwood, Jeffy," she replied. "We've got a surf lesson we're going to be late for." Then she pulled Bea with her, leaving him behind.

"A-right, a-right. See yous girls! Have a nice swim."

He turned to head back inside, probably to mop up the sweat pooling in the center of his chest, and that was just fine by Bea.

She and Diane whispered together like schoolgirls as they strode to Surf's Up.

"He was so much sweeter back then, right?" Diane remarked. "Like the hapless third wheel sort of rattling behind Craig and Doug.

"Diane," she replied, her voice low. "Whatever happened between him and Craig? And your *wedding*? I don't remember Jeffy being there. I would *definitely* remember if he were there."

"He wasn't," she spat back. "Craig broke up with him—if that's the right phrase here—the week before. Turned out he'd swiped Craig's dad's credit card and booked them a private night at the Red Garter for the bachelor party. It was the sort of thing that ends a friendship, I suppose. I didn't divulge everything because Craig told me not to. He probably won't care anymore now—I mean about me telling, not the credit card thing. He was livid. Still is, I'm sure. It showed Jeffy's true colors. Who would have thought, though. You know? Jeffy's nice enough. Always was. But that was low. I mean really low, Bea."

"Yeah." Bea nodded, satisfied after all. To see him there, though, so close to Aunt Lil's... so close to her... it was unnerving and still captivating, like finding a human time capsule, dirt-clogged and time-worn but still remarkably familiar.

And that he *knew*. He *knew* Sophia had died.

The whole interaction made Bea's skin crawl. Not because of sweet, well-meaning (if a little slimy) Jeffy. Anyway, to run into a blast from the past was one thing.

But to run into one of those three boys—the boys that rocked their worlds—was quite another.

She took a deep breath as they wove through the racks of Surf's Up, and the muscles in her back began to release. Her pulse returned to normal. Having her friends around her proved to be therapeutic. Maybe they would stick around the boardwalk all summer like she wanted. Maybe Diane could get a job there to help with bills. Maybe Sue would give up the California trip. Maybe they could spread out across the boardwalk like old times, like queen teens, unafraid and ready for an adventure.

Maybe the summer could be about more than Sophia's death and the sale of Aunt Lil's house. Maybe it could just be about the three of them. Bea, Diane, and Sue.

"Say, where's Sue?"

"Inside," Diane replied. "I told her to take my card and get us each a wetsuit quick, before it's declined."

"What's declined?"

"My credit card," Diane replied, laughing. "Now, come *on*. We're gonna spice this trip up. No more talk about debt or Jeffy or Joe-the-cheater or even perfect ol' Soph."

Bea's chest took the blow, but her heart was somewhere else.

And that was the first step, really. The first step away from the depths of her tragedy.

The first step away from a lifetime of living for someone else, and the first step in the direction of finding something… or some*one* new.

Even if it was only for fifteen minutes.

"Bea!" Brooks Morgan greeted her from the open door of his shop, Darla yawning at his side.

Their trip to the second floor of Aunt Lil's could wait a little longer.

Bea squatted down, accepting wet-nosed kisses from the sweet golden retriever. Then, she smiled up at him. "Just to warn you, I'm not used to being the student."

Chapter 23

Diane

Diane didn't expect Bea to do a one-eighty, but she was game for a surfing session after all. Maybe it had something to do with the sandy-haired stud. Who could say?

And if Sue—nervous Nellie Sue—could woman up and get out on the water atop of a piece of foam, then maybe the impromptu trip down the shore was going to be more than a mope session after all.

Diane needed something more than a mope session. She needed a chance to have fun and clear her head.

Because the plan that was brewing in her brain was going to turn her life upside down. Truly, it was.

So, they spent the morning where the water kissed the sand. Diane's only regret was that Craig wasn't there to laugh with her—and at her. She loved that about Craig, that he saw the light in Diane. It bounced between them. On her sixth (and last) attempt to stand up in the water, that's what she pictured as she managed to get upright—just in time to be taken down by a wave.

Never mind that Diane's attraction to her husband had waned. Never mind that he knew how to push her buttons and that he could be annoying and too affectionate and that she firmly believed their chemistry had run out just a year after their marriage.

Never *mind* that he built an empire and let it come crashing down around them.

Those happy moments were all that she could summon now.

Water-beaten and heavy-limbed, she called it a day. "I'm too fat and too old for this!" Diane cried out, her frizzy hair in tangled clumps around her shoulders as she dragged the surfboard back up to the shore, where Sue sat.

Sue had only made one attempt so far. Thirty minutes into their fifteen-minute freebie (the Surf's Up guy told them Darla could watch the shop, but he'd actually just locked it up with a sign that said he was out to lunch), Diane, too, was ready to call it.

The only problem? Bea had turned into a full-blown beach babe.

She and Brooks—what a name! like a hippie-surfer-dude-country-star or something—had been waist deep in the water for the past twenty minutes together at her board. He sat on the back, steadying her as she tried, wobbling, to stand up, only for them to crash into the water together, laughing like teenagers.

"Has she been working out?" Sue asked Diane. They sat together like a couple of beached whales. Well, Sue was more like a scraggly knot of kelp slung up on the shore; Diane was the whale. She was okay with that, too.

Diane lifted her shoulders. "I don't think it has

anything to do with cardio. I think that right there is pure adrenaline. Who knew saltwater was an aphrodisiac?"

"Saltwater has nothing to do with those two," Sue added. "But I'm waterlogged, and my eyes are burning. Can we just leave them here?"

"You were in the water for thirty seconds!" Diane cried back.

"I'm not fit like you," Sue whined.

Diane raised her eyebrow. "*Fit?* I'm one slice of pizza short of being the barnacle-covered Shamu carcass from *Jaws!*"

"You think I'm skinny and in shape, but I'm actually just weak. You have muscles, Diane," Sue pointed out.

Diane accepted the compliment. She did have muscles, actually. Her defined calves ascended into thick, strong thighs, and even despite the paunch, her core muscles weren't anything to sneeze at. Of course, being a few sizes thicker than average, Diane took full advantage of being an XL woman. It gave her something to joke about. But the jokes hid reality.

In reality, she walked every morning and poked her way into yoga classes at The Club three days a week. She played tennis on Fridays, too. So what if she liked to eat? Life was meant to be lived, right? And, hey, she tried to get up on that board six whole times. Who was to say she might not give it another go the next day?

"Alright, let's go. We can shower up and make lunch for when Bea comes back."

"*If* she comes back," Sue pointed out as they stood and wiped sand off their butts before helping one another peel the wetsuits off their skin. It was more of a workout than the surfing part, truth be told.

"She'll be back sooner or later," Diane said as they

walked the wetsuits up to the house. They could rinse them there and hang them out for Brooks to return to the shop later.

Sue mentioned her surprise that Bea was taking so quickly to the water, but Diane cackled in response.

"She's not taking to the water. She's taking to the sexy instructor. Mark my words."

"True. Maybe that's what she needed, you know?"

"One hundred percent. *That*," Diane said, thrusting her finger down the beach as they entered Lil's, "is what Bea Russo has needed since she was thirteen years old."

"Diane, why do *you* think Bea never married?" Sue asked like a kid who never found out why the sky was blue or the grass was green. One of those stumping sorts of questions whose answer was readily available but still devoid of good and basic sense.

Diane just shrugged. "Bea has always been too serious. She took every date too seriously, you know? Hell, it's hot in here." She fanned herself as she strode to the thermostat at the front of the house. "Was it always like this?"

"Like what?"

"I mean, we're never going to dry off. I think my butt is going to prune up or something."

"Yeah, it was always like this. That's why we slept downstairs all the time, remember?"

"True," Diane agreed. And they had, too. "Listen, you can take a shower first. I gotta make a phone call." Sue agreed, and Diane grabbed her purse, digging inside for her phone.

Her grand plan wasn't so grand, in truth. At least, it wasn't elaborate or anything. But it was a big call to make. Something she really could not go back on.

But spending the day back at Gull's Landing and

catching glimpses of the life she thought she'd left, Diane learned something about herself. It was still possible to have that girlfriend gossip and hard memories and friendly teasing. That depth and lightness, together at once. And having that was far better than having awkward acquaintances who happened to join the same clubs as Diane.

It wasn't pity for Craig or seeing history through rose-colored glasses. It wasn't an ache for company in the face of loneliness, either. It was the fact that, quite plainly, she loved him. It took her a trip to the past to remind herself of that. A trip to see Craig and her marriage to him through the people who knew her the best.

So that was her plan. To call him and tell him just that.

That she loved him.

But right when she opened her phone to tap his number in, she got a text. It was something from one of the gals in Book Club, the one who was so *worried* about Sophia's death and the *implications* and the *context*.

It was a screenshot of the front page of Briar Creek Independent's website.

The headline stopped her heart.

Local lawyer and respected community member to file Chapter 7 bankruptcy; million-dollar estate up for grabs.

Beneath the words was a tabloid-style photo of Craig —five o'clock shadow, mussed hair and dopey-faced— holding his sunglasses beneath his chin as he walked from his driveway into his house—the one she'd been to just days before.

Diane wondered how in the world she could stand to be the center of her own small-town scandal. How *Craig* could be wrapped up in all that... Solid, affable Craig whom everyone adored and respected and admired.

Swallowing, she tapped out a quick reply, her gut reaction: *Don't believe everything you read!*

Her so-called friend wrote back immediately. *I know! I know! Just thought you should be aware. It doesn't affect you, does it?*

Diane growled under her breath and searched the recesses of her brain for something she'd read about some businessman-turned-politician. *"Ah-ha!"* she whispered, then sent her reply.

It was a strategic financial decision. Like I said—don't believe everything you read! We're doing fine. He was listing the house before all this.

A white lie could be the difference between total reputation annihilation and a return to innocence.

And it was, because ol' Book Club gal wrote back, changing topics on a dime.

I figured as much! I'll tell the girls. By the way... how's the shore? Any more news on your poor sweet cousin? XO!!!

Like an underhanded softball toss, the solution floated into her lap.

Diane had an opportunity. She could easily and swiftly tear all the focus from Craig, preserve his image and hers. She could do it right then, while Sue was in the shower and Bea was flirting with Brooks in the tides of Gull's Landing.

She could go upstairs, snap a few photos, tell the Briar Creek crew to keep her name out of it, and *poof*, Craig and his financial woes would be last season's Louboutins. And if she did that, then her grand plan could remain intact. She could still tell Craig: *you know what? I still love you. Even with all this crap and your muddied name and mine, I still love you and we can sail into the sunset together again, like we tried to the first time*

She *could* do it.

But *would* she do it? Was her wonky divorce-marriage worth a different betrayal?

The problem was this: to Diane, Craig was worth everything in the world.

If only she had known as much before she agreed to follow the trends and sign on the dotted line and split up their assets and believe the lie that a quiet, boring marriage was a bad one.

Now, in Diane's mind, she had one of two options: be a good friend—*cousin*—or… be a good ex-wife.

Chapter 24

Sue

She may not have been in surfing shape, but that didn't bother Sue. Every moment that ticked by was time savored, even if she spent the last hour sitting in sandy swim bottoms, wet and salt-stained like Darla-the-dog. Physical discomfort had never been so, well, comfortable.

New life warmed her body as she let the hot water run down her skin, and Sue began to consider what things might be like now that she was about to be a Single Woman.

Examining the collection of bath soaps and face scrubs, Sue considered the fact that they were probably left behind from the summer before—from Sophia's trip there. Funny that she'd have taken a shower at all. How long had she stayed in the house before she died? One night? Two?

Sue shuddered at the thought and squeezed her eyes shut, tilting her head back to rinse her face and hair.

189

There were better things to dwell on than what had happened to Sophia in the house. She forced herself to think of the last time she—Sue—took a shower in that shower. But the memory wasn't there. The bathroom and shower were all too familiar, but any memory of using it had vanished. Perhaps showers and the like weren't the sorts of things a memory bothered with.

Opening her eyes again, she studied the neat shelf of bottles, where the luxe-looking facial wash beckoned her like the serpent in the Garden of Eden. If she used it, she was all but consorting with the devil himself. Who did that? Who stole skincare products from the dead?

Not Sue. But then, what was the harm? Sophia wouldn't be back to claim it. And Sue always wondered what it was like to clean her face with expensive soap.

Maybe it would be okay to tread there, on those haunted leftovers. Maybe it would embolden her, too, to stick around long enough to go upstairs, for one. To do lots of other things, too. Like, for starters, begin to think of herself as a divorcee. Maybe she could set aside the annulment and be a little bit glamorous for a while.

Oversized black sunglasses and manicured fingernails came to mind. A fluid, floral jersey-knit dress, loose about her hips and thighs and skimpy up top—showing off her delicate shoulders. Maybe Sue could pull that sort of look off if she tried.

Now was the time *to* try, after all. She had her friends. She had the summer off. She had a little extra money that she'd purposefully cashed out before blasting out of town like a woman on the run.

The funny thing was, Sue had nothing to run from. Only a new life to run *to*.

After guiltily sampling every last one of Sophia's fragrant washes, she shut off the water and wrung her hair. The smell in that cramped tiled stall was divine, and Sue swore to herself that she'd make the switch from unscented generics to the good stuff. Then she reached for a towel—one of Aunt Lil's originals with long faded pink strips down a bleach-white rectangle. It was too small and too threadbare to adequately dry her off, especially in the humidity, but that was okay. More moisture was better when you were north of fifty years old. But there was one thing Sue could not stand. It all started when she was a little girl. After bathing, her mother would twist her hair into a long braid down her back—a long, wet braid. At the first peep of a complaint, her mother swatted her butt and shooed her off. She'd learned to use bobby pins all by herself at the ripe age of six—sneaking into her mother's ceramic pin jar and taking as few as possible—sometimes only two—then turning the braid into a braided bun. Funnily, her mother never commented on the style change. Not that Sue could recall. It became her signature style until she was older and allowed to use the blow dryer.

Sue still hated the feeling of wet hair on her neck and back. It gave her a chill and turned her mood foul, and now wasn't the time to let such a thing in. Not when she was riding high on the adrenaline of a fresh start.

She scrunched her shoulder-length hair (not since her wedding day had Sue let it get any longer than that) with the old terrycloth (did it smell a little musty? It might have smelled a little musty—oh, well). Then, she pulled out her linen shorts and white tee.

"Diane!" she called as she opened the door, letting the steam out of the small bathroom. "Your turn!"

No answer came and Sue slipped back in, searching for a blow dryer.

She raised her voice again as she opened and closed

the cabinet drawers. "Did you bring a blow dryer?" In the rush to pack and leave, it was the one item Sue had forgotten.

Again, no answer, but she remembered very distinctly that Aunt Lil had one. That was a long, long time ago. Maybe it broke. Maybe ol' Lil had sold it off at a yard sale. Maybe she never replaced it and didn't need one when her hair turned to cotton candy.

Maybe it was upstairs.

It was the summer of 1985. Their last summer together in Gull's Landing and at Lil's. Or, at least, the last before Lil's funeral.

Sue didn't know then that it would be the summer to mark the end. If she had known, she might have done something special to mark the occasion. She might have begged the others to organize a tea party, like when they were little girls. Or maybe she'd have turned over a new leaf and announced that the best way to commemorate such a thing as The Last Summer Down the Shore Together would be with a formal dinner at Gil's on Gull's, a surf-and-turf joint known for its lobster rolls and cheesy biscuits.

But she couldn't have predicted the future and she did not know it would be the last, so the final night they were there—after Bea pried them away from Pelican Pier—they simply went back to Aunt Lil's, the boys as their escorts until all four of them—Diane, Bea, Sophia, and Sue—were tucked away inside, sunburnt and content after another successful summer at the shore.

But Diane didn't stick around, and only Sue knew it.

That's another reason why Diane didn't want to

sleep upstairs, in the hot second bedroom down the hall from Aunt Lil. She was going to sneak out.

It all started when they crowded quietly together in the living room, arguing in hushed tones, as usual, about who would sleep where.

Sleeping was the worst part of summer at Aunt Lil's. Technically, they were assigned to the upstairs bedroom. That's where Lil had always set them up. It had two twin beds framing the window that looked out over the beach.

As little girls, they easily fit two to a bed up there— Sue and Soph in one and Bea and Diane in the other.

Back then, Aunt Lil hadn't yet invested in air conditioning. She didn't care, because she was skinny enough to be one of those middle-aged ladies who was always cold.

And as little girls, none of them even realized it was hot. They were too busy giggling and telling stories and chatting late into the night until they were so worn out that sleep came like a thief, robbing them of their waking hours together.

But as those little girls grew up, things changed of course. The sisters turned into long, lithe young women, and as Diane filled out (as she liked to say), more often than not one of them would stay downstairs. And then they all (even little Sue who didn't get too far past five feet and a hundred pounds) became red-blooded teenagers with sweat glands and heartbeats, and there was not enough deodorant to last any of them through the summer.

Downstairs, in the living room, there were box fans propped against the windows. Aunt Lil forbade the girls from moving them up, because that's just where the fans stayed—downstairs. They were the downstairs oscillating fans, and the only upstairs fan (save for the ceiling one) was kept in the bathroom, because of mold. You couldn't argue with Aunt Lil. At least, not if you wanted to stay the whole summer long.

So, some nights, the four girls set up camp in front of the TV, taking turns on which two would get to share the big sofa and which one would claim the love seat and who would be left on the floor.

Sue hated being on the floor. She hated being downstairs. It scared her. They were right next to the front door—an easy entry point for ne'er-do-wells—and Aunt Lil left the windows open, of course.

"Can we sleep upstairs tonight?" Sue whined.

"*You* can," Diane replied.

That was the other problem. Sue also hated to sleep alone when she was away from home. So even though she felt safer upstairs, up there she had to battle the sound of the ocean and the gulls and the errant beach drunk calling out obscenities into the night.

"Will you come up with me, Soph?"

Sophia blew out a sigh. "Sue, it's too hot up there. I don't think I can stand to sweat through my clothes again. Come on. Just sleep down here with us."

Sue sulked. "Sophia, you *like* the bedroom upstairs. You always say so. You like the view and the quilt. Remember?" She was playing off of her best friend's early-summer comments. Those moments when they first arrived each year, full of energy and hope and fondness.

"I won't be able to sleep." Sophia crossed her arms over her chest. "And I really need to get a few hours. I'm still exhausted from this week."

"It's our last night here," Bea reasoned. "Soph, you can sleep on the ride home tomorrow."

That's how they often ended, those arguments. With

Bea encouraging her little sister to do right by her best friend and head upstairs.

And Sophia did. She dragged herself up, irritated but wiped out enough that once she flopped into her own bed, it only took a few whispers back and forth with Sue until she fell asleep.

The last thing Soph had murmured before falling quiet was "Sophia Victoria Hurley; whaddya think, Susie Q?"

Even though she smiled at Sophia's longtime nickname for her, Sue hadn't thought much of it. She figured Sophia would do better to stick to a romantic last name like Russo. But if there was one thing Sue knew, it was that Sophia was falling hard for Doug. And no one could have changed her mind on that. Not Sue. Not Diane. Not even Bea. Deep down inside, actually, Sue wondered how the two would keep their fire going. Would they meet up in the pre-dawn hours? Secretly? Would Doug drive to Philly and steal her away? Anything was possible when S.E. X. was at stake. Sue sensed it.

As Sophia's breath grew heavy and rhythmic, long shadows stretched across the upstairs bedroom walls.

Sue wouldn't have the luck of falling asleep so quickly. She never did. Her father used to claim it was because she wasn't tired and she ought to do more physical activity. Her mother wondered if she was too tired—overtired. *If you get yourself too worked up in the day, you'll never fall asleep! It becomes a vicious cycle, Susan. You need to take a nap after school.*

In all likelihood, Sue never slept because she was always worrying.

Once, years earlier, her grandparents had taken her to church at St. Augustine's in Philadelphia. Afterwards, on the sidewalk outside, another pair of parishioners came over to them, chatting pleasantly until the husband introduced Sue and her grandparents to the fragile-looking Mexican child that stood between him and his wife.

Sue remembered the girl remaining frozen, but still they quietly befriended each other as their parents swept them off to the family hall for doughnuts and coffee after mass.

The little girl, whom the couple had adopted only two years before, still didn't speak a lick of English—according to her well-meaning parents. Even if she did, Sue had figured, they still would have sat quietly together at the fold-out table.

But Sue made an effort. She appreciated her unfamiliar role as the older one—the leader of the two. *"I get nervous when I come to the city,"* Sue had confessed in a whisper to the little girl, trying to relate but still posing as stronger, more confident. Being honest could do that for her, she thought. *"I worry I'll get hit by a car or kidnapped or something."* She raised an eyebrow down at the child, unaware it was the wrong thing to say.

Or perhaps, the right thing.

Because that's when the girl tucked her small hand into her dress pocket and pulled out a piece of folded fabric.

Carefully, the child unwrapped the cotton and revealed a row of miniature figures.

Sue squinted and lowered her head. *"What are those?"*

"Muñecas quitapenas," the girl had replied.

"You can understand me?" Sue had asked.

The curious little child gave Sue a look, and it made her feel all of six inches tall. *"Oh."*

"Put them beneath your pillow at night. They will take your troubles for you."

And that's exactly what Sue did.

All the way until that last night in Gull's Landing, when she tossed and turned for an hour or more as Sophia snored softly nearby.

Finally, when Sue couldn't handle her restless legs and the sweat on her back, she rose from the creaking wooden bed and crossed the room, wide-eyed in the dark. Carefully, she crept on her tiptoes to her suitcase.

She wasn't sure what she was more frightened of just then, as she blindly rummaged in the front pocket for those two little Mexican charms: waking someone else in the house and bearing their wrath, or the nakedness of walking through the moonlit room where shadows crossed through the lace-curtains.

It had to have been later than Sue even realized, because outside of their window was now quiet. Only the sound of the water remained against the empty night. No more drunkards. No more birds—at least none that Sue could hear.

And so, when she alighted upon her two little dolls—ridiculous, really, that a seventeen-year-old was *that* scared—then clutched them against her chest preciously and turned to tiptoe back into her bed, the sound sent a quiet scream up her throat.

It was a set of voices. Just below her window, in the backyard. *Not* out on the beach or up on the boardwalk.

In Aunt Lil's *yard*.

Kidnappers. Had to be.

Sue dashed to her bed, sinking far against the wall, deep beneath the damp sheet and heavy quilt, trembling and breathing so hard that she feared her heart would burst from her chest and draw attention.

"*Soph*," she whispered tearfully. "*Are you awake?*"

Sophia continued to snore. The voices came again, quiet and conspiratorial.

Sue did everything in her power to tame her thudding pulse so she could make out what they were saying. She dared not creep to the window and peek out.

What if they had a gun!?

"*Sophia!*" she hissed more urgently.

Again, her best friend breathed heavily through her nose in response.

That's when Sue started in on the Rosary (except, without her Rosary it was more just a jumble of prayers that Sue couldn't remember in such a scary moment). She'd made it halfway through the Apostle's Creed when the voices returned. They were louder but also more distant, somehow.

Sue squeezed her two tiny knit dolls and edged toward the window, knowing that if she didn't act, that it could be too late. She had to be brave. Whimpering to herself, she scootched and scootched until she was on the far side of the gossamer lace, peeking with great care from the corner.

And that's when she saw them.

They weren't kidnappers.

It was Diane and Craig, running out to the beach, hand-in-hand like something out of a movie. The moon lit their path down the sand, and Sue watched with awe and confusion as they fell together, in a heap. Laughter trailed up toward the window, and suddenly Sue wasn't afraid any longer.

She wasn't afraid at all. She was captivated.

Craning her neck to get a better look, it occurred to her that perhaps they wanted their privacy. She slowly eased back into her bed, wide awake, giddy over her view to her friend's secret escape.

And perhaps just a little bit… inspired.

Ashamed, now, of the worry dolls and her several minutes of pure, unmitigated fear, she stood from her bed, tossed the dolls into her half-open suitcase then flopped back down.

Anxiety stabbed again—or perhaps superstition— and she stood, went and collected the dolls, and returned them more carefully to their pouch before falling into bed again.

Her head still pounded from their earlier tour of Pelican Pier and the wild moment where the Canadian boy twirled her and dropped her on the ground. And now her heart was pounding again, too.

That was the night that Susan Jean Merkle decided she was too old for worrying. And it was also the night she decided that she would stop saying no all the time and start saying yes. And it was all Sophia's fault.

But maybe, if she said yes, she would have a midnight walk on the beach and fall into a tangle of bodies on the sand, laughing and happier than ever.

And so, the following summer when Joseph John Bleckert proposed marriage, she had no choice.

She had to say yes.

But back then, on that fearful moonlit night, if she had stayed up just half an hour longer, waiting and listening, then she would know that her first intuition was right, after all.

Chapter 25

Bea

Dragging herself and the surfboard through the squelching sand as it smacked the arches of her feet, Bea was elated.

There was no other word for it.

"I'm *starving*," she moaned dramatically, heaving the board onto the dry shore and falling to her knees on the crumpled towel she'd brought from Lil's.

Sue and Diane had left half an hour earlier. She'd watched them make their way back up to the house, and she was grateful for it.

So was Brooks. She could tell.

"Don't you have to be back at the shop?" she asked him, as he rolled onto the sand next to her.

He smiled. "I told you, Darla's got it under control."

"Need I point out that Darla is a dog?" Bea joked.

"Well, she's not manning the cash register or anything, but she's supervising my clerk."

"Clerk? I don't remember—"

"My son, Bennett. His shift started right when we took off down here. He'll be a senior next year. Loves to surf. Hates to work. I'm trying to break that."

"You have a son?" Bea bit her lower lip, her brows furrowed.

"Yeah. You sound… disappointed." He threw her a sidelong glance.

"Oh, not that you have a son—" Bea squeezed her eyes shut. She had never been good with flirting. And here she was, stuck with a dad on the beach, her hair matted to her head. The elation was beginning to slip.

Brooks frowned. "So you *are* disappointed?"

Bea buried her face in her hands then came up, laughing. "I'm sorry. I didn't mean that at all. I mean—" she turned to him, finding it in herself to face the question. "Are you married?"

"Ah." He wrapped his arms around his knees and rocked back. "No. But I'm not divorced, either." Again with the sidelong look.

She frowned and swallowed. "Oh." It occurred to her then that she could say the same exact thing. So she did. "Me, too."

"Really?" A small grin curled his lip. "What does that mean?"

"I could ask you the same thing," she shot back, tickled by the playful back-and-forth. It hadn't been long since she'd been in Gull's Landing, and there she was like a teenager with a summer crush on a townie. She shook her head and looked down at her legs—long and dead with exhaustion. They weren't bad legs. Not for someone her age. Not quite as toned and smooth as Sophia's, but if Brooks happened to notice, he'd see she wasn't too flabby. That's the one thing Bea had going for herself at home—a strict exercise routine. Three miles a day, two days a week, and laps at the community center pool four days a week. Sundays off. That's how she kept her mind busy in the lonely hours of the afternoons. Laps in the pool, however, didn't compare to an hour in the surf—not in terms of muscle fatigue, at least.

Even with the regimen, Bea never could keep up with Sophia, who added kickboxing and yoga to her routine.

Brooks unzipped the top half of his wetsuit and leaned back on his elbows. "I met a girl... oh, I guess about eighteen years ago now. We had Bennett. That's mostly the extent of it."

"Sounds like you're leaving out some details." Bea lifted an eyebrow.

Brooks laughed, and Bea decided then and there that she liked his laugh as much as she liked the rest of him. So far, at least.

"Fair enough," he replied, his gaze on the water. "She was a Shoobie."

"Shoobie?" Bea turned to him, grinning. "I haven't heard that word in ages."

"Ah, yeah," he answered. "I guess you're a Shoobie, too, huh?"

"Hey, I've been coming around here longer than you've lived here. So if anyone is going to call anyone else a Shoobie, well—"

He raised his hands in defeat. "All right, all right. Anyway, it was my first year here. I got a little carried away with my newfound local status, I suppose. And my new business. Anyway, she was a sweet girl, and I got Bennett out of the deal, so all's well that ends well." Brooks sat up and twisted toward the boardwalk, stretching. "He stays here for the summer. Has since he was a tyke. That's our deal, mainly. It works, you know?"

Bea nodded. She did know. "That's why we're here. When we were all girls, we came and stayed at Aunt Lil's every single summer. Until I was eighteen."

Brooks smiled but stayed quiet.

"Does Bennett bring friends?" Bea figured it was best to wrap up their conversation on a light note. Hearing about his affair or discussing her childhood felt a little too deep for a first surf lesson.

"Nah. He's made them here. He got hooked up with the locals when he was young, and they took him in, I guess you could say."

Bea smiled. "He probably had to earn that spot. It's not easy, you know."

"Oh yeah?" Brooks answered. "Sounds like you have personal experience."

She laughed. "Not me, no. But my cousin, Diane, she met her husband here. That last summer. He was a local, you know. Craig Bettancourt. Did you know the Bettancourts? His folks worked on the boardwalk, too."

Brooks frowned. "Sounds familiar, but—oh, wait, did they happen to get in a bit of trouble a few years back?"

Bea winced, forgetting about what Diane had told her. "Yeah. They were good people, I'm pretty sure." It occurred to her that she did not, in fact, know if her cousin's former in-laws were decent people or not.

"I didn't know them. I heard about it. All over the papers. The general vibe in the paper was negative. But people around here were pretty defensive of them. Such a pity, you know?"

"What's that?"

"When good people lose their good name."

Looking out across the water, Bea nodded. It was the worst that could happen. Worse than death, even. Losing your good name.

It's why, when Soph died, Bea wondered a little bit if it wasn't such a bad thing that Greg kept mum. Maybe there was something to be said for discretion. For keeping other people's secrets for them.

Maybe, like Bea, Soph had secrets, too.

———

SHE PARTED ways with Brooks after agreeing to a second lesson at some point in the near future. She'd be around all summer, she told him, to which he replied again that if she needed anything, he was just next door.

Once Bea was inside, frigid air hit her, chilling her skin and sending her into the living room to the thermostat. It was one thing to use the AC in a reasonable way. It was another to turn the place into an icebox. She'd rather be eternally damp and muggy than send a four-hundred-dollar electricity bill to Greg. He'd pull the plug sooner than Labor Day, that was for sure.

As she stabbed the rubbery arrow to 78, she turned and noticed the living room *and* kitchen were empty.

Where was Sue?

Where was Diane?

"Girls?" Bea called out, walking to the downstairs bath. Empty. "You here?"

Certain they must have left, she called out once more. "Sue? Diane? Are you here?"

No answer came, but a rustling sound stole Bea's attention.

It was coming from the second floor.

No, Bea screamed internally. *You can't go up there! Not without me!*

She dashed to the staircase and pounded up the narrow wooden steps, hesitating halfway, "Diane?" Bea rose her voice as she ascended higher. "Diane did you come up—"

She stopped at the top.

"Bea, I'm so sorry. I just—"

But Bea had looked past her and down the hall to the open door. The room with two little twin beds and heavy quilt sheets and gauzy lace curtains.

Sophia's favorite place in the whole house.

The room with the view of the ocean.

Chapter 26

Diane

"I know, I know," Diane said, pacing as her heart pounded. She'd made the choice, and there was no going back now.

The four words came again, as if on repeat. "You *cannot* be serious."

"Do you want an apology? I can apologize if you want," she answered. "I mean, I expected you to be *surprised happy*, but… *surprised angry*? You're joking, right?"

Suddenly, the tone shifted. Softened.

"I'm not angry, I swear. Well, I'm stressed as crap, but not at you. I'm not angry at you. I'm angry at *myself*, Di." A pause. Then, "Are you *sure* this is what you want?"

"It's what I need, Craig. And it's what you need, too. We can fix it together. Okay? We'll follow the letter of the law—we'll sell the place to my mom. She can rent it to us until everything blows over."

He didn't answer immediately, and Diane's breath hitched in her chest.

Then, his voice lowered. "I figured you'd never talk to me again."

"Well here I am. On the phone in Gull's Landing, talking to you. And I want to talk to you every day for the rest of our lives, Craig. Really and truly."

"Oh, Di. I could drive down the shore right now. I'll pick you up. We'll get ice cream or a slice of pie—tell me what to do, what you want. I'll do it now. And every day."

"Listen. You don't need to make any ridiculous promises, Craig. We can just... do what we used to do, okay?"

"Di, what is that supposed to mean?"

"We share the house. We share dinner a few times a week."

"How about our lives, this time? Can we share them too?"

"Don't get cheesy on me, Craig. You never were cheesy. Now's not the time." Even as she said it, she was grinning like a fool. Butterflies in the stomach and everything. "Let's start fresh," she went on. Sweat broke out along her forehead as she paced in front of Aunt Lil's. She'd just told her bankrupt husband to move his butt over to her house. That they were going to live together. They were going to fix the mess.

"A fresh start," Craig agreed.

Then, he told her he loved her—nothing too out of the ordinary, actually, and they ended the call. With the snap of her fingers, Diane had successfully dragged her ex-husband from the depths of despair. She'd not only offered him lodging for when the time came to give up his house to the bank, but she offered him more than that. She'd offered him a second chance. In fact, though, it wasn't just Craig who Diane was giving a second chance. It was herself, too. Sometimes in life, you had to do that. Give your own self a second chance.

As she cradled the phone in her hand, ruing the fact that she might have to cut back on manicures, the image from the text reared back into her mind.

Craig's reputation, his professional *future*—and hers, if you could call quasi-volunteer gigs professions—was still at stake. Sure, she could divert the attention, but at what cost? Pimping out her dead cousin? Subverting her living cousin's single request?

No way. Diane was better than that. She'd have to do things the right way. And to do them right meant to do them the hard way.

Assured in the promises of her future, she rubbed the back of her hand along her forehead and stepped back into the house.

Inside, the air was stuffier than before, and she could hear voices coming from above, but that couldn't be.

Unless…

"Bea? You back?"

Diane strode toward the staircase. "Sue?"

Two faces appeared at the landing above.

Bea's, grief-stricken and pained. Sue's, red and tear-streaked.

"I was outside for *ten* minutes! What happened?" Diane climbed the stairs, carefully and one at a time, suddenly nervous about the very thing she was most anxious to do once she'd arrived in Gull's Landing.

Sue shrugged and pushed her fingers into her wet hair. "I needed a blow dryer. I figured *you* were up here. I don't know what I was thinking." She shook her head mournfully.

Diane's eyes flew to Bea, who stood staring, her eyes

red-rimmed and bloodshot—from the surfing lesson or crying, who could tell? "I wasn't ready," she whispered.

Diane looked past her friend and down the hall. In the near distance awaited the room where they slept as girls.

Through the open door, Diane could see the corners of two twin beds and the window that connected them along the wall. Outside the window rocked the Atlantic Ocean, expansive and impossibly blue.

"You will never be ready." Diane set her hand on Bea's shoulder and squeezed it, then took the other and turned her friend one-hundred-eighty degrees. "Come on. It's time."

Chapter 27

Sue

S ue stood glued to her spot in the hall. How she wound up on the second floor was a mystery even to her. It was as if a hot shower had morphed her back into a girlish seventeen-year-old. Like she lost her sense and floated up there, transported in time and space.

Then, as she made it to the top of the stairs, she saw the bedroom. Light glimmered off of white caps in the water like a moving postcard, framed by the gaping door. Her immediate reaction was to wonder about those white caps.

Had the weather turned since they quit their lesson? Was a storm brewing off the coast and making its way to Gull's Landing? Had a rash of speedboats jetted across that rectangle of ocean, churning the shallow stretch of sea for her view? Was she imagining it or misunderstanding what she saw?

Then, in an effort to make sense of her view, Sue's peripheral vision kicked in, and she noticed more than just the ocean beyond. She saw the foreground of the still-life painting that was that old bedroom.

She saw the lace curtains. One hanging loose at the edge of the window, the other hooked back.

There was the shag carpet, dingier perhaps. A vaguely familiar rug hid a swath of it, but even the rug couldn't tame the thick piling and reared up in little hills across its length.

And the edges of the two beds—just slivers—one neatly tucked and the other a mess of fabric and pillows and even, it appeared, a clump of clothing. *Clothing.* When had clothing become a horrifying thing?

Shock took over at that point and she froze, her body immobile as her mind raced painfully through what she was seeing.

From her vantage point and with the whole of the setting now coming into focus, it looked like a picture from the annals of history. Apparent facts began falling like a deck of cards. Aunt Lil never touched the girls' summer bedroom, for one—at least not in terms of redecorating. But, contradictorily, whoever was there last —Greg or the police or the EMTs—they didn't even have the decency to shut the door. How could they just leave everything there? Wasn't there a cleaning crew? Wasn't there someone who came along and tapped a magic wand over the place and *poof*, it was different and clean and absolved of the God-awful tragedy?

She much, much preferred to think of Aunt Lil's just the way she saw it when she left that room for the last time.

———

1985

Sue conducted a mental review of the night before. Worry dolls, shadows, secrets. It was eventful, that was for sure.

First, she had agreed to go to Pelican Pier so long as her friends didn't bug her about riding anything too scary. Then, a strange Canadian boy dragged her to the dance floor, tried to flip her over and smacked her head on the ground. It hurt, but she survived to live through a round of Diane and Soph and Bea arguing about how much longer to stay out and where to spend their final moments.

They'd settled on the Ferris wheel, which was fine by Sue, who rode it with Bea.

Bea complained the whole time about how Sophia was too interested in Doug and Doug was too much of a loser for Sophia. Usually, that sort of conversation would draw Sue in and hold her there. She rarely got to partake in intra-Society gossip, despite the fact that she was named secretary of The Summer Society not four years earlier.

Apparently, however, now that they were *grown up*, the club didn't matter anymore. Not like it used to, back before the boys came around and ruined everything.

Even so, Sue would have felt like a hypocrite if she didn't at least try to stir it back to life. "Bea," she'd said as their passenger car crested the top of the wheel. It was dark by then, but the lights of the Pier and those of the boardwalk illuminated their stretch of earth. Sue was emboldened, if only for a moment. "Call a meeting if you're so peeved. You know?"

"A meeting?" Bea had replied. "We aren't thirteen anymore, Sue."

Sue shrugged, but she had nothing to lose. "I feel the same way, honestly. I could call the meeting."

"You do?" Bea's eyes had grown wide in the dark. "You hate Doug, too?"

"Well, I don't *hate* him, but he's a creep. There's no doubt about that. Seems like Sophia doesn't realize it. But tonight's our last night here. Does it really matter? They'll never see each other again."

"Sure they could. He could drive to Philly. She could drive here if she wanted to. And I just know how it's going to be when we get home. She'll hog the phone. She'll need stamps for letters. She'll talk about him nonstop."

"But Bea," Sue had argued softly. "You'll be at college in the fall. You won't even be around to have to deal with all that."

Bea had shifted her weight in the passenger car, leaning closer and turning in, her face grave. "That's what I'm most scared of, Sue."

Sue had frowned, confused.

"That I won't be around. Just in case."

"Then that settles it. We're calling a meeting." Sue got worked up about those things. By that point, Bea had her scared.

But once they got home, the meeting was brushed off. And that's a big part of the reason that Sue had lain awake and afraid until the moment she caught Diane and Craig in the surf like they were reenacting *From Here to Eternity*.

Now that morning was upon them and Aunt Lil had served up pancakes and bacon and excused herself to the backyard for a cigarette—as if she didn't also smoke *inside*—Sue had drummed up enough courage to follow through on the plan she and Bea had hatched the night before.

"Now that you're all here," Sue said, her jaw parallel with the kitchen table. She swallowed and looked at each girl in turn. First, Diane, whose uncharacteristically sheepish expression did little to hide the hickeys on her neck. Then Soph, whose snoring the night before had meant little, apparently, because she looked as tired as Diane, who probably didn't return home until the wee hours of the morning.

Lastly, Bea. Bea, who Sue was so certain would clear her throat and say something along the lines of *Yes, we need to talk. Sophia—your relationship with Doug is unhealthy and unwise. It's time we all conducted an intervention for your sake, my dear sister.* But she didn't. Instead, she kept her eyes on her pancakes, pushing them around in the syrup with a slow, weak hand.

"What is it?" Diane asked, bored already.

"Well, um." Sue batted her eyes and tried to stare hard enough at Bea to gain her attention, but it didn't work. "Um." She licked her lips and glanced to Sophia. "It's about our futures. All of us. Okay?"

It wasn't Sue's place to make an issue of Doug, that was becoming clearer by the second. Still, Bea kept quiet. Bizarrely so.

"What do you mean our futures?" Sophia answered through a yawn.

"Did you finally give into a tarot card reading?" Diane ribbed.

Sue shook her head, but the idea wasn't entirely bad. "No, but we can talk about that, too."

She felt Bea's eyes flash on her and glanced over. "Bea? Did you want to begin?"

"No. This one is all you, Secretary Susan."

Sue flushed, but in that moment she was mature enough to see something. Bea was acting odd and mean, but that only confirmed how much she *needed* Sue to open the conversation. Though they weren't best friends, they were close enough. And if there was one thing in life Sue was pretty good at, it was being a good friend and making good decisions. A teacher even told her once that she had *uncommonly sound judgment*. Sue carried that compliment in her heart, until it was contradicted years later, of course.

"I'd like to call a meeting of The Summer Society to discuss a serious concern."

"You're joking." Diane's eyebrow crept up on her forehead and she shoveled a forkful of pancake into her mouth.

Sophia, who had yet to touch her breakfast, offered a sweet smile. "The Summer Society, oh my *goodness*, Susie Q! We haven't done Summer Society stuff in *ages*."

Sue blinked. "I know, it sounds silly. But it worked back then, right?"

"Worked for *what*?" It was Bea who responded, her tone callous and searing.

"Whoa, Bea. What crawled up your butt?" Diane pointed out, setting her fork down and crossing her arms over her chest. That was Diane's defensive pose. It's exactly the way she looked when a random sleazeball hit on one of them, or if they got turned down for anything ever—like the time Sue was ten cents short at Mack's. They got an extra breadstick for free out of that whole debacle.

Bea shot back, "Nothing. At least, nothing *important*."

"But Bea," Sophia said quietly. "We did make a pact."

"We made a pact for *everything*. Come on, Soph. We

made a pact to come back here if we were in trouble, and guess what? Diane was in trouble in February when she cheated on that math test. Did we all come back here? No. We made a pact to keep each other's secrets, and guess what? When Sue admitted that her Barbies kissed, I—" Bea pointed at Sophia, "—told Sister Ann at CCD." Her face took on a pain that could only come from someone confessing to a grave sin, but that was little consolation.

What sort of a Catholic tattled on her friend? Sophia reached across the table, but Sue flinched. "Well, then," she said. "You're right, Bea. I guess those days *are* over." Sue's voice trembled as she said it, and tears stung the corners of her eyes.

"No. No. No. You know what, Sue?" Diane asked, her voice high and falsetto and every bit the dominating force. "I think we *do* need a meeting of The Summer Society. To overthrow our so-called *president*."

Bea, for her part, leaned into the table. "Yeah. Maybe we do need a meeting. Maybe we need a meeting to discuss how *reckless* some of you behave."

"Oh, gimme a break. You could use a little reckless-ness in your life, Bea." Diane uncrossed her arms and drew her coffee mug to her lips. Sue thought she looked about ten years older just then. And she sort of liked it. She and Sophia exchanged a look before Sue remem-bered that she had started the whole conversation *against* Soph. She looked away.

Bea shoved her chair back from the table and shot up. "You don't know a thing about *my life*, Diane De Luca."

Sue cowered beside her, but Diane stood up too, ready for battle. "This is a whole tub of bull crap if I ever saw it." She glared hard at Bea then turned to Sue, then Soph, and added, "Summer Society. On the beach. *Now.*" She swung her pointer finger like an industrial-sized fishing hook and turned on her heel, leaving half a pancake on the table.

That's when Sue knew things were serious.

Without another word, the other three of them followed her, Bea huffing audibly and Sophia keeping abnormally quiet. Sue wilted into herself. She'd made a huge mistake.

Or maybe not.

They passed Aunt Lil, who sat at her patio table with a hollow-cheeked man, reading his cards as he stared at her in awe. Sue was distracted by the bizarre scene, but only momentarily. She quickly skipped back up to the others and soon enough found herself sitting in her traveling outfit in one of the Adirondack chairs on the beach just outside Lil's fence. Sand had already slid inside her shoes, but now was *not* the time to lodge any complaints.

Diane rose a hand. "As… wait a minute. What was my job?"

"What do you mean?" Soph whispered.

Sue replied, "Treasurer. You were the treasurer."

"Oh right. Just because I got a hundred percent on that math test."

Bea scoffed, and Sophia giggled.

A little smile tugged the corner of Diane's mouth, but Sue watched her force it down. Those tiny memories, the ones that meant nothing and everything—that's what they had. As a group of friends. And that's what Sue didn't want to lose. Not after Diane and Bea went off to college or wherever. Not after Sophia fell too far down the rabbit hole of young love, either. She needed those memories. She needed her friends. It was the reason she was willing to speak up for once.

Diane went on. "As treasurer of The Summer Society, I hereby call a meeting to discuss Bea's witch attack on the last day we're here."

Bea's mouth fell open and her eyes flashed. "What? No. Sue is the one who called the meeting. And she called it to discuss our *future*. Isn't that right, Sue?"

Sue gulped and nodded.

"So just because I'm having a bad morning, well that's not a… that's not a *thing* we need to *discuss*. Okay?"

Sniffing, Diane folded her arms again. "We'll see about that. Sue? You have the floor."

Sue squinted around the beach then back up at Lil, who was leaning over the table toward the small grayish man. From what she could see, the cards were pushed aside, as if they didn't matter at all. Could Aunt Lil hear the girls now? If Sue submitted her grievance there, in the circle of chairs on the beach, would Lil hear her and come down and defend her nieces and make Sue leave or something?

She had no choice. She had to speak up. If not for Bea, then for Sophia. Clearing her throat, she swallowed and studied the charred wood of a fire they'd killed off two nights before. "I think Sophia should break up with Doug."

There. She let out a breath and squeezed her eyes tightly shut. She did it.

Half-expecting another outburst of some size or shape, Sue tucked herself to the far back of her chair and pulled her knees up to her chest. She finally peered out at her friends.

Diane's face was blank. She sat quiet. Perhaps, Sue liked to think, in agreement.

Bea was studying Sophia with the focus of an eagle.

Sophia glowered and, like a serpent, twisted her head to Sue. "You're joking."

Sue shook her head, tears stabbing the corners of her eyes yet again. She brushed them away, angry that she was so quick to get emotional. "You're better than him, Soph," she managed weakly, praying for divine intervention.

It came. Bea joined in, at last. "Sue's right. You need to dump him, Soph." As she said it, gone was the seething rage. Gone was the edge and broodiness from breakfast. It came out softly, like a pillow for Sue's idea, breaking the fall of the words.

"No." Now it was Sophia's turn to cross her arms. She met Bea's gaze, and Sue and Diane looked at each other. It was a stand-off. They'd been down that road before. It didn't happen often, but when it did, Sue wanted to crawl in a hole and not come out for a month.

"Why not?" Bea replied, her tone belying the otherwise reasonable question.

"Why *would* I?" Sophia spat back.

"Because he's not good enough for you."

Sue caught Diane rolling her eyes. "Hey, listen. I want in on this, Madam President."

Bea held her hand up to Diane. "This is serious. Diane, you and me? We're going to college. We're eighteen. Soph's still in high school. She's still a kid."

"I'm one year younger than you!" Sophia roared, life returning to her.

But Diane shook her head. "Hush. You *are* still a kid. And Doug isn't the cream of the crop, here, Soph. I agree with Bea."

Sue watched in awe at the shift in power. Now it was three against one.

Diane went on. "But it's a summer fling. It's harmless, Bea. Doug's harmless."

Sue caught Bea flinch.

"It's not a fling." Sophia was gripping her armrests, her eyes now on Sue, who thought she was absolved of the mess once Diane got involved.

She wasn't.

Peeking from the corner of her eye at Bea, Sue tried to communicate telepathically. *What do I say now? HELP!*

Bea's face hardened. Her gaze narrowed on Sue and she nodded her head.

Sophia would listen to Sue. She would listen to Sue when she wouldn't listen to Diane or Bea.

Sue had the power now.

But she hadn't the slightest clue about how to wield it.

She searched her brain for the right thing to say. The right question to ask. Where was her sound judgment now? Miles away, in her suburban home on the edge of Philly.

"Um," she uttered at last, thinking of the situation as though she were a parent and Sophia was her daughter. As if Sophia was an unruly teenager who needed to see the light. When had the whole matter grown so huge? Sue wondered. Sure, she knew that Doug was scum, but maybe Diane was right for once in her life. It was just a summer fling. Even if they stayed in touch, Sophia would snap out of it.

Maybe.

Maybe not.

Then again, Sue realized, treating her best friend in the world like a child could not possibly be a good way to get down to business. She had to meet Soph on her level.

As a peer. Peer pressure. It could be a good thing, she once heard.

She licked her lips and went with the only thing that could come to mind.

"Are we still The Summer Society?" Her eyes flitted around the others.

Bea and Diane nodded. Sophia did too. "We'll always be The Summer Society, Sue." Her voice was a low rumble, her face earnest. There was a break in the momentum. An opportunity.

"So, we're safe, then?" Sue probed gently.

She saw Diane roll her eyes, but Bea leaned in closer and put her hand over the dead fire. "If any one of us is ever in trouble, then we come back here. Right?"

Diane threw her hand over Bea's. "Of course."

Sue pressed her hand on top of Diane's but looked at Sophia. "And we're here right now. At Aunt Lil's shore house. Together. All of us. Right, Soph?"

Sophia frowned but pressed her hand on top of the pile. "Well, sure. We're The Summer Society. We made a pact. We're here for each other, girls." Sophia squeezed their pile of hands in hers and broke away. "So what does any of *that* have to do with Doug Hurley?"

Sue eased back to her seat, satisfied to know they were still one. Still a sisterhood, even if she wasn't one of the sisters. Even with loudmouth Diane who figured a summer fling couldn't hurt.

And she asked the only question that came to mind.

"Sophia," Sue began, growing bolder.

"What, Sue?"

"Truth or dare?"

Chapter 28

Bea, 1992

For a wedding, it was perfection.

For the beginning of a marriage, it was a disaster. At least, according to the girls' mother.

Despite Dolores's pleas and Bea's lackluster reasoning, Sophia refused to wear a white dress.

"Cream-colored dresses are white enough," Sophia argued when she revealed the gown on the morning of.

That was another problem. Sophia went out and bought the dress on her own. No bridesmaids. No meddling aunts. No mom. No Bea, either.

"Why, though?" Dolores implored. "Won't Greg be disappointed?"

"*Mother*," Sophia hissed beneath a head of hot rollers.

Bea let out a sigh. "There's nothing *to* be disappointed about, Mom. This isn't 1950."

"And besides," Sophia added, her lips stretching into a phony smile, "Greg *knows* me."

"Oh, for the love of God, what's *that* supposed to mean?" Dolores was full-on wailing and fanning herself, her green lace fan ineffectual at best and tacky at worst.

Bea tried her hardest to defuse the situation, but it was Diane who bounced her way in. "Aunt Dolores, the color of the dress has nothing to do with Sophia's purity and everything to do with fashion. Take it from me, that's about all that matters to this girl right here." Diane slapped Sophia's back and guffawed, and it did help.

Dolores clapped the fan on her thigh and gave up the fight, leaving their cramped hotel room and taking off to check on something else—something more within the realm of her control.

"It's a controversy," Sue whispered. "I'd never wear anything other than white on my wedding day."

"Sue, gimme a break," Sophia replied edgily. "It's not like I'm trying to broadcast to the world that I'm *not* a virgin."

"You're *not?*" Sue gasped.

"Sophia *is* a virgin," Bea reassured everyone before settling her hands on her sister's slight shoulders. "And even if you weren't, you could wear white. And virgins, by the way, can wear cream-colored dresses if they want to." Bea threw a pointed look at Sue.

The others exchanged quiet glances, but Bea ignored it. She was doing her best to ease Sophia's wedding day jitters. Not compound them.

Diane joined them in front of the mirror, lifting Sophia's hand and studying her manicure. "All that matters is that you love Greg. And anyway, you'll have confession before you make your vows. So, you'll be as pure as newly fallen snow."

Bea recoiled. "Let's talk about something else. This is getting ridiculous."

Nodding urgently, Sophia agreed.

"So, Cancun? For your honeymoon? I'm so jealous, Soph," Sue cooed.

"I'd prefer Gull's Landing, actually."

"You're joking," Diane answered. "Why would you want to have your honeymoon down the shore?"

"Why wouldn't I?" Soph shot back. "It's my favorite place in the whole wide world." As she said it, Bea detected something in her voice, though she wasn't sure what. A tremble? A shudder? Grief?

Soon after, the hairdresser returned to pick and push at Sophia's hair. The others prattled on about what a catch Greg was, how well Sophia had done for herself, the bright future she had.

And for Sue and Diane—that was enough. It was enough that Greg came from money. It was enough that he had a thick head of dark hair and glimmering green Greek eyes to match Sophia's Italian ones.

It might have been enough for Bea, too.

But then, just minutes before their father meandered in from outside to sweep his youngest daughter up the aisle and into the handsome arms of Gregory Matthias Angelos, Bea went to retrieve the blushing bride in her cream-colored dress and soft blonde curls.

At the time, what she saw had confused her, but she'd accepted Sophia's bungled answer.

Years later, though, looking back, Bea wondered if the little baggie of pills weren't Tylenol. If the glass of amber fluid wasn't Cola.

And if Sophia's heart didn't belong to someone else... still.

Chapter 29

Bea

In the stretch of time since Sophia's wedding, Bea could calculate exactly how often she'd seen her little sister.

Every major holiday, save for two. The year Sophia and Greg spent Christmas in Acapulco and then the year that Bea couldn't make it to Easter brunch because of a flu. Then, of course, they had their bi-monthly luncheons. Their daily phone calls.

What Bea could not calculate, however, was what their relationship had become.

Once Sophia married Greg, he'd filled the role of Sophia's partner in crime. No longer did it belong to Bea. Not Sue, either. Or Diane, obviously.

Bea wasn't Sophia's *first* emergency contact. And even Sophia's *second* emergency contact went to Greg's parents, inexplicably.

Sometimes, she thought about the miniature

moments that acted as shards of evidence in the break-down of their sisterhood. Like when Bea and Soph were on the phone gabbing and Matt had rushed into the house, wailing with pain. Bea could recall how serious it sounded. How loud the boy was. Instead of asking Bea to come over right away, and instead of describing to Bea right then and there what she was seeing, Sophia had hung up.

Everything turned out fine. Matt had fallen from the top of his backyard swing set, broken his arm, and Sophia called Greg who rushed home and drove them off to the ER. Bea brought a get-well bucket for him—toys and books, but she wasn't the first on the scene. It didn't belong to her, that special role. It belonged to Greg.

That was all just fine, really.

But then there was the time Bea and Sophia went shopping. Sophia selected a glimmering red cocktail dress with big silver polka-dots and heavy crinoline. The very top of her cleavage pressed together tastefully above the cinched bodice and when she twirled in front of the dressing room mirror and Bea told her how perfect it was, Sophia agreed. Two days later, Sophia returned it, claiming one of the other moms from Matt's school thought it was *too* much for Parents' Night Out.

Bea might not have recalled that particular memory if Sophia hadn't told Bea that her judgment was off. Bea hadn't known the dress was for a school event. She felt attacked and it turned into one of those silly fights that never should have been. Something had cracked between them—their sisterly bond couldn't withstand the demands of motherhood, perhaps.

Neither one of those small moments in time could have compared, however, to the night that changed the course of history, though. So while Bea did not know where she stood with her best friend, her sister, her *soulmate*, at the time of Sophia's death…

She knew where those tiny fissures began. Even if Sophia hadn't known.

Chapter 30

Sophia, 1985

I t was just after midnight. Sue never did learn that I had mastered the pretend-sleep.

Fooling her was easy enough, she was too scared of the dark or worried about getting kidnapped or something. That was Sue. A worrywart. Not me, though. I found ways around my fears.

But as for that particular night... well, how could I sleep then?

On the heels of not only that crazy summer, but after the week I'd just had... sleep was an impossibility, that much was true.

In fact, I was one-hundred-percent positive that I would never sleep another night in my life. Not on my own. No way.

There was supposed to be the distinct and charming *tap* of a pebble on the kitchen window. For my part, I had to keep a close ear on the kitchen from the living room, where I'd planned to sleep, of course. That was the deal. Doug was supposed to find a small, smooth sea stone so as not to break the window. He wasn't supposed to accidentally break my heart, either, but how could you really trust a man to follow through on matters of the heart? You couldn't, plain and simple. Something I didn't learn until I met Greg, and even then... well, wasn't it too late by then?

So the pebble thing, well, that was a bust, after all.

Sue had to go and beg me to sleep on the second floor which meant that I'd never even hear any pebble. All I had was Aunt Lil's bedside clock, a wing, and a prayer. So every little while I peeked out at the clock. Finally, after listening to Diane and Craig take off into the night like a couple of lovebirds, I heard Sue start to snore. Sue didn't realize I wasn't a snorer by nature. But I knew for a fact that she was. Reddish-blonde hair and braces? How could she not be a snorer? I checked the clock for probably the millionth time and *boom*. Six minutes past midnight.

If he wasn't waiting down there patiently, searching the dimly lit sand for tiny pebbles, I was liable to jump out that window right then and there.

How could I possibly handle being stood up? At that very moment in time was when I needed Doug the most. More than after our first date. More than after our *third*. And even more than after "it" happened.

If Doug Hurley didn't show up like he promised, then I would never leave Gull's Landing. I couldn't face the rest of the world without him. And even despite his wandering eye and his absentee folks and irritating sister who talked too loud and wore too much makeup... I was all in.

I'd even begun to picture myself there, on the board-walk. Maybe me and Doug would start a little Italian restaurant, and he'd want to name it after me, as sort of a consolation prize since I'd be stuck with Hurley for a new last name.

Russo's.

Or maybe instead of a full-blown restaurant (which would probably be a lot of hard work), we'd do a bakery or something and call it *Sophia's. Sophia's Sweets: Specializing in Cannoli and Cheesecake.* I loved cheesecake more than anything in the world. I could've used one lately. Really, I could. It occurred to me that that summer was the first me and the girls hadn't had our annual cheesecake bake-off.

It was a tradition we started when me and Sue turned twelve and Aunt Lil gave up on telling us we couldn't use the electric hand mixer. Each of us made our own take on New York cheesecake. Having never had the real thing, we weren't entirely sure if we were doing it right, but Philly and Jersey were so close that how could any of us have been wrong?

Mine always came out the best, which pissed Bea off. She hated to lose. She really did.

I peered down through the window, totally certain Doug would be standing there, hands shoved in his pockets, real peeved that I was late. Maybe he'd have gone through a dozen pebbles. Maybe Aunt Lil had woken up and—no. She'd have heard that.

But he wasn't there.

Talk about peeved. I glanced back at Sue, who was snoring like an old mom-mom, then pushed the window open so I could hear if he walked up.

That was the main problem with Doug, you see. He was one of those chronically late types. I didn't learn this until recently. Like within the last week when I started expecting him to meet me when we said we were going to meet. That's when I figured him out. His hair took too long to gel or maybe he was pressing his shorts—I really don't know. But I started to notice he was late. Either that, or he started to be late. But I pushed that thought so far out of my mind that it couldn't be true.

So, at first, the fact that he wasn't down there, like Romeo, climbing up Aunt Lil's trellis bugged me a lot, but it didn't freak me out.

I thought back to that cheesecake idea. It was a pretty good one, and I could really use a good idea just about then. A distraction. Something to look forward to and take my mind off of things, you know?

I spotted my duffle near the closet and tiptoed to it. God forbid I wake Sue. That would have ruined everything, of course.

It was dark out, but the moon and the low lamps of the boardwalk still let in a bit of light, so all I had to do was shove my hand into the bag and grope around for half a second until I found it.

My personal diary.

Bea never knew I had a personal diary. Neither did Sue, for that matter. Of course not Diane, either. You see, when we started The Summer Society and I was named Vice President, I had to take notes somewhere. So I re-assigned this thing I got for Christmas one year. It was originally *supposed* to be a diary, complete with a miniature key and a lock that you could jimmy open if you were really desperate to get in there. Initially, in those early days, I jotted down the different ideas we, as a club, came up with.

One year, we tried to get a babysitting service off the ground. Turned out parents down the shore were happy enough with the lifeguards on the beach.

Another year we decided to rake leaves, but most of

the houses in Gull's Landing didn't have any leaves come June. Maybe they never did at all.

Later on, the pages turned from business ideas to paper games. The girl kind, where you worked out a math equation to learn if you were going to have three kids or four or even zero. There was another one where you were awarded points based off the alphabet and *boom* you could tell if your crush was a good match or not.

When our games ended, I still had over half a diary of space left, and I'm not one to waste *anything*, you see. Really, truly, and like I said earlier I was starting to need a little help to fall asleep by that time, so, *boom*, it couldn't hurt right?

I grabbed a pen from the cup on the dresser and perched like a stork on the corner of the bed, facing the window with just barely enough light to see the faint pink lines in the diary.

It was only eight after twelve by then. Sue continued to snore. The backyard continued to sit empty in the glow of the moon. And, I could still hear and now even *see* Diane and Craig, rolling around in the sand. I can swear to God that they were not *doing it*. They were mostly being really silly and loud. The bigger shock, to me, was that no one else had come down the beach yet and yelled at them to go home.

Another minute ticked by and (speaking of *ticked*) I was getting really ticked. I watched Diane and Craig walk further down the beach, maybe toward the Pier. Maybe they were going to sneak in there, who could tell? Not me, because by then I was furiously scratching out my idea about *Sophia's Boardwalk Sweets* (same catch phrase as above, by the way).

I glanced again out the window, and again at the

clock, and by then I hated the idea of a bakery and even the very thought of a cheesecake made me want to gag. I threw down a few more words about turning full rebel, stealing Aunt Lil's tarot cards and turning into a board-walk gypsy before I went back and re-read the last couple of entries I'd added just days earlier.

It wasn't as sad to reread as it was to write. I mean, hell, I could even see the smudged lines where a few tears must have dripped down onto the thin pages and blurred the words. What was more sad, it occurred to me, was how I went from all *that*—all that drama and that huge, incredible secret—into *Sophia's Boardwalk Sweets*. It was maybe the first time I found myself to be a little younger than I always felt.

What a wonder that none of the girls had stumbled across it. In some ways, deep down, I hoped they would. I hoped they would catch a glimpse of the notebook and recognize it and dive into my duffle bag, grab it out, and dance around as I screamed and kicked and screamed some more. And then one of them would accidentally turn to the second-to-last and third-to-last entries and stare at me in shock and braid my hair and rub my back like we all used to do to each other in our quiet moments together.

But if that happened in real life, if the girls really found the book and really read it—I don't think they'd braid my hair and rub my back. If they really found it and really read it, then what would happen would be this:

Sophia Victoria Russo wouldn't be so perfect anymore.

And *that* was the best-case scenario. The worst-case scenario would mean I'd lose my best friend forever (Sue already hardly tolerated me), and my sister would never see me the same. Perfect or not, I'd be broken to Bea. Pathetic.

A teenage nothing who used to have everything.

Then, after that, they'd tell Mom. And if Mom found out, then there was no way I'd get to come back to Gull's Landing.

I ended up hiding that diary and hiding it well. And after it was hidden, and after everything happened, it was as if *nothing* happened after all.

Chapter 31

Sophia, 1985

At sixteen minutes after midnight, when my stomach was starting to hurt all over again, I saw the figure of someone walking up from the south end of the beach.

Alone.

It was him! It was my Doug!

I debated seriously whether to slip outside before he got there or just sit tight and wait.

Well, obviously I realized that the smart choice was to wait. After all, then I could pretend I had fallen asleep and forgotten all about him. Yes. I could pretend I'd forgotten that his kisses were ecstasy and his tan body was something out of a magazine, and that when he tickled my ribs I wanted to fall into the ocean and float away. I could pretend that he didn't have me wrapped around his finger.

With new energy, I dug my boobs out of the bottom of my bra and pulled them up, pinched my cheeks hard, bit down on my bottom lip until it nearly bled, and teased my hair with my fingers as best as I could.

Then, tossing my hair about my shoulders, I started to lean out and look down, hoping to catch him as he just finished tossing that darn little pebble against the kitchen window (and trust me—I *knew* the risks of keeping the second bedroom window open: without a screen, we'd all be eaten alive by mosquitos come sunrise).

When I did, though—when I hovered dangerously beyond the sill, my body still on fire, my heart pounding —I didn't see just Doug down there.

I saw another girl with him. A tall, familiar girl with dark hair. A girl who had no business talking to my boyfriend.

But that wasn't all I saw.

———

I watched in horror, really I did. You know how they say you can't tear your eyes away from a car wreck, but it wasn't the sort of thing you ought to be staring at in the first place?

Yeah.

That's exactly what it was like.

The only problem was that I didn't have a good angle at all. From my seat on the window, so long as I didn't give into the temptation to jump and end it all there, I could see the kiss and I could hear a scuffle—a really quiet conversation with lots of hissing and all that. Then they were apart again and Bea's figure had disappeared back inside and Doug was walking back to the yard.

I almost died right there.

How could your sister do that to you? And why?

My gut reaction told me that it was a mistake. That I didn't see what I saw. And if I did see what I saw, well it was *over* with Doug. And it was over with Bea, too. No way could I stick around for her.

But then, before he got to the little white gate at the back of the yard—the one that sometimes got hung up on sand if the tide rose particularly high and pushed beach-walkers closer to the house—he turned and looked up at the house and saw me.

And he waved frantically.

I was sort of stuck. How could I go downstairs and face Bea? And anyway, would she let me out? She had to, because if she didn't then I'd call her a tramp and a backstabber and maybe I'd even slap her square on the cheek.

I didn't wave to Doug, but I tore away from that window and downstairs and when I made it to the first floor, Bea wasn't there.

The light in the bathroom glowed in a strip beneath the door, and I was safe.

Safe, but still seething. Still confused.

Until, of course, I got outside and Doug explained everything.

Yes, Bea tried to kiss him. No, he didn't like it.

And lastly, the clincher on the whole thing, Doug told me that there was no reason to talk to Bea about it. He told me she was obviously sad and jealous, and if I said something, then I'd be worse than her, because those sorts of things *happened* and it was *no big deal*.

I believed it all. Every last word of it.

He rewarded me for accepting his explanation. For choosing his side over Bea's and letting bygones be bygones. He apologized that I had to see the whole stupid thing, and he swore up and down that he didn't like Bea. He swore up and down, too, that I'd be a real jerk if I made her feel bad over what boiled down to one little kiss that meant absolutely nothing.

That night, Doug Hurley told me in no uncertain terms that despite what happened to us that summer, he loved me.

I loved him, too.

For one more day.

———

After we walked the beach and cuddled together on a bench, Doug brought me back to Aunt Lil's. The plan was to stay together forever, of course. I was still in school for another year, but he had a car and could make it out to Philly on the weekends or when he didn't have to work the bowling alley—his newest job.

With the promise of forever settled in my heart and a softer stance toward my hopeless big sister, I slipped back into the house and crept upstairs, past a snoring Diane and a tossing and turning Bea. But once I was back in the little twin, sweating beneath the sheets and wondering if my stomach cramps would ever go away for good, I tossed and turned, too. Sleep refused to come.

Eventually, I looked at the clock, starting to feel a new sickness—that sort of sickness you get to feeling when you haven't slept in a really long time. It was well past two, and if I was going to make it home to Philly the next day, I had to get some sleep. I was desperate for it.

I knew about Aunt Lil. I knew what happened with Uncle Sammy and how those years were no good, no good at all. And I knew that in order to survive the length of his life, she'd turned somewhere for help.

I knew all this because I needed that help, too, just two weeks before.

You see, I couldn't tell Bea what happened. I definitely couldn't tell Sue. And what was I going to do? Head to a Gull's Landing walk-in clinic, a Shoobie with a secret and a funny feeling in her gut?

But Lil, you see, despite her years of warnings and the time she almost called the Coast Guard when Bea went missing, well—she was the sort of aunt who could hold your worries for you.

Back then, the first time I went to her, my tail between my legs as she sat shuffling her cards on the fold-out table, she knew just what to do.

And now, I knew just what to do. So again I crept, — feeling like a real prowler now—to the second-floor bathroom where I quietly closed the door, flipped the light, opened the medicine cabinet, and read each and every single bottle of prescription medication, stopping only when I'd found the one that would work. The one that Aunt Lil said I didn't need then but that I might need one day.

I ran a stream from the faucet, tossed the pill onto my tongue, and cupped water into my mouth, washing it down in a quick, painless swallow, and *poof.*

Since then, I never had trouble sleeping ever again.

Maybe that's why I married a pharmacist.

Maybe that's why I got over the summer of 1985.

And maybe, just maybe, that's why I didn't care if my big sister kissed my boyfriend.

Chapter 32

Diane

Now Diane and Bea stood facing each other outside of the second-floor bedroom. Bea had spilled everything, going over exactly what happened that last night so many years ago. Doug. The kiss. Bea's commitment to keep it a secret from Sophia.

"It's not a big deal, Bea," Diane whispered in reply to her old friend's confession. She was torn between grappling with Bea's sudden and pain-stricken revelation and with gawking in at The Summer Society room.

It was the best way she could describe that little space that looked over the beach, especially now that it carried so much more weight.

Fleeting, intangible memories shuffled through Diane's mind's eye. The summer they pierced Sue's ears on the carpet. The time they couldn't find Bea anywhere —not on the boardwalk, not on the beach—and Sue had wandered weepily upstairs as Lil was about to put a call in to the Coast Guard to drag the ocean or something.

Bea had been in the tiny closet with a romance novel, asleep. That's when they found out about Bea's hidden library. The closet of the second bedroom met up with the second-floor bath. And, oddly, Bea had used the bathtub access space—hidden only by a removable piece of plywood—to hide a small hoard of similar books, each cover more sensual and sweeping than the last. Ol' Lil laughed her butt off, but Diane was seeing red. She was genuinely scared that something had happened to Bea. And all for what—*Fabio*?

Now, she was seeing blue. The ocean lapping like a moving picture in the window. She looked back at Bea, sad for her.

"How can you say that?" Bea pressed herself against the doorjamb, unmoving.

Diane let out a long breath.

Bea's eyes flew to Diane, and Sue finally made her way down the hall, taking up the space along the wall by Diane.

Diane replied, "Because we were *kids*, Bea. We were *eighteen*, and you weren't a bad sister. You were the best sister. Doug was the loser. You know he was. And anyway, Bea, Sophia obviously didn't even know."

But Bea shook her head. "If that's true, then how come things changed?"

1985

"Dare," Sophia answered, and if Diane wasn't so over the moon with giddiness about the night before and sadness over leaving, she might have been better able to tell that Sophia's face was greenish and sallow. Her quiet moodiness extended far beyond the illness she'd been battling. But now, as she replied to Sue, she seemed to muster a little strength.

Sue took a deep breath and settled her gaze (as well as someone like Sue could settle a gaze) on Sophia. "I dare you to tell us why you won't break up with Doug."

Diane tried to get Bea's attention and see where her mind was, but Bea kept her gaze on Soph.

"Because I love him, that's why." Sophia's eyes welled up and she held her arms over her chest protectively.

"And you think he loves you?" It was Bea who asked the question, and though the question itself was bold and accusatory and even cruel, Diane could see that Bea hated to ask it. Bea pressed her hands against her face and shook her head.

Then, Sophia caught them all off guard. "Yes, I think he loves me. It's *you* three I'm wondering about."

But before anyone had the chance to call her out on making a baseless accusation, a sharp whistle cut across the beach and bells began to clatter. A siren blared.

And their final meeting of The Summer Society came to an abrupt and traumatic end.

Chapter 33

Sue

They hadn't budged from the doorframe, and Sue's back was starting to cramp with the tension.

"You *kissed* Doug Hurley?" Sue asked Bea, bewildered.

Bea took in a long, deep breath. Her chest rose high and shuddered back into place. "No. *He* kissed me."

"Wow," Diane breathed. "I thought he and Sophia were supposed to be soulmates or something."

"Soulmates? We all told her to break up with him. Don't you remember? It was our last pact." Sue frowned, unsure if the subsequent events that day had muddied her memory. No, no, no. She was sure of it. "I held a meeting of The Summer Society, remember?" she prodded.

"Oh, yeah." Diane nodded. "I do remember. Of course. You and Bea were worried it'd turn out badly. But Sophia, she was so head over heels for him, you know?" She glanced down. "I guess it *did* turn out badly."

Bea nodded. "That's why I never said anything after it happened. I couldn't do that to her."

"Why not? Maybe it would have helped her, you know, move on?" Sue tried to be useful, but Bea looked up as though she'd been slapped across the face.

"It would have started World War III." Diane shook her head. "She'd have turned all her anger onto Bea, and then what?" Diane looked at Bea. "You made a good decision, hon."

"But you know what? Sometimes I wonder if she did know. The way she acted that next morning, all sulky, as if the world was ending…" Bea started, but Diane cut in.

"She didn't want to leave him here. I remember that clear as day because I felt the same way about Craig."

"Was Doug all bad?" Sue offered, against her own instincts. "I mean, he was a kid, too. Just like us." In her heart, she knew Doug Hurley was smarmy. He was a womanizer, and the fact that Sophia was in love with him said less about him and more about the innate problem with teenage biology and how it was so willing to quell red flags in the face of tan bodies.

Bea gave her a look. "I think you know the answer to that. I mean, Doug was basically a younger Joe. Sue, he *grabbed* me that night and *kissed* me. I told him no. I told him to stop."

"Is that why you never got married?" Diane asked, blunt as the broadside of a cement block.

"Okay, whoa," Sue broke in, stepping in, not as the meager interloper but as the leader, for once. "This is too big of a conversation for the hallway. If we are going to grill poor Bea on her life choices, then we need to do it over a slice of cheesecake. Not here. Not now." As she took her stand, the other two offered nothing but hardened expressions.

At last, after Bea and Diane exchanged a look, they both shook their heads. "We can talk about it later," Diane declared. "Because I'm going in there."

Chapter 34

Diane

Stepping into the room was both overwhelming and underwhelming. Underwhelming in that, frankly, there was no "crime scene." There was no blood spatter or yellow tape or signs of a struggle.

Of course, there wouldn't be.

And it was overwhelming for a whole slew of other reasons.

One, there *was* a scene, of sorts. A subtly gruesome tableau, really. A picture of who Sophia, perfect blonde Sophia with her green eyes and olive skin and handsome husband, really was.

The bed to the left was made, its quilt folded down and pillow untouched. A shadow bled across it. Or perhaps that was a layer of dust.

Diane turned from that and examined the rest of the room. The second bed, to the right of the window, was unmade, its covers bunched in a swirl. A heap of clothing fell from the edge to the floor in a sort of waterfall of dirty laundry. Surprising to see, considering Greg had been there. He'd had a chance to wrap it all up in his arms and breathe in his dead wife one last time.

Maybe he had.

Shoes, unfamiliar to Diane, lay at odd angles, half poking out from beneath the bed, at the foot of which stood the tall dark wood dresser. The top drawer was cracked open, strange since it was empty. Diane strode across the room and peered inside. In her mind's eye, she was a policewoman, called to the scene to help Greg go through Sophia's personal effects, perhaps. She'd have been curious, too. Maybe another cop had left that drawer open in a search for something nefarious. For something to explain the unexplainable.

Behind her, Bea eased onto the unmade bed, and Sue stood by the door, her hand over her mouth.

"How can you bear it?" Sue whispered.

Diane looked at Bea, whose face was blank. White. She passed her hand over the bed, over the rumples of wrinkles, her fingers moving up and down them as if she was gliding overtop of the ocean in a boat, cutting through swells, the white caps hitting her palms.

"Are you okay, Bea?" Diane asked, leaving the dresser with its incriminating evidence on top, unexamined.

Instead of replying, Bea lay back onto the bed, pulled the wrinkled blankets up and over her body, and tucked herself deep into the waves of fabric.

Chapter 35

Bea

She put herself in Sophia's shoes.

A final night there, in Aunt Lil's with the love of her life. Suppose Sophia didn't know that Doug kissed Bea? If not, then there was no question about the events of the next morning and what they would have done to a foolish girl in love.

And in fact, there was no question.

That's what happened when a young person died. They were frozen in time and place as a perfect version of what a human being could have become.

Doug Hurley was not perfect. He would have become a lecher or a bowling alley creep or a boardwalk bad boy, hitting on younger girls until the end, no doubt.

And Bea had realized it. Maybe others had, too.

But Sophia never did.

As far as she knew, he was the sweet, attentive, handsome boy of her dreams. The one who first told her that he loved her.

What was a girl to do with that sort of love? Encapsulate it? Store it away? Bury it like a dead pet only to forget where, exactly, the homemade grave marker was supposed to be?

From Bea's vantage point, that's what Sophia had tried to do.

She'd taken her first love, silly though it may have been, and stowed it some place only to revisit it in fits and spurts over the rest of her life. Initially in her head. Lastly in person, there, in Gull's Landing.

But what Bea could not understand was why everything had gone to total and utter crap. Why had Sophia never amounted to the perfect version of herself? Wasn't that supposed to be the flipside of the tragedy? The survivors find a way to press on and make their lives better? Weren't they supposed to understand the fragility of life and go forth and conquer and come out as a great human-interest piece for TIME Magazine? *On the Tails of Tragedy... One Girl Survives the Death of her First Love.* And then the article to follow details painstakingly just how beautiful that girl's life became after all. How she did *not* fall into despair or depression. How an early introduction to mortality fortified her rather than destroyed her.

Bea wondered very privately and very guiltily *what the big deal was?* So Doug was Sophia's first love. Was that really magazine worthy? No.

But had his drowning really changed her sister's very being? Was it enough to do that sort of long-term damage? Or was there more to the story?

Sue and Diane spoke in hushed voices around the room, but Bea squeezed her eyes tighter. She had not seen what was on top of the dresser, and she didn't want to. Didn't need to. She knew.

"Can you believe they just... left it all here?" Sue

whispered. "Don't you think Greg would have cleaned it? Or hired someone to clean it? Or even the police could have bagged it up."

"Greg was devastated. She was the love of his life. He just couldn't face it," Diane answered.

"But the police could have helped," Sue reasoned.

Diane lowered her voice another octave. "Aunt Dolores told me that Greg demanded they just leave things the way they were found. He'd handle it."

"But he didn't. He let Bea come out here and *see* this," Sue hissed.

"Sleeping pills," Diane said quietly. "Wine? I mean maybe—"

Bea shot up in the bed. "It's not what it looks like."

Sue and Diane turned their horrified expressions on her.

Bea found the reserves to continue. "She didn't *kill* herself, okay?"

Again, they just stared. Bea looked past them, verifying their observations.

On top of the dresser stood a bottle of wine, its label unrecognizable to her. Next to it, two orange pill vials and a Costco-sized bottle of Tylenol.

Nothing new. Nothing surprising. And nothing deadly. Not for Sophia.

Satisfied that she was right, Bea let out a breath and untucked herself, swinging her legs over the side and holding on to the bed post. "She started taking sleeping pills a long time ago. And drinking, well, of course she had a glass every night. Tylenol, come on. Who doesn't take Tylenol? This whole thing was an accident. That's what Greg said. He said she wasn't suicidal. And I know he was right. It was an *accident*." Bea's jaw set and her gaze hardened. She lifted a hand, growing angry. "So stop… stop *whispering* and *gawking* and turning this whole thing into gossip. You knew Soph. You know she wouldn't kill herself."

But their faces said it all.

They didn't believe her.

And now she was beginning to wonder if she believed herself, either.

"But, Bea, if she'd been taking sleeping pills forever, didn't she have her own?" Sue asked, holding an orange bottle between two fingers like it was a scorpion that might rear up and sting her.

Bea frowned. "Of course. She had a prescription. She didn't… *overdose* or mix drugs. She just couldn't sleep. That was all."

Sue's face remained pained, but her voice turned softer. "Bea, these aren't even Sophia's." She took a step closer, turning the bottle in her hand so Bea could read the label, but her vision was blurry and her head pounding. "They're Lil's."

Chapter 36

Diane, one week later

"It was such a mess in there. I don't remember Sophia being disorganized or anything, you know?" She was sitting on a picnic table on the boardwalk. Craig sat opposite her, sipping a Long Island iced tea and nodding sympathetically.

"Maybe she wasn't messy," he offered. "Maybe she just hadn't cleaned up that morning. Or the cops made the mess during their search."

Diane stared past him at the water. Craig came down a couple of days after they'd gone into the second-floor bedroom. Since then, not much had changed about the summer vacation. After the few moments in The Summer Society room, Bea had shooed them all out and closed the door, declaring it was a project for another day. After that, they resumed the morning ritual of coffee and breakfast, took to the boardwalk or the beach for the day, and played cards at night, Sue and Bea sleeping on the downstairs sofas.

Diane, however, had moved up to Lil's room. It was non-negotiable. She said she wasn't staying on a corduroy sofa with Bea's feet in her face for the rest of the summer. What she didn't say was that she was ready to leave then and there. Diane was all for lending a hand or a shoulder to cry on, but she had her own stressors in life, and sleeping on a musty sofa for two more months would only compound her tensions, not ease them.

The proceedings for Craig's financial issues had slowly begun to take shape, and it wasn't as bad as they'd originally figured. He'd hired a good friend to represent him, and with some careful navigating, Diane's folks could quietly buy her house and then rent it back to them. So that was the plan for when she returned back home to Briar Creek: she and Craig would rent from her folks and sleep in separate bedrooms and drink wine together at night and laugh like old times. Maybe Brittany would even come over for dinner and act weirded out as usual.

In the interim, Craig took a leave from his practice. He felt it would come across as problematic if he didn't settle his personal affairs before resuming, and so he called Diane in the middle of a perfectly normal day and asked her if they needed any help at the house on the shore.

They did, actually. Lil's bedroom ceiling fan was broken. The downstairs showerhead popped off, leaving them to use the upstairs bath, but as if there was a domino effect in play, that faucet had developed a significant leak.

And then there was their sisterhood, their society. It was something a handy guy like Craig could not help with. Even more worrisome than the leaky faucet was the women's inability to reconnect as old friends. Sophia's death had drenched them in discomfort.

The breakfasts were silent. Beach walks awkward. And every last card game ended in an argument. And that was just in the span of seven days.

Even Sue had threatened to leave. The only problem was, she had nowhere to go. The tickets to San Diego had expired and the money had been wasted. Joe had texted her that *If she wasn't coming home to fix things, then why did he have to end his affair?*

It was one of few moments in the past few days that had pulled laughter out of the women.

So it was logical for Craig to come down and break up the tension, and neither Bea nor Sue objected.

"Are you really going to stay the rest of the summer, Di?" Craig asked, picking at one of her French fries.

"I don't know. I guess we need to figure out the plan for the house, and Bea needs to get back up on her feet first. Maybe I'll give it another week, and if she doesn't turn the corner, then I'll leave. Sue's staying, anyway. At least for the month."

"What are her plans?"

"She'll probably go to her mother's house. Although, I think Sue has enjoyed being here. She's tanner than I've ever seen her. And happier, too." That much was the truth. Even with quiet breakfasts and awkward walks and angry card games, Sue had settled into herself.

"And Bea?"

Diane shrugged. She knew what Bea's plans *ought* to be.

One day among the blur of their spur-of-the-moment reunion, Diane had wondered aloud to Sue if they should start packing up the little remnants of Sophia's last visit to the shore house—maybe it would help, but Bea had overheard and promptly stormed up the stairs to the bedroom, locking it and pocketing the key.

But Sue, to her credit, found new purpose in the idea of tackling even the smallest of projects.

Diane watched her make a go of organizing Aunt Lil's side table. It was where she'd kept her tarot set and stationery, address book, stamps, pens, bills, and so forth.

After sorting through a thick stack of unopened mail, Sue had uncovered nothing of interest. She had, however, made several comments on how it was a wonder the house hadn't fallen into foreclosure with the level of oversight.

Diane happened to agree with that and pitched in a bit, reading through the junk and ascertaining that nothing was out of order. Lil knew important documents from disguised ads all the way up until her death. Sue commented that she was surprised not to find even a speck of something that might have been left undone. Impressed, too. Still, it begged the question of how, exactly, everything was settled in the end.

That was the point at which Bea finally gave in and agreed to discuss the matter of the house.

Now, Craig asked Diane about it again. "What will Bea do with the house? I mean, what *has* she been doing with it? Who technically owns it?"

"It was all handled back when Lil died. The deed transferred to Soph and Bea. Greg stepped in and set up autopayments for the utilities. He covered the taxes. He ran everything through his own finances. It was all there, settled."

"And now?"

"That's why we're here. He told Bea that it was time

to let go. I guess he and Matt don't want to keep it, if you can believe that."

"Of course I can," Craig replied, scoffing. "I hate coming back here as it is."

"What do you mean?" Diane studied him. "You hardly knew Sophia."

"I'm not talking about Sophia. I'm talking about Doug," he replied, twisting in his seat and looking out over the water. "After he died, I swore to myself I'd never come back to Gull's Landing. I didn't want to be near that, you know? I was so scared, Di. I was scared that even touching a toe into that water his ghost would swim out from the deep and drag me down, you know? And he was just a buddy. If it were *you?* Or, God forbid, *Britt?* I'd burn the whole city down just to erase those fears."

Diane considered this and figured it was reasonable. Just because she had a morbid interest in Sophia's death wouldn't mean that she would if, say, Brittany had died. Or Craig. God forbid, indeed. If something happened to either of them, Diane probably *would* list it immediately and drop the price to a hundred bucks just to kiss the place goodbye. And she'd never look back.

"But," she reasoned, "Bea doesn't feel that way. She is sort of pulled here. Trapped, even."

"Trapped?" Craig answered. "She's not trapped. She's got a career and a house, doesn't she? I think she *wants* to stick around, you know? You see, Bea's the opposite of Greg. It's clear as day, Di. If Bea's ever going to live her own life, she's got to say goodbye to Soph. For good."

"She could have done that at the funeral. She can't say goodbye if she spends a summer here."

"She can if she can put the past in the past. Sometimes, that's what people need in order to move on. They need to sort of relive it. Own it, you know? Instead of running away from it. I may agree with Greg, but that doesn't mean I agree with running away."

"Your parents ran away," Diane pointed out.

"No. They ran home."

"They went on vacation, Craig," she argued.

"Some people prefer paradise."

"My paradise is home. In Briar Creek." Diane loved vacation, sure, but she was a creature of habit, deep down. Which was why, even through their divorce, Diane and Craig kept to a routine.

He reached a hand over the table and covered hers. "Mine, too, *Princess.*"

Chapter 37

Bea

Her grand plans to reconvene The Summer Society had fallen apart. Sure, they'd settled into a pat beachside routine, complete with card games and margaritas and the essence of summer down the shore but gone was the energy and enthusiasm. Gone was the comfort.

The second-floor bedroom hung above them like a gray cloud. A heavy reminder of why they were there and how their summers would never be the same. At least, not Bea's.

And now they were sort of inadvertently stuck. Not because of Bea's stubbornness. Not because of Diane's developing circumstances on the home front with Craig —who'd joined them for a few days to help with repairs but seemed more interested in stealing his ex-wife away —but because of Sue, surprisingly.

Days after they first entered the bedroom—or as Diane had taken to calling it again, The Summer Society room (which Bea liked, since it meant it wasn't Sophia's room or the death room or the second-floor bedroom. It was the room where they'd stowed away as innocent girls. Nothing more, nothing less)—Joe had tracked Sue down to Lil's and had her served there.

Sue had sobbed over it. She was humiliated and angry and sad, and Bea appreciated each of the emotions. Mainly, though, it meant Sue either had to go back to her mom's house or find her own place.

"Why don't you stay the summer? Like you planned?" Diane asked one morning over coffee in the backyard. They sat at the patio set, the sun rising above the lip of the ocean as they quietly drank.

"I planned to go to San Diego, remember?" Sue pointed out. She'd pointed that out every single day since the day she was supposed to leave but hadn't.

"Remind me why you didn't go?" Diane pressed, shoveling a forkful of eggs into her mouth.

"Because you two needed me here. And because who wants to fly across the country alone? Not me, for one."

"So again, why not stay?"

Sue remained quiet, thoughtful.

"You figured Joe was going to come and sweep you away, didn't you? Reclaim his tickets and his wife… his life, too?" Bea was forming the theory as the words took shape in her mouth. Though they had lots in common—quiet lifestyles, a love of books and alone time—she didn't always understand Sue. And she definitely didn't understand what Sue and Soph had that bonded them so closely as kids. She added, almost as a question: "You'd have gone back to him."

Sue shrugged in response, which was enough to prove out Bea's theory.

"Let's tackle the room again," Diane said, diverting

the conversation. "While Craig's here. He's an outsider, he'll make it easier. He can bring in some bins and we can organize her things and—"

"No," Bea replied. "That's not why we're here."

"Then why *are* we here?" Diane asked, letting her fork clatter onto the plate.

Bea shook her head. "We're here because we made a pact. We agreed to meet up and be there for each other. And if this place is going to be sold, then we only have one last shot."

"Well, here we are," Diane answered, holding her arms out. "We're here for each other, right? Why not make a little headway. *Before* Greg sells, Bea," she added.

"I don't care about that," Bea replied, crossing her arms. "I just want it to be like old times, okay?"

"Bea," Sue joined in, "it can't be exactly like old times, but we can do our best. And like Diane said—we *are* here. For each other."

Bea met her gaze. "Well, we might be here now, but where were we for Soph? We weren't here for her, were we?" She was arguing now. Nothing Diane or Sue could say would satisfy her. She knew it and still pressed ahead, uselessly. Angrily.

An undercurrent raged just beneath the surface of Bea's skin. Their accusations that Sophia had purpose-fully mixed drugs and alcohol. That she came to Lil's to take medication and drift out to sea like Virginia Woolf.

"You know what?" Diane asked. "That's a load of crock."

"Excuse me?" Bea replied, her blood turning to a low boil.

"It's a load of crock to say any one of us wasn't 'here' for the others. We've done it all. We were best friends forever. Right? Then life hit. Right? Weddings and kids and jobs. The same crap that all adults go through—we've done all that. And you know what, Bea? Yes, our little club fell apart. Of course it did. You and Soph went and lived your lives just like Sue and I lived ours. That's how it goes, hon. We lived our lives. But we're back now, aren't we?"

That's when it hit her. Like a load of bricks.

Bea did not have a wedding or even a crappy marriage. She had no kids.

She had no life.

And without a life, she never developed the motivation to even once try and overcome that ill-fated summer of 1985. And all those times she met Sophia for a luncheon or scheduled a sister mani-pedi—none of it made up for the dissolution of what they had as girls. What they should have had as women.

Their sisterhood.

Their club.

———

"Bea it's for you!" Sue trilled from the back door. At Aunt Lil's, the back door was as good as the front. They were interchangeable, really. You knew you had an old friend at the back door. And if the front doorbell rang? It was a stranger. A solicitor. Or Sue.

After coffee, Bea had gone for a solo walk on the beach where she thought hard about who was right. Diane and Sue? Who wanted to press ahead and wipe away history? Wipe away Sophia? Or Bea, who was still hurting.

When she got back, Diane and Craig were working on the upstairs fan, and Sue was cleaning out the fridge. She'd been bound and determined to recreate their

261

cheesecake bake-off, and it seemed that cleaning the kitchen was the only way she knew how to move everyone in that direction.

Bea peered from her seat on the sofa, a rerun of *The Price is Right* on mute as she read and reread the same page from her current book—a delicious Elin Hilderbrand title that deserved much better than Bea Russo, distracted and deflated.

She glanced at her wristwatch, then smacked her hand against her head, groaning.

"I'm not here!" she called in reply, sinking back into her sofa.

"It sure looks like you're here," a man's voice answered from a close distance.

Bea flipped around to see Brooks Morgan standing behind her. Diane was in the kitchen throwing a thumbs up and waving ridiculously.

There was no hiding her messy frizz or magically erasing the bags beneath her eyes now. Or, of course, the fact that she was sitting in her pajamas at two o'clock in the afternoon.

"Oh." It came out on a long sigh. "I'm supposed to be on the beach right now, huh?"

He tapped his own watch, a chunky black diving number. "I don't normally make house visits, but you're on the way to my classroom."

Bea laughed. "I'm sorry," she said, tossing the book onto the sofa and standing, smoothing her flannel shorts and trying as well as she could to disguise the fact that she'd sling-shot her bra into her suitcase just minutes earlier.

"It's all right," he replied, fiddling with the zipper on his wetsuit. She was starting to wonder what he looked like in normal clothes. "I don't charge unless you miss the lesson."

"And what's the fee for a missed lesson?" she answered, crossing her arms firmly over her chest.

"A slice of pizza from Mack's."

She narrowed her gaze on him. "I'll get you a gift certificate, then."

"I don't accept that form of tender."

"I'll pay cash."

"Nope."

Bea drummed her fingers along her arm. "So either I take the lesson or what? You sue me for a slice of pizza?"

"Either take the lesson or I'll take you to Mack's." Brooks put on a crooked smile, and it was enough to send a thrill up Bea's spine and shake her out of her doldrums, momentarily at least.

"I suppose I'll get ready."

"I'll wait in the kitchen." He turned easily and rejoined Sue in the kitchen, and Bea wondered exactly what in the world she was going to do with this imposing, easy-breezy, boardwalking, single-dad surfer.

Maybe it was her depression—which she fully admitted to struggling with. Maybe it was the humidity. Or the fact that four people were stuck in a two-bedroom house with only one bedroom available to them—by Bea's own subjugation.

But she realized it didn't matter. Because at least it would be different.

Chapter 38

Diane

"Wear this." Bea stood in Diane's room with Sue at her suitcase, pulling out every last piece of clothing Bea had packed.

Diane grabbed a white linen dress from Sue's outstretched hand and handed it off to Bea, who held it limply against her body.

"I think you've lost five pounds just since we got here." Diane clicked her tongue at Bea's trim build, admiring it and disapproving it all at once.

"I can't wear this," Bea protested. "I can't *do* this."

"Do *what?*" Diane asked. "Go get a slice of pizza with a hot surf shop owner who just so happens to be a teacher, too?"

"No," Bea hissed.

"Well, you have another option. Go surfing again," Sue pointed out helpfully.

Bea shook her head. "It's bad timing. I'm not here for *distractions*," Bea reasoned, nibbling her lower lip.

Diane smiled. It was her old friend's most obvious tell. Bea wanted with all of her being to go out with Brooks. That she conveniently forgot about the surf lesson would add up *if*, the day before, she hadn't returned to the house from up town with a box of Roots-be-Gone and a new tube of lipstick.

"You're a trip, Bea Russo." Diane grabbed a pair of strappy flats from the corner of the suitcase and pushed them to her. "You were just waiting for him to turn up. I know it."

"I was *not*." Bea strode across the room and ducked behind Lil's folding screen. Diane and Sue had just enough time to look at each other excitedly. They alone couldn't seem to shake Bea loose of her funk. But maybe a local hottie could help.

"Ahem," Bea cleared her throat for effect and appeared from the side of the shoji.

Diane's eyes fell down her friend's length. The dress glowed white against her summer tan, and she scrunched her newly touched-up hair into funky waves above her shoulders.

The gloom that had encapsulated Bea in the past days still clung about her, but it was weakening, Diane was sure.

And as Bea sauntered with a new energy from the room, Diane realized that her cousin's grief could be no match for a grain of hope.

———

BEA HAD LEFT, her feet light and her eyes glimmering as she followed a hapless Brooks over to his shop, where he needed to change for their impromptu dinner-date. Yes, it was a date, Sue and Diane agreed once she was gone.

"Let's go in the room," Diane whispered. "We can get it all cleaned up and surprise her when she gets back. She'll be in a good enough mood that she'll be grateful."

Sue shook her head. "No way. Violate her trust? I'd just as soon keep chipping away downstairs. We're making progress, Di. She's out with Brooks. Craig is here helping with repairs."

"Speaking of which…" Diane started as they left the kitchen and went back in pursuit of Craig.

"Hon?" Diane called. Sue threw her a sidelong glance, but Diane ate it up. Reconciling with her penniless ex had fortified her. Anything could happen and it wouldn't matter. The world wouldn't end, because Diane had her one-and-only. As boring and bland as Craig Bettancourt was, he was exactly what Diane needed. She'd been wrong to follow through with the divorce. He had, too, but it was Diane who gave in first. To the trend. To the temptation to date around and add a little spice to her life.

Fortunately for her—and for Craig—none of that mattered.

"I'm done with the fan," Craig replied, working a rag into a wrench like a regular handyman. Diane grabbed his butt through his jeans and leaned in to kiss him. He kissed her back before asking, "What's next?"

"The leaky faucet in the upstairs bath, if you have the energy."

Sue added, "Or the downstairs showerhead."

"The rest of my tools are upstairs. But let's take a break. I could go for a cool drink right about now."

Chapter 39

Sue

Sue had been waffling lately. To go back to Philadelphia or stay. And if she went back to Philadelphia, then what?

If she were honest with herself, she missed Joe. At least, she missed the thought of him. The familiarity of him. Sometimes, even, the thrill of him. The thrill of wondering if *today* would be the day she'd arrive home to catch him in the act.

Sure, that thrill was gone once she *did* catch him in the act, but it returned in full force once she left.

There was the highly viable option of taking back up with her mom. It'd be safe, physically. She'd have three square meals a day and a clean bed. She'd get the joy of reading the paper every morning. Then there was the library—just down the street. And her mother's own library, filled to the brim with all of Sue's childhood favorites—*Anne of Green Gables* on up through *Pride and Prejudice.*

Maybe, though, it was time for Sue to broaden her horizons. She'd phoned in to work to see about the summer session—did they need her for audio recordings? Or anything else?

Her boss told her that the requests were slow. Apparently, few blind students had enrolled, and one of the student aides had pitched in.

She missed the kids.

When no solution came to her, she wandered back into the kitchen to take back up with prepping for the cheesecake bake-off. Sue found that next to reading and working with students from the university, baking was where she found her peace. She could work in isolation *or* with others if she wanted. She had total control of the end product, so long as she followed the directions, and by and large the entire endeavor was sweet.

Sometimes, as she worked a new batch of dough or pulled a hot sheet from the oven, she imagined her own young daughter was there, shoulder-to-shoulder with her, listening intently as Sue shared all her best baking secrets.

But now Sue was north of fifty, and a child was out of the question. And even if it wasn't, a child meant bringing a man into the picture, and despite the pang she sometimes got about Joe, Sue came to recognize one truth: she wasn't entirely certain she wanted a husband —or a boyfriend, or a fling—*at all*. She quite liked sticking to her own company. And since she quite liked her own company—her quiet time and alone time— would she really want a child twenty-four seven?

And at her age?

Quite possibly not. So maybe returning to her job was the best answer. There, she could work with kids—or at least, young adults. Maybe that was the best Sue could do. Sitting in a dark room with a tape recorder and a textbook and handing off the finished product to the nineteen-year-old at the front desk.

Or, maybe not.

She finished wiping the butter shelf and slid the plastic door back into place. The fridge was done. It was time to review the ingredients they'd cobbled together. The cheesecake bake-off could commence as soon as Diane and Bea were ready.

Chapter 40

Diane

Diane clicked off the phone, catching the chip in her red manicure. She made a mental note to book herself at the boardwalk nail salon, then flicked a glance over to the other side of the bed. Craig was snoring softly. No, she supposed a manicure might not be a smart move.

That was fine. She could do it herself. She had seen Lil's collection of nail polish bottles on the dresser. Then again, were they dried out?

Who cared if they were? Diane was on cloud nine. Elated.

"Craig, guess what?"

He rolled toward her, growling like a bear cub. "Hmm?"

"I just talked to Britt."

"Huh?" His eyes fluttered awake. "Is she okay? What happened?"

"No, no, no. She's *fine*." Brittany had worked at

Craig's law firm as a legal assistant before joining a criminal defense team across town. She wanted to stay with her dad, but when the opportunity arose, Craig and Diane agreed that she couldn't pass it up. Not if she wanted to soar. That criminal defense team happened to be the one representing Craig in his bankruptcy proceedings. "They are bumping up our case to the beginning of next month. There was an opening, and the judge remembered you from something and squeezed you in." She shook his shoulders with glee, but he moaned again.

Craig hadn't been optimistic about anything lately.

Days earlier, when he set about fixing the fan and the leak in the upstairs bath, they got a call regarding their plans to sell Diane's house and settle some of the debt. There was some problem with that—something that flew high over her head—and talk about their options started to grow tangled. Craig had packed up then and there, declaring that he was going back to handle it.

But his lawyer and Diane had convinced him that there was nothing he could do. To stay on the shore and enjoy the time he had. Soon, things would heat up. He'd need to return to work and start digging his way out of the hole he'd made.

Diane and Craig had fought. He'd halted operations on fixing the upstairs bath after spending a whole afternoon on the downstairs showerhead, and his crushed energy turned her mood sour, too.

Sue's unending proposal of a cheesecake bake-off couldn't turn the tide. Even Bea's news about the best date ever couldn't.

Diane was starting to wonder if the summer really was doomed. If they really should pack it in and let Greg hire a real estate agent to flip the place. Maybe they were all on the wrong track. Diane for falling back in love with

Craig. Sue for giving up on her marriage. Bea for wanting to spend *months* in Sophia's crypt. In the last couple of days, that's what it had felt like: that the four of them were stuck there together.

Craig stirred to life, sitting up and dragging his hands through the tangled sheets. He reached over and pulled Diane in for a kiss on the cheek and a tight hug. Then he leaned away and frowned, his hands still clutching her shoulders. "This means I've gotta get back to town, Di." His eyes searched hers, hope dancing in them. "I've got to get back and prep. If I have everything in order, and we can still rent your place, then it'll work. If I drop the ball, then everything falls apart."

"Don't be ludicrous, Craig," Diane chided. "Nothing will fall apart. I mean come on, it already did, right?"

And she was right. They'd already divorced. He was already bankrupt. His parents were already in Jamaica on the heels of their own scandal. What else could go wrong for them now?

"As long as you and I stick together, we're going to make it through this time."

"Hang on," he told her, twisting away and leaning over to grab the overnight bag he'd brought along.

"What is it?" she asked, frowning as he dug around.

"Sticking together," he said over his shoulder, still digging. Aunt Lil's bed hung low to the floor, which Diane had never much liked. But it did offer a cozy effect, which she was getting used to. Maybe she'd consider removing the second box spring on her own bed at home. See what that did for the feng shui.

Craig found whatever he was looking for and twisted back up, his hand a fist against his chest. "Diane De Luca," he began. "You said you wanted to stick together. You mean it?"

She nodded, confused.

"Then marry me again, Di." He held out a thin band. It could have been white gold or silver. It could have been nickel. It didn't compare to her wedding band or her chunky engagement ring—with the upgrades he'd bestowed on their ten-year anniversary eons ago. The same set that she still wore, just on the opposite hand.

"We did everything right before," Craig went on, holding her gaze. "But somehow we let the world convince us otherwise. People said we were too young to get married, remember? I think we made the mistake of listening to them." With that, he slid the ring onto her finger. Her other hand flew to it, nostalgia gripping her by the chest. Craig added, "But we aren't young anymore, are we, Di?"

"*Plastic?*" she asked, laughing. "Where did you get this?"

"Last night," he replied. "While you were on the Tilt o' Wheel, I won enough tickets playing Skee-Ball."

She laughed again. They had gone to Pelican Pier the night before, mainly out of boredom. They'd even taken a ride up the Ferris wheel, talking quietly about life —Brittany and the bankruptcy, Diane's various vapid clubs and the relief of getting away from it all even for just one summer.

Diane studied the ring and then eyed him, a smile creeping up her lips. "I'm not running away to Jamaica with you, Craig."

"We aren't running from anything, remember? We're going home."

"Home," Diane whispered back, nodding and smiling like a fool. "I'll go home with you, all right, Craig."

"For good?" he asked.

"For good," she answered. "But not until Labor Day." She narrowed her gaze on him, lifting her eyebrow.

But Craig leaned in, cupped her chin and planted a big kiss on her mouth. "Labor Day it is. After all the work we'll have done this summer, we'll have earned it."

They fell into the sheets together, husband and wife all over again—for good this time. It was frumpy but exciting, comfortable but new. Just like old times. In fact, that it was so familiar made it a thrill of another order. Because for Diane—who was always looking for the next trend, the next thing to do, the next connection—that familiarity was exactly what she never knew she always needed: that familiarity was her true love.

———

AN HOUR LATER, Craig was packed and about to hit the road back to Briar Creek.

Diane stood at the door, ready to usher Craig to his car.

Sue was fussing over setting out three baking stations, excited to return to a girls-only trip (which Diane and Bea were excited for, too).

Bea appeared from the downstairs bath, wearing her swimsuit with a towel tucked over it. "Heading out to the water?" Craig asked as he crossed from the kitchen, where Sue gave him a to-go cup of coffee and a store-bought croissant.

"Surf lesson," Bea replied. There was a solidness that had taken hold of her, something Diane respected. Admired. It was the old Bea re-emerging. Independent and assured, her head higher than the others'.

"Enjoy it," Craig told Bea. "Brooks is a good guy. Don't make the same mistake I did, Bea."

"And what was that?" Diane asked as he joined her at the door. "Letting a good thing go." He winked at her.

Just as they were about to walk to his car, Sue called out. "Hey, what about the faucets?"

He never did fix them. In the span of time since he and Diane took care of the fan, Craig had merely assessed that they needed more parts, and they'd just made do using the upstairs bath. What the other two didn't realize was that they never really needed Craig for repairs to begin with.

It was only Diane who needed him. For something else entirely.

Craig stopped, exchanging a look with Diane. "My wife is going to handle it. She's good at fixing things."

Chapter 41

Sue

Sue had declared that as soon as Bea was back from her surfing date with Brooks, they were having a girls' night. She wanted to host the bake-off and go back to the good ol' days together.

Diane declared that she was going to spend the morning on the downstairs bath first, since that was Bea's preferred shower.

As for Sue's part, she had the morning off. So she took to the boardwalk.

It did her good, a morning of fresh air. She strode by the surf shop and *Clothing by Carly*, taking a peek inside before continuing on. Mack's Pizzeria smelled like heaven, of course. Then there was Licks on the Landing, the same ice cream shop from their youth. Kids walked away from the to-go window, heaping mounds of sweet cream about to topple onto the beach as they tripped down the steps.

The Italian restaurant didn't open until four, and that

was just as well. Sue didn't need another temptation to tuck away inside and devour a five-course meal of nothing but carbs and cheese. But she could do with a small snack. Maybe something fruity or something sweet.

After walking the length of the boardwalk, it occurred to her that no such grab-and-go joint existed. There was the Quick Stop with candy bars, but who wanted a candy bar when you were on vacation? Even if the vacation had turned into a months-long project.

Gone was the Banana Stand from the eighties, where you could get a smoothie. Surprising, really, since the world had turned into a bunch of health nuts.

Sue's only options were ice cream, candy bars, pizza, or a burger. None of it sounded appealing. She saved her appetite for the cheesecake they'd be having that night and turned to head back to the house.

As she made her way down, slowly, she people-watched. Sue had never been a people-watcher in her life. She always felt she was the object of others' people-watching, in fact.

Lots of kids clamored around in groups. Many probably tourists. Some locals, too. They mixed so easily down the shore. Sue wondered what the local schools were like. Did Gull's Landing have a college? She didn't think so, but she couldn't be sure.

Even so, did it matter? Sue wasn't about to give up a stable job for the tourist trap of her youth. And she wasn't accredited to teach much of anything, anyway. Sue didn't want to be a teacher like Bea. She didn't even know what she wanted.

"Excuse me, miss?"

Sue snapped to attention. She'd been standing in front of *Carly's*, gawking, in all likelihood. A big red *Going Out of Business* sign flapped on the storefront space above the doors. *What a shame*, Sue had thought. She hated to see anyone failing ever. It struck her like an arrow to the chest. Someone's dream was dying right there on the boardwalk.

The voice came again. "Can I help you find something?"

Sue pinned it down to a pretty blonde at one of the boardwalk racks of clothing, shuffling them with long, clacking fingernails.

She shook her head. "Oh, no. I'm sorry. I just—" Sue thought of an explanation for her goobery staring. "I know a man who works here is all," she said, pausing and wondering if she ought to buy something, after all.

But the woman replied quickly. Suspiciously. "No man works here. Especially now that we're closing."

Sue held up a hand to wave her off apologetically, but the woman was persistent.

"Unless you mean my brother? Jeffy?"

Groaning inwardly, Sue just smiled and shrugged. "Oh, well yeah. I heard he worked here or whatever. He probably doesn't remember me." She wanted to scream and sprint away. Firstly, Sue had no interest in talking *about* Jeffy or *to* Jeffy. It was just a ploy to extract herself from her uncommon attempt at taking in the local sights and making observations—getting out of the house while her two friends were otherwise engaged. Sue looked out to the water, shielding her eyes.

She couldn't spot Bea or Brooks.

"Jeffy helps out sometimes, but he sticks to Wildwood. How'd'ya know him?" the woman asked.

"Oh, from when we were kids," Sue answered. She found her footing and pointed to the house just yards off. "We stayed there growing up. My friends and me. We're back for one more summer before my best friend's husband sells the property." As she said it, Sue realized the gravity of her words. Her best friend was dead, firstly. Secondly, they hadn't been much of best friends in many, many years.

"Greg Angelos?" the woman answered, her eyes wide. She stopped sliding the metal hooks along the metal ring. The sound of a gull squawking loudly cut through Sue's senses and she felt unanchored again.

"You know Greg?" Sue asked meekly.

The woman encroached upon her like a snake. "Not personally, no. But I read the news. I saw him when he came down, you know."

Sue swallowed.

"Was it true?"

"Was what true?" Sue asked.

"Did she slice her wrists?"

Recoiling, Sue shook her head violently. "No. Oh my God, no." Gumption returned and Sue shook her head again. "It was an accident."

She began to walk away, deciding firmly that she would *not* make a purchase from this tactless woman who'd all but accused Sue's very best friend of something so awful as that, but the woman called out after her, cackling. "That's not what the locals believe!"

Sue's jaw set as she walked away, and her gut clenched.

For her best friend's memory to sit like a suicidal ghost on the boardwalk of Gull's Landing... it was repulsive.

Carly—or whoever that woman was—was propagating a rumor, plain and simple.

But then again, Sue realized as she made it back to Lil's house and stomped the sand off her feet at the doormat, even she had believed that very rumor.

And so did Craig. And Diane. And maybe even Brooks.

But not Bea.

And maybe not Sue. Not anymore.

Sue realized that she hadn't been such a good friend to Sophia after all. She couldn't fix that now, but she could do her best, at least, to honor her memory.

The only problem was, Sue had no clue where to begin.

Chapter 42

Bea

"I'm home!" Bea called out, glowing with saltwater-streaked hair and sunburnt shoulders. She'd wear more sunscreen the next day. Brooks' orders. She didn't want to turn into a full-blown hag. Not anymore.

Bea strode to the scrap of paper where they'd begun keeping a running list of groceries. Her eyes flashed down the items and she grinned, newly excited to tackle's Sue's little beachside dream of bringing a splash of their childhood back.

Everything was rosier now, with Brooks in the picture. They were just friends. He talked a lot about his son. She talked a lot about teaching. And together, they shared new experiences—eating on the boardwalk like a couple of longtime locals. Her flopping uselessly off of her surfboard while he tried in vain to keep her standing up.

She was beginning to wonder if she was going to need lessons for another five summers before she could do it. Or if somewhere inside, her body was refusing to cooperate in order to prolong her time with the whimsical, easy-going Brooks Morgan.

It was nice to have a new friendship to nurture. And nice to have her old friendships to nurture.

Bea realized that even if she was physically incapable of going upstairs in Lil's, she'd at least gotten over the hump of being there at all. In the last couple of weeks, they'd overcome the awkward breakfasts and forced beach walks. Card nights were occasional, and when they did play, Diane busted out the margaritas and suddenly, Bea was having fun.

She wasn't sleeping well, but she *was* having fun.

And as for the sleep, both she and Sue had taken to sneaking in midday naps. But on that particular afternoon, Bea began to wonder if she might not steal away upstairs. Now that Craig was gone and Aunt Lil's had become some kind of marital refuge, it changed things. Instead of Lil's old room, that upstairs space—in Bea's mind at least—was less a historical monument and more a vacation rental or something.

"I think I'm going to take my nap upstairs!" Bea hollered, waiting for a reply.

None came. "Hello? Diane?"

Nothing.

"Sue?"

"We're up here!" Sue's voice floated down from above.

Bea sucked in a deep breath and glanced back out the kitchen window. Brooks was ushering two teenagers down the beach. He wasted no time in working through his lessons, but he also made sure to save her a daily slot for whatever. It was his prerogative, he'd said. He owned the business, he set the hours.

She liked that about Gull's Landing. The sense of self-destiny. Of commanding one's own life. She wondered if there was more space there for other people who were looking for that.

Then she remembered it didn't matter. Greg was selling the place.

Climbing the stairs tentatively, she replied to Sue. "What are you two doing?"

Sue's face popped above the landing. "Diane's fixing the faucet in here." She looked away then back at Bea and made a face before whispering, "Or trying to."

Bea joined them both in the cramped bathroom.

"Do you even know what you're doing, Diane?" she asked her friend, who was squatting in the bathtub, her fingers shoved in the round silver plate.

"Yes, as a matter of fact. I took a workshop on basic home plumbing. I just fixed my own a few years ago. With Craig's help, but…"

It was a wonder to Bea that Diane and Craig had the relationship they did. It was also a wonder that for all the money he'd made (and lost) they still did their own repairs. Diane once said it was she who'd inspired them to become more self-sufficient. She liked her luxury, but she also liked her projects.

"I can't get access to the back of it on this side. I need to replace the unit. It's totally shot." Diane rubbed her hand across her hair line and pointed near Bea to the sink, where a new faucet sat in a cracked clamshell case.

"How do you get access then?" Bea asked, her pulse quickening.

Diane knocked on the shower wall and pointed.

Directly into The Summer Society Room.

Chapter 43

Bea

"I'll go in. I'll go in and make the change and pop right back out. You'll never know I was in there." Diane stood in the tub and reached across to the sink to grab the new set.

Bea's breath hitched, but she agreed. "Okay. But will you need help?"

Diane hesitated. "Yeah. I will."

"I'll go," Sue said, her voice even. Strong.

Bea gave her a grateful look. Then she replied, "I'll stay here. I can help from this side."

Diane lifted an eyebrow. "The key?"

"Oh, right." Bea left the bathroom and skipped downstairs to grab it from Aunt Lil's wooden box.

In a rush to get it and go back up, she knocked the box over and postcards skittered to the floor.

Sighing, she called out that she'd be right up. Then she shuffled them all into her hand, tarot cards mixed in too, and tossed them onto the table before jogging back upstairs where she handed the key off to Diane.

Seconds later, they were both in there, and Bea was stuck in the bathroom. She could hear rustling in the closet and decided to sneak a peek at the medicine cabinet.

Opening it slowly, she winced at the creaking of the rusted-out hinges. Inside were three shelves, each one full. Aunt Lil had medications for days. Bea frowned as she examined each label. Some vials looked more like elixirs than pills, dating as far back as the seventies. She started to wonder what else there was about Aunt Lil she didn't know —tarot cards and tinctures? She lifted an eyebrow, but then heard one of the two women gasp loudly through the wall.

Bea turned to it, pressing her hand along the space above the towel rack. "What happened? Are you okay?" she called through the plaster.

"Bea you gotta see this!" It was Diane's voice, loud and excited.

Bea shook her head. "No, just tell me. What? Is it a rat's nest?"

"It's not a rat's nest!" Sue hollered. "It's way better than a rat's nest!"

Swallowing, Bea replied, "What is it?" Her mind's eye flew to Sophia. What had she worn on that last visit? What had they taken her back home in? How could Bea have forgotten to ask such a basic, important question?

Did Diane find her purse?

No, Greg had that.

Was it something else?

"Bea, look!" Sue was back in the bathroom doorway, a book in each hand.

Bea smiled.

Chapter 44

Sue

"Your old romance books," Sue said to Bea. "There's a whole stash of them."

Bea marveled at the tattered covers. They were damp and yellowed and basically ruined.

"No wonder there's a leak!" Diane called through the wall.

"I've got to get back to help her. You must have shoved over a dozen back there."

Grinning warmly, Bea kept her gaze on the books. "I can't believe I forgot. I wasn't sure if Aunt Lil would have let me keep them if she knew about them."

"She would have," Sue said. "She read them, too, remember?"

"Yeah, but she wouldn't have wanted to get in trouble with my folks."

"I'll be back in a bit. We'll get them all out of there and set them on the side table to dry, okay?"

Bea nodded and Sue took off.

Within fifteen minutes, impressively, Diane had swapped out the old faucet for a new one, and the bath was fixed. To Sue, this was magic.

By the time they locked Sophia's room back up, she had brought two loads of old books down to the kitchen table, setting them along the side table like they were ready for show.

The day had washed into a pleasant mood, all three repairs were complete, and Diane had led the charge. Sue had cleaned the entire kitchen and was looking forward to her little baking plan.

And then there was Bea, charmed by a happy bit of history—picking up each book and turning it in her hands, marveling.

"Jeanne Bowman, Emma Goldrick. I remember these!" She held up a thick, tattered, nude-colored book. "Diane, look! *Wifey!*"

"Oh my," Sue breathed. "How did you even get your hands on a copy?"

Bea shook her head. "I think I got it at the library and forgot to return it." She studied the book and opened the cover. "Oh yes, look!"

Sue squinted. A faded stamp read *Property of Gull's Landing Public Library*.

Diane laughed. "Little Bea Russo, desperate romantic and rule follower. But a thief? That's a new low I never even considered."

She'd set aside her pink tool kit—the one Craig had schlepped from her house in Briar Creek—and was going through the books, too.

"This one has no cover. It must be *really* bad."

Sue rolled her eyes and started back toward the fridge. "So, what do you gals think? Ready for cheese-cakes or what?"

"Wait."

"Oh, come on," Sue nagged. "I've tried your margaritas and walked three miles on the beach. It's my turn to pick the—"

"No, wait."

Sue turned.

Diane was holding the coverless book, still shut, facing the edge of pages toward them. Bea frowned at Sue.

"What, Diane? What is it?" Bea asked.

Diane's eyes flew back down. She fiddled with it and then glanced from Bea to Sue and back to Bea again. "This isn't a book."

Swallowing, Sue felt a line of sweat crawl up her spine. She looked again at the book. It was faded now. Not so pink, more orange. The silver lock had rusted to match the dull cover.

"That was Sophia's," Sue whispered.

"Sophia's *what?*" Bea asked.

"Her diary."

Chapter 45

Sophia

May 22, 2018

Wow! I sure had a lot to say back then. Less so, now. I suppose that's why I'm back. I'm lacking something lately. The drama, maybe? The craziness?

It's a miracle I didn't come back and burn this thing when I reread the past. It's a wonder I didn't burn myself, actually, or do something more extreme. That pain was so visceral. I can remember it.

I never did take to writing in here after that last day down the shore.

It's hard to forget, now. The frenzy on the beach. All that.

He was supposed to come back that day and give me a "see-you-later" kiss. We promised to meet in Philly. He'd never had a cheesesteak, if you can believe that.

I remember when I met Greg, that was the first thing I asked him. "Have you ever had a cheesesteak?"

The first thing I thought of when they found his body, crumpled and bruised in that rocky crag south of the house, was not "poor, dead Doug." Not poor me, either. I thought about Bea. I wondered if her heart was broken, too. Then I started to wonder why, why, why? Why would my sister do that?

I guess that's when I began to reconsider the whole entire summer.

It didn't change my heartache. It didn't change how I felt toward her. It just happened to be the first thing that came to mind.

How sick is that, when you think about it?

How sick is it that when the love of my life turned up dead on the beach, drowned (later reports cited a blood alcohol level double the legal limit to drive), my mind flew to her? Not him or his parents or me.

Not our little baby—the fledgling life that slipped like a ghost from my body so soon—soon enough that I was okay. Soon enough that a medical doctor would call it "a blip on the radar," as Lil had declared when I came to her, sobbing and struck by the dramatic change my life had taken.

A blip on the radar to an old spinster like Lil, maybe. Barren for life and a single widow save for her weird affair with the mortician. But not to me. Not after a summer of lying to the three girls that meant everything to me.

The police said they thought Doug was walking home and wandered too close to the shore, tripped in the dark, hit his head and was carried out. He probably drowned in less than an inch of seawater.

I never got over that. I never did. Not even when I met perfect Greg or had perfect Matt! Can you believe it? Talk about stuck in the past.

Another thing had come to my mind in those early days after the tragedy.

I wondered how we could ever go back... I mean, how we could ever come back?

How could we fulfill our pact?

I knew we couldn't. And of course, we didn't.

Maybe that will change now. I hope so. I hope that after I finish this little diary entry and tuck it back into the wall with Bea's tacky old romance books that one of us will dig this out years from now. Or maybe it won't even be one of us digging around in this old house. Maybe some other girl will. Maybe Sue will adopt after all. Or maybe it'll be sweet little Brittany. Not so little anymore, I know. I know.

Maybe Matt's future daughter—can you imagine me? A mom-mom?

Maybe there will be another generation of *us*. Young girls who form their own Summer Society.

Chapter 46

Bea, one month later

She didn't kill herself.

They figured it out after discovering the diary and poring over Sophia's private tragedy. And the public one, too.

There was evidence there, yes.

But not as much as they found in Aunt Lil's postcards.

Not right away, however. First, Sue made them do the cheesecake bake-off. They invited Brooks and his son, Bennett, over to be the judges. Brooks voted for Bea, which felt obvious. Bennett immediately chose Sue's, which was far more sincere.

The ensuing weeks were better. Bea mustered the courage to allow Sue and Diane to talk her into cleaning out The Summer Society room. They even washed the sheets and Sophia's left-behind outfit, which Bea wrapped in the quilt from the bed to take home. She wasn't sure what she'd do with it, but she felt better just knowing it was hers.

They took Lil's bottle of sleeping pills and Googled it. Nothing much came up. It was a standard-issue prescription sleeping medication. Expired, but only by twelve years. Its efficacy probably hadn't worn down much, but when Bea texted Greg to ask about any medical findings after her death, he reminded her that he had waived his privilege to learn about the autopsy results. Surprised that the coroner had ordered an autopsy, and even more suspicious that Greg wanted to ignore it, she learned that she could request the results. And she did.

But it would be weeks until she received that information.

In the meantime, all they had to go by was the mess Sophia had left behind—purposefully or not.

Then again, finding the diary, with that timely entry that suggested Sophia would be back to check on it… meant that she hadn't planned on dying.

And that was all Bea really needed to know to move on. But then there was the news of her kid sister's pregnancy and miscarriage. And her knowledge about that unwanted kiss, and those facts crumpled Bea all over again.

It was Sue and Diane who pulled her back from the depths, convincing Bea that Sophia died without anger toward Bea and having had what so few ever really got to experience: that sweet young love. The kind that Bea herself never even enjoyed.

That's when Bea decided it might be okay to keep meeting Brooks for surf lessons and Mack's pizza and even a glass of wine here or there.

Still though, even with the diary, Bea and the other two wondered what in the world Sophia was doing back at Lil's. Secretly.

So, there they were: a month later, as Sue sat down to sort through Lil's box of cards and bills in earnest—this time with the mission to start throwing things away since the house would go to market on Labor Day weekend.

Bea had just sent off another text to Greg, this time letting him know that they were running out of time and may not get everything moved out by September.

Craig had texted Diane that he'd officially moved into her house, with the help of Britt.

And Sue had stumbled across the stack of postcards that Bea knocked over the day they discovered the diary.

"Wait a minute," Sue whispered, aligning three postcards in a neat row across the kitchen table. "Look, these aren't new."

"What do you mean?" Bea leaned over from her lunch setting—caprese salad with half of a cannoli on the side (they'd been eating a lot of sweets lately—the benefit of long walks and surfing sessions).

Her eyes focused on the backs of the three cards. Diane leaned over, too.

"Look at the date," Diane pointed out, her finger tapping the upper righthand corner.

"Two-thousand eighteen?" Bea asked. Then she glanced down and across.

Three greetings.

Three notes.

One signature.

Bea grabbed the first one and read silently, her eyes flashing across it.

She looked up at Sue, her heart pounding in her chest. Diane grabbed the second card.

Sue finally grabbed the third and read aloud. *"Dear Susie Q, It's been way too long, don't you think? I'm here in Gull's Landing at Aunt Lil's. I was thinking about the old days, and I just sort of got swept away. I didn't even tell Greg, if you can believe that. I feel so dangerous. Anyway, consider this your official invitation to reconvene The Summer Society. I expect to hear back from you by way of phone or mail within forty-eight hours of receipt. Don't let me down. Your old best friend, Soph."*

Sue looked up, and Bea's eyes were filling to the brim. She shook her head and brushed the tear away. "How can it be?" she whispered. Sue covered Bea's hand in hers and squeezed.

Diane cleared her throat—her eyes were glassy, too—and her voice trembled as she read hers. *"Dear Diane, Guess what? We're doing it. We're taking a summer together. Right now. Pack up, kiss your book club goodbye for a month or two and meet me at Lil's. I'll even treat you to a margarita. The Vice President of The Summer Society, Sophia Russo-Angelos, AKA your favorite cousin."* Diane laughed through her tears and rested her hand on top of Sue's, squeezing it and smiling and dipping her chin toward Bea. "What about yours?"

Bea started to shake her head. How could she share the message with anyone in the world? It was her last private conversation with her sister. Meant for her eyes only. But then she remembered why she was there, and she considered what the message said and she realized she had no choice. She had to.

Dear Bea, What happened to us? We turned into these cranky old sisters who keep their appointments and gossip about their friends. When did that start, anyway? Listen, Bea. I'm worried about you. I know. I know what you're thinking. You hate it when I say crap like that. Anyway, I have an idea. Let's get you out of town, okay? I have just the place. Meet me down the shore. If we don't start using Aunt Lil's, Greg is going to make us sell it. So here is my plan. We're going to reboot our old club. You can still be president if you want. I'll make sure Diane doesn't gripe. Okay? I'm here now. Come on down, the water's fine. Your sister, Soph. P.S. No excuses! We made a pact. Remember?

Epilogue

The Fourth of July, two years later

"Sparklers, little American flags, graham crackers, marshmallows, chocolate squares (the good kind), and roasting sticks." Bea finished her appraisal of their grocery cart and directed Diane to the cashier. "We're ready."

"What about sunblock?"

"We've got four bottles, I swear," Bea replied. She shook her shoulder-length waves back and paid before they loaded up her car and headed home.

"Craig's bringing hot dogs. Brittany's doing watermelon, and Brooks is bringing beverages. So that leaves Sue—"

"—with dessert, yep."

"Will she need help bringing things over?" Diane asked, checking her makeup in the mirror.

"Bennett and Greg agreed to run a cart."

Life as they knew it had changed dramatically in just two years.

Since their initial reunion, Sue got a job at Gull's Landing Community College as a part-time Student-Faculty Liaison. She helped to resolve conflicts as they arose and generally offered academic counseling and personal support to the student body.

But that was just on Mondays, Wednesdays, and Fridays.

Every other day of the week, she was the co-owner and full-time baker at *Sophia's Boardwalk Sweets*, specializing in cheesecakes and cannoli on the Gull's Landing Boardwalk. Her business partner?

Recent retiree and the celebrated woman of the night: Beatrice Russo.

They'd rented out Carly's former clothing boutique, running the boardwalk bakery (a runner-up name, to be sure) right next to Surf's Up.

Everything had settled in. Bea was dating Brooks, and Bennett and Matt had become best friends—Shoobies in Crime, as they called themselves.

Greg read Sophia's diary and her postcards, wept like a baby, and changed his mind about selling the place. He agreed to cover expenses indefinitely, which allowed Sue and Bea to turn into roommates just as soon as the ink dried on Sue's divorce papers and letter of resignation.

Bea and Diane arrived back in time for the retirement party, and Bea headed up to her room to get ready.

She pulled on a loose, white linen dress and the shoes they'd discovered wedged beneath the bed two summers before.

And then she stood at the window with the view. Soph's favorite spot in the house—when it wasn't too hot and when she wasn't expecting some wayward local to come and toss a pebble at the wrong window.

Bea saw more than the ocean, though. She saw

Bennett and Matt laughing with a small group of local boys off down the beach.

She saw Diane and Craig canoodling like teenagers in the corner of the yard.

She saw Brittany with her new boyfriend, helping Greg light a fire on the beach.

Then there was Sue—walking triumphantly down the boardwalk steps, a fresh platter of desserts teetering in her hands as Darla-the-dog darted around her and dashed off to the beach toward Brooks.

Brooks Morgan and his last lesson of the day: a group of giggling preteen girls—a little too young for their bikinis, too wise for their years, and too weak to lug an old red Coleman cooler across the sand.

And Bea wondered if those girls, too, had their own little summer society.

Surely, Bea, Sophia, Diane, and Sue wouldn't be the last to ever establish a secret club in Gull's Landing.

Maybe they weren't even the first.

———

Gull's Landing continues with Aunt Lil's story in *The Garden Guild*.

If you enjoyed this novel, order Elizabeth Bromke's bestseller, *House on the Harbor*, available where books are sold.

Stay up to date with the author by joining her newsletter. Visit elizabethbromke.com for more details.

Also by Elizabeth Bromke

The Birch Harbor Saga
The Hickory Grove Series
The Maplewood Series

Acknowledgments

Elise Griffin, I owe this story to you! Your careful analysis was critical, and I know that it made *The Summer Society* into what it needed to become. So grateful to God that we met and that you agreed to come aboard. Thank you!

Vicki Fiorillo, Lela Fiorillo, and Kara Beck: thank you for all your insider information on the local experience of the Jersey Shore. I couldn't have hatched this book without your help.

Thank you, Mrs. Leyva-Otis for the history on worry dolls. And again Vicki—for going above and beyond and *sending* a set to me.

Lisa and Krissy—thank you for your work and time on shining her up, so to speak. So wonderful to have a great team whom I can rely on with great confidence.

Ed, what can I write here that I haven't already told you? Nothing, but still. Without you, I couldn't... I *wouldn't* write books. Little E. *always* for you.

About the Author

Elizabeth Bromke writes women's fiction and sweet romance. In her free time, she reads, bakes, and walks her dog with her husband and young son in the mountains of Arizona.

Join Elizabeth reader group, Bromke's Bookworms. Visit elizabethbromke.com today.

Made in the USA
Monee, IL
15 March 2021